C000093737

ABOUT THE AUTHOR

Carol Cooper is a doctor, journalist, and author.

She graduated from Cambridge University where she studied
medicine and her fellow students. On her path to general
practice, she spent years in hospital medicine, worked at
supermarket checkouts, typed manuscripts in Russian, and
proofread manuals on rebuilding dual-diesel engines.

Following a string of books on childcare and an
award-winning medical textbook, she made her fiction debut
with *One Night at the Jacaranda*.

Carol lives in Hampstead and Cambridge and has three
grown-up sons and three step-children.

HAMPSTEAD
FEVER

Carol Cooper

HAMPSTEAD FEVER
Copyright © 2016 Carol Cooper
Cover design by Jessica Bell

Published by Hardwick Press 2016
London, UK
ISBN-13: 978-0-9954514-0-7

The right of Carol Cooper to be identified as the author of this Work
has been asserted by her in accordance with sections 77 and 78 of the
Copyright, Designs and Patents Act 1988.

No parts of this publication may be reproduced, stored in a retrieval
system, or transmitted in any form or by any means, electronic, mechanical,
photocopying, recording, or otherwise, without the prior written permission
of the copyright owner.

This book is sold subject to the condition that it shall not, by way of trade
or otherwise, be lent, resold, hired out, or otherwise circulated without the
publisher's prior consent in any form of binding or cover other than that in
which it is published and without a similar condition being imposed on the
subsequent purchaser. Under no circumstances may any part of this book be
photocopied for resale.

This is a work of fiction. All characters and events in this work, other than
those clearly in the public domain, are entirely fictitious. Any resemblance to
any persons, living or dead, is purely coincidental.

HAMPSTEAD FEVER

Carol Cooper

CHAPTER ONE

DAN

Dan nibbled Laure's earlobe as his fingers wandered over the contours of her breast.

In the cot one foot away, the baby gave a cry. The cot death guidelines said it was OK for babies of eleven months to sleep in their own rooms, but no point trying to tell Laure that again.

"It's only a testing cry," said Dan.

She said nothing. He could already feel her thighs and stomach clench. And not in a good way.

The moment was gone. He'd have to sort himself out. Again.

"Stop it." She reached across to the baby. "Not in front of Jack."

"Why? It's not like he knows what I'm doing."

"Babies are very intuitive." She must have read that somewhere. The flat had more baby books than Waterstone's. "Anyway, you're making the whole bed jiggle."

"He's a bloke. Never too soon to learn essential skills." Still. Dan covered himself with the sheet. It reeked of milk and sweat and stuff, all getting high in this ridiculous heat. Eleven at night and not a breath of air in the flat.

Dan closed his eyes. He usually did. Tonight it would also help avoid her steely gaze. The warders used to have that look. Loosely translated it meant, 'I know your game, sunshine.'

He could hear their son, sucking. Now she was cooing at Jack, like she used to coo at him. His hand speeded up to a frenetic pace.

Actually, she'd never cooed at him, but never mind. He thought of her magnificent breasts. Way better than Page Three or a lads' mag. Or the National Gallery. He'd spent a lot of time there after doing bird. Education they were, galleries and museums. Free, gratis, and for nothing as well.

Now Dan was wilting a tad. He opened his eyes. She returned the gaze over Jack's head. You could hardly see where the boob stopped and their baby's blond head began. His little hand stretched out over Laure's ribcage under her breast.

Before the baby, Laure had loved Dan. Never mind that he wasn't as posh as her. She'd loved him unconditionally. Or so he'd thought. Then little Jack came along. The much-wanted baby who mewled and puked.

Shakespeare, that was. Class.

Their baby also pooped and needed feeding, changing, cuddling, and a zillion other things that added up to twenty-four hours a day. And that wasn't counting visits to the doctor, because Laure wasn't going to take any chances when Jack sneezed or brought up a bit more milk than usual. That little scrap of baby had totally rearranged their lives.

He'd gone soft now. Which never happened to him.

GEOFF

Fuck progress, thought Geoff.

He jabbed F5 then F1 to save the consultation. Now he

wondered if he should have pressed F8 instead. Or as well. As it was, it only made the previous consultation re-appear. He was running late. No surprise there. With the new patient database, it took twenty minutes to do a simple little thing like print a chest X-ray form. Back in the day, all he'd had to do was yank open a drawer, grab a form, scribble *CXR*, and sign it. Job done.

Bloody hell, life was easy when he first qualified, fifteen years ago, burning with zeal to make a difference. Turned out he'd been trained for a lifetime of sorting out computer problems and hordes of patients with minor symptoms.

Fuck the new database.

Fuck the commissioning group that brought it in only months after the previous change in software. And, today, fuck the entire NHS management.

He gazed at the screen. It was filled not with the patient's medical details, but with irrelevant guff like *Pt consent given*, *Pt address changed* (which it actually hadn't, unless you counted a new comma), and perhaps the most common entry of all, *DNA* for *Did Not Attend*. Stuff that mattered like *coughing up blood* lay hidden below reams of pointless entries.

A young man sat there in front of him. Unemployed, with a squat nose and tats up one arm. A sleeve, they called it. There hadn't been a single patient without tats all morning. One very attractive patient, job in some investment firm, had a tattooed swallow below her knee. What was that going to look like when she got saggy skin and osteoarthritis? But then these days even the prime minister's wife had a tattoo. Jesus!

Geoff asked, "What can I do for you?" You never asked patients what brought them to the health centre today, unless you wanted to hear all about the 232 bus.

Meanwhile the computer was firing a range of tasks at Geoff: check the patient's blood pressure, calculate his risk of a heart attack in the next ten years, and get his consent to share info. It was also reminding him that, come the year 2060, said ugly git would be due his elderly health check.

The patient (whose name Geoff had instantly forgotten) had pain in the left testicle.

Might be a torsion. Uncommon in adults, but, unless treated promptly, it could lead to gangrene of the testicle.

"Right. I need to take a look," Geoff said, pulling the paper curtains across.

As he waited for the fellow to undress, he wiped the photo on his desk with a tissue. It was Davey, aged five, at the beach. Brancaster Staithe, Norfolk. Happy days before the divorce. Before Australia.

"Ready yet?" Geoff called out, aware of how late his clinic was running.

"Yeah. Course."

Turned out the man was sitting fully clothed the other side of the drapes.

As patiently as possible, Geoff explained again what he needed to examine. Another three minutes passed while the man undressed. Back in Camp Bastion, every second counted. Military medicine had pushed forwards the frontiers of many specialities, like resuscitation, trauma surgery, anaesthesia, and plastic surgery. No visible impact on general practice, though.

On examination there was nothing abnormal about this patient's tackle, apart from the pong. The heatwave did little to improve patients' personal hygiene. Geoff peeled off his gloves and dumped them in the bin. "Hmm. All's well there. When did you first get the pain?"

The man shrugged. "Maybe a week ago. But I ain't got it no more, like. Not since I pulled that bird the other day."

"Fair enough," said Geoff, even though there was nothing fair about it. The ugly, unemployed fucker got laid just like that, while he, Geoff, had been celibate for ten months and counting.

KAREN

The bench was hard. So was he.

Twenty-five minutes, thought Karen as she flung her knickers into the corner of the changing room. No point wearing your best underwear when it ended up with the abandoned socks and shin pads.

Footie Dad, still in his Charlton Athletic shirt, dragged her on top of him on the bench they'd hauled into the middle of the changing room. Karen was getting the hang of keeping one leg either side of the narrow bench.

The place whiffed of Dettol and trainers. On the plus side, the windows were too high for anyone to see in. The door was locked and they'd jammed a chair against it too, just in case.

Twenty-one minutes left, according to the clock. They gathered pace.

Squeak scrape, squeak scrape went the bench on the floor tiles.

She hoped the rickety old thing would last their weekly encounters, because she planned on many more.

In a perfect world, Karen wouldn't have been banging the children's football coach. But she'd become resourceful since her marriage broke down. While her four children were parked with friends, she got nearly thirty minutes on a Sunday at about 5 p.m. It was simpler than having real boyfriends who met the kids, came into everyone's lives, and eventually turned out a disappointment all round. She and Footie Dad rarely bothered to speak, so, in the six weeks they'd been at it, he'd not once told her that his wife didn't understand him, or that they'd slept apart for years.

That was fine by her. Time was short and Karen had no interest at all in the state of his marriage, or much else about him.

After all, she was just using him for sex.

HARRIET

Even now, a good five minutes after rushing out of the flat and slamming the door, Harriet's pulse still throbbed in her temples. She would sit here on the wall until she felt cooler and calmer, and perhaps by then Sanjay would be more subdued too.

She moved into the shade on the wall. It was another blazing day and the bricks were fiery hot through her skirt. Over the road, a children's birthday party was going on. It was a party for children who could not walk, Harriet concluded. Parents aimed to park as close as possible to the gatepost with the blue balloons, gunning for any hint of a space whether their car fitted into it or not. One woman stopped her 4x4 right in the middle of the street to let out two little darlings, each carrying presents bigger than themselves.

A van had been abandoned across next door's drive. According to the livery, it belonged to Smarty Marty, your top choice in children's entertainment in the whole of North London.

Harriet was still seething. She would phone Virginia. Her best friend would understand.

Virginia answered on the second ring and let Harriet tell her all. The row had started with chest hair.

"He's driving me nuts." Harriet's voice was louder than she'd intended. She glanced towards Sanjay's flat to check that he wasn't looking out of the window.

There was a pause. "Are you still having sex?" asked Virginia.

"Of course." Harriet didn't add that it was less often these days.

From inside the house with the party came a right din, and on the pavement a late arrival was howling his little head off because he had missed pass the parcel.

"Well. Guess I'd better go back in," Harriet told her friend. It had been a silly argument. They would make it up in the end.

Sanjay had been changing out of his shirt when Harriet asked if he'd ever thought of waxing his chest, especially as it was so hot this summer. As soon as the words were out, she knew she should have kept quiet.

"No." He paused for a moment, his face set. "It would remind me of my fucking cancer treatment."

"But you didn't have cancer after all," she pointed out. Besides, the hair had all grown back, lush, lustrous, and coal black.

"I still lost my hair with the chemo, didn't I? For nearly eighteen months I was treated for cancer. I got all that bollocking poison, and for nothing. I loathed being bald. My hair was already growing back when we met two years ago, so you obviously can't appreciate what it was like."

"There are lots of bald men." Harriet had written plenty of features on male pattern baldness.

He fixed on her with huge dark eyes. "There aren't that many with no eyebrows, eyelashes, or nose hair."

"What about ear hair? You always moan about hair growing like triffids out of your ears."

"No ear hair. And no chest hair, obviously."

Harriet took this in. "You know, I never figured out why you didn't want to sue the hospital."

"Bollocks! I got my life back. Suing takes time, and costs the NHS money. Maybe people don't realize this, but compensation doesn't come out of the doctors' pockets."

"Maybe it should."

"Maybe. I don't know. I mainly wanted an apology and the promise it wouldn't happen to some other poor sap."

Harriet had heard this before, but still didn't see how a mere apology had been enough for him. "But it's left a scar."

He was shouting now. "Of course it fucking has! It's left a shed-load of scars." He pointed to his neck and his groin simultaneously like a maniac. "And those are just the scars you can see."

"OK." She should have put her arms round him, but right

now he was as huggable as a box of fireworks.

"So now you know why I like having chest hair."

He'd disappeared into the bathroom, still fuming.

They always did make up in the end. Harriet knew that from the two years they had been together, but every time it was another chip in your favourite mug. You couldn't ignore it.

CHAPTER TWO

DAN

When had he realized something was wrong between Laure and him? Dan grabbed denture glue from the cabinet and gave it some thought. Fixodent made him feel like an old man, not a thirty-eight year old. But no way could he afford an implant for that missing front tooth. Not when there was barely enough to live on. Dan pushed the plate back into his mouth and grinned at the mirror.

There was one night in particular. Probably when Jack was just a few weeks old.

Dan had washed his hands again before putting on his baseball cap and leaving work. You didn't want to pick up your brand new baby with garlicky hands. He cleaned his hands a lot after work.

He sniffed his fingernails as he waited for the night bus. It arrived after just ten minutes. As Dan touched in with his card, he made no eye contact with the driver who appeared resigned to an unpalatable shift.

Dan gave a wide berth to some geezer who was barfing noisily into a plastic bag.

He remembered there were seats free behind two pretty teenagers, barely clothed, and a couple of gobby Turkish lads chatting them up. Dan installed himself across the aisle from an old bloke slumped onto a pile of carrier bags and got his book out. You could learn a lot from good writers like Tony Parsons. Maybe one day enough to feel educated.

A skanky guy got on at the next stop, wheezing and spluttering as he made his way down the bus. Dan turned away, sure of catching something if he breathed in. Laure wouldn't let him near their baby if he got ill. And if Jack actually caught something, she'd probably never forgive him. That was her new job, trying to stop Jack getting ill. Took him to the doctor or the baby clinic on an almost daily basis. As if that was going to help. Everyone knew those places were riddled with germs.

When he got in, he said, "I love you, gorgeous."

Laure turned over and pretended to be asleep. "Don't," she mumbled when he touched her.

He peered into the cot by the side of their bed. Jack was fast asleep, fists curled tight. Dan spent a couple of moments just watching the perfect little boy. The most amazing thing that had ever happened to him. And to Laure.

Dan undressed in the bathroom, readjusted his top plate as usual, and crept into bed.

Laure shrugged him off.

"Why can't we?" he pleaded.

"Because, in case you hadn't noticed, I pushed a baby out eight weeks ago, that's why."

He let several minutes go by before stroking her bare shoulder. "Remember when we did it the other way?"

She was still awake. Didn't reply.

"You liked that," he whispered. It was an understatement. She was wild about it. "And I don't have to go anywhere near your cunt."

"That was then. This is now." Seemed to be her new mantra, that.

She tucked the duvet around her breast and closed her eyes tight, a clear message that everything was shut.

Now Jack was nearly a year old. They'd moved to North London. Dan got the job at Lolo's, *the* place to eat. Pay wasn't brilliant, though.

Everything down there must have healed now. And still Laure hardly wanted to be touched. Then there were her shaking attacks or whatever you called them. He wasn't that good with words. He could see she tried to control her fear. Even so, she would tremble and her breathing speeded up. Those attacks were another worry on top of shortage of money and sex.

She'd read masses about looking after babies. By the time she was seven months gone, Laure had read every single book on pregnancy and baby care. To her, poring over *Mother and Baby* or *The Essential First Year* was no different to studying, he supposed. She wanted to be the best.

"Bet you passed your law exams first time," he said.

She'd looked up from *Baby and Child Questions and Answers*, her face knotted with concern. "I did. But this is different. You only get the one go."

Best not to push it, Dan thought. Here she was fretting about one baby. She'd throw a wobbly if he suggested having two. Especially as she was already forty.

"See? We'll be fine," said Dan when they got in from a scan at the hospital. "Drink?"

"I'm not drinking, remember?"

"Sorry. I forgot. You're being ascetic."

"Not ascetic. Teetotal."

"Right. Teetotal." He wished she wouldn't be so quick to correct him. So far that day his use of parsley in the soup had been ascetic, as had the amount of toothpaste he had applied to his brush. Useful word, ascetic. Well, it would be when he figured out how to use it.

During pregnancy she'd worried about the birth. Only natural. Dan couldn't see how any woman could be happy at the prospect of something like a cantaloupe forcing its way out of her fanny. Obviously human openings stretched over time—what lag didn't know that?—but birth seemed to happen painfully fast.

Course, Laure's past didn't help. Abused by her dad in her teens. Not full rape, but still traumatic. Dan understood trauma. He figured they'd need an extended family when the baby arrived. But he didn't try too hard to persuade her to call her parents.

He'd only read *A Dad's Guide to Baby Stuff* and he felt prepared. Damn it! He wasn't just ready. He was excited about being a dad. A six-year stretch for a crime he hadn't committed was behind him now. He had the woman of his dreams, and a baby on the way. Life couldn't have been better.

Once upon a time, she could get pretty excited too.

LAURE

"Is this the colour you wanted?" Dan displayed the little bottle.

"*Purple Passion*, isn't it?"

He peered at the label. "It says *Lilac Love-in*. Will that do?"

"It's fine." Laure stretched out one foot and lay back on the sofa cushions. At this stage of pregnancy, she couldn't reach her feet. This was going to be a luxury. As she repositioned a cushion, her belly shifted from left to right.

She had forgotten how much she loved having her toes stroked. Stretching out the other foot, she let her legs fall slightly apart.

Dan looked up from his nail painting. "You're not wearing any knickers."

"Got to prevent thrush," she lied. She cradled her belly. All was quiet in there. It was unreal how peaceful the baby was during the day when he was such a hooligan every night. "The other foot can wait, if you like," she added as she licked her upper lip.

She'd never seen Dan put the top on the nail varnish and remove his jeans so quickly. Actually she'd never seen any man carry out that particular sequence of movements.

He knelt by the sofa and pulled her gently towards him.

These days she was moist all the time. 'Getting ready for baby,' the midwife said, explaining the engorged labia and swollen mons Venus as if all pregnant women were simple.

Just one easy movement and there they were, locked together. Laure spread her legs wider to feel all of him. Bliss.

As their rhythm accelerated, a surge of heat enveloped her. She lay beached on the sofa, unable to move.

Now Dan was studying her belly. "I think the little guy might be playing football."

He was certainly doing something. Her womb had turned from dormitory to athletic stadium, and the shape of her abdomen changed dramatically with each kick. Laure reclined and shut her eyes as Dan continued with his running commentary. "Will you look at that! It was practically a somersault there."

Laure grunted. "Normally it's the woman who talks after sex while the man snores himself senseless."

"I'm in touch with my feminine side, me." The gymnastic display had become frantic. "Uh-oh, I'm not sure the little person liked that shag," continued Dan.

"But I did."

Now little feet were beating a tattoo against her flank. "Doesn't it hurt?" asked Dan.

"Not at all."

The right foot was still unvarnished when Jack was born twelve hours later and turned their world inside out.

CHAPTER THREE

DAN

"Likely to be late, is he?" asked Dan as he shuffled dishes in front of the oven.

"I doubt it," said Laure.

They were having Sanjay and his girlfriend, plus Eliot and his lodger Daisy.

The dinner party was all Dan's fault. "You know what your trouble is?" he'd told Laure one morning when she was feeding Jack. "You don't see enough people."

"I see lots of people."

That was arrant nonsense. Good word, *arrant*. "I'm not counting the health visitor and the mums at toddler group. Which you hardly ever go to."

"That's because I don't want Jack to catch all those viruses." By which she meant every single virus in existence, and then some.

"Let's have people to dinner. Soon. I'll cook." He wouldn't just cook. He'd take care of the menu, the shopping, the lot. Didn't often cook at home. This would be great. There were dishes that could be served on a big wooden board. Maybe something topped with thinly sliced roast beef. Or carpaccio of salmon. People would help themselves. With fingers if necessary. Helped break the ice.

"What about the cost?" Laure had asked.

"Don't worry. I know where to shop."

"Who would we invite?" she asked.

"All your ex-boyfriends of course. Have we got enough chairs?" It was a joke. Not a very good one, granted. "Sorry. We could invite the neighbours."

"Oh, God, not the Freemans. They're odious."

"Not the Freemans. I was thinking of Eliot, and that flatmate of his, what's her name." Eliot was gay, so no threat there. And the lodger was well fit.

Laure said she wanted to ask Sanjay as well, along with his partner Harriet.

"Who's Sanjay?"

Laure explained over a nappy change. Turned out she and Sanjay had been an item years and years ago, before her job in The Hague. Long before she and Dan had even met, but still. Wasn't a good thing.

"Why?" Dan asked.

"Why what?"

"Why would you want to invite him?"

She picked up Jack and plopped the nappy sack and contents into the bin before answering. "Sanjay's a nice guy. And he's funny. You'd like him."

That sounded pretty unlikely to Dan. The whole idea began to stink like a nappy.

"He was at speed-dating the night we met, two years ago. And he's only got one testicle," Laure added. As if that was supposed to make him harmless.

Dan couldn't remember him from the Jacaranda bar, and didn't even want to know why he'd only got one ball. Not his circus, not his monkeys. But Laure told him anyway. Long story about a misdiagnosis. He'd been treated for cancer with surgery and everything. Then the doctors figured he'd had TB all along, not cancer.

Sounded a bit unlikely. Perhaps she just wanted to make him feel sorry for the guy.

Well, not going to happen. Arrantly.

While Dan got dressed for work, she jawed on about Sanjay and his fundraising job with some wonderful charity for kids, and his girlfriend Harriet who was a freelance journalist, and how they had meet speed-dating too, and had been an item about the same length of time he and Laure had been together, and they were totally loved-up and everything.

It irritated the crap out of him. It also reminded him that Laure had been a hot-shot international lawyer, while he, Dan, was an uneducated fella who'd been in jail and now had a job in a kitchen. A kitchen in Lolo's Restaurant in Hampstead Village, no less. But a kitchen all the same.

They ended up inviting Sanjay to their first dinner since the baby was born. Dan could see that would lead to trouble. He just didn't know what kind.

"That's the door now," said Laure. "I'll get it."

HARRIET

Across the table and the tea lights, Sanjay looked so hot, exactly like that Indian film star people raved about. Armaan Kirmani. That was it.

Want the recipe for a perfect dinner party? You can't go wrong by dimming the lights. Candlelight creates an atmosphere that soothes the senses and adds a hint of romance, especially if you choose the right scents.

Nobody had asked Harriet to write a feature on dinner

parties. There had been few commissions of any sort lately, but that didn't stop intros breezing into her head. She paused from her mental composition to drain her glass. Dan passed behind her and refilled it immediately.

The flickering flames and the two glasses of Merlot she'd had so far were enough to convince Harriet that she had everything she'd ever wanted, apart from a steady income. So what if she and Sanjay sometimes had differences of opinion? He was funny and kind as well as good-looking. No wonder she'd fallen for him even when he'd been really ill at the time.

Thank you, God. Harriet wasn't sure she believed in God, but she might need to revise her opinion, seeing as He'd given Sanjay new life and all.

Harriet beamed across the table at nobody in particular.

It was a little weird being at Sanjay's ex's for dinner, but that relationship was totally in the past. Now Laure had someone else. She even had a baby that clung to her like a barnacle. Harriet could barely imagine Laure and Sanjay together.

Laure. Pronounced *law*, Sanjay had said. It was the French version of *Laura*.

Here was French Laura breastfeeding again, with her baby's long legs stretched out towards the dining table. Harriet didn't know much about babies, but at that age weren't they meant to eat from a bowl or something?

The other two people at dinner weren't a couple. Daisy had just shimmied back in, enveloped in a haze of expensive perfume. She went out to vape almost as often as Laure fed her baby. Daisy was this über-glamorous woman who managed to look super cool despite it being the hottest day for ten years. She lived with Eliot, next door but one to Dan and Laure, and she said she was an actor. A lot of people said that. Didn't mean they did any acting.

Right now Daisy was talking to Sanjay. Harriet hoped to God he wouldn't tell her all about his testicles.

That left Harriet with Eliot who would have been a dish if he gave up gurning. He said he worked in commodities.

"So is that Eliot with two Ls?" She couldn't think of anything to say about commodities.

Eliot pulled a face. "One L, two Ts, at least on my passport. Trust my parents not to realize it's an anagram of *toilet*. That's why I spell it with one T. Like TS Eliot."

"Good thinking," said Harriet.

Eliot grinned and stuffed the rest of his bread roll into his mouth.

The starter had been fabulous, especially the carpaccio thing. Well, Laure's partner Dan did work in a trendy restaurant. Maybe one day Harriet could afford to eat there.

Laure wasn't helping with the meal at all. She was sitting with her hair draped across her face, clutching the baby as if her life depended on it. She had barely let go of the little mite all evening. Was this a dinner or an NCT meeting?

Harriet got up to see if she could give Dan a hand in the kitchen.

"Nah. I'm OK, thanks." He shooed her out with a smile and an oven mitt.

SANJAY

Sanjay refilled Daisy's glass as soon as she sat down. "Are you a model?"

She placed an elbow on the table and faced him full on. "I'm an actor."

"Wow. Would I have seen you in anything?" He knew he came across as a flirt. Harmless, though.

"I've been in *Holby City* twice, though you'd have to be very observant indeed to spot me." She took a sip of Merlot and licked her lips. "They were non-speaking parts."

"I'm very observant." He beamed. "Not of Hinduism though."

"As a matter of fact, most of the time I work in a real hospital. With medical students."

"Wow," Sanjay said again.

It turned out that Daisy did what she called simulated consultations, with doctors-to-be quizzing her and trying out their interview skills. "They get it wrong quite a lot," she added.

Adele was letting rip from the speakers behind them. Sanjay wasn't a big fan. On the plus side, *Rolling in the Deep* meant he had to lean in to hear what Daisy was saying.

"Last week I played a woman with appendicitis, and two of the students sent me home with just a prescription for painkillers."

Sanjay nodded. "I can believe that. Good job you didn't really have appendicitis."

"They didn't even ask to examine me," she continued with disdain in her voice.

"They examine you?" Medical school sounded a lot of fun.

She shook her magnificent head, sending her tight curls dancing. "No. I have a slip of paper in my pocket with the appropriate examination findings. So when a student wants to examine me, I hand over the paper."

Sanjay wasn't surprised medical students got things wrong. Fully-fledged doctors did too. Before he knew it, he was telling Daisy about how his TB had been misdiagnosed as cancer, and all the hassle it had caused. It was her fault that he ended up telling her he felt he should now make the most of life. She encouraged him by nodding a lot, which made her earrings and her dark curls quiver. Every so often she came out with, "Oh my God!" Her generous mouth was most delectable when she used long words. He willed her to say *simulated consultations* or *testicular cancer* again, but she didn't, so he looked at her blouse instead.

"Have you got survivor issues?" she asked.

"I don't think so," replied Sanjay. He wasn't sure what he had, apart from all kinds of expectations. When told he didn't have cancer, the extra years felt like a precious gift. Turned out that his new life was very like his old life, but with a plastic testicle.

HARRIET

Oh God, thought Harriet. Now he was telling her all about his testicles. Had the man no shame? He was clearly pissed. Asians really shouldn't drink. They had no head for booze, especially in this weather.

Harriet turned to Eliot who was grimacing at his spoon. His random facial movements were a bit off-putting, but who else was there to flirt with? She twiddled a lock of hair as suggestively as she knew how and asked, "Have you lived in Hampstead long?"

He sucked his teeth. "Three years."

They compared noted on their favourite places, like the Hampstead Providore in Rosslyn Hill. Talk inevitably turned to the sweltering heat and the bathing ponds on Hampstead Heath. They were normally far too cold except for the hardiest souls, but Harriet declared she was tempted to cast caution and clothes to the wind and throw herself into the water.

Trouble was, Sanjay didn't look in the least perturbed, let alone jealous. Not even when she fed Eliot a grape from her salad. Maybe Eliot could have looked a bit more interested too.

"Who do you write for?" Eliot asked.

"I'm freelance, but I do a lot for *RightHere!* magazine."

"Never heard of them," said Eliot.

"It's a lifestyle title. But I write features for anyone who'll pay me." That was getting harder and harder. As old publications closed down, new ones sprung up but never quite took their place. Last week one of them had offered her a regular column before saying they had no budget but the exposure would be great. As if exposure would pay the looming rent demand. "I'm also writing a novel," Harriet added. Maybe saying it more often would actually make her book happen, beyond the ten thousand or so words she had written and re-written so far.

"Oh, right," said Eliot. Instead of asking what her novel was about, he said NW3 was crawling with writers, like that clever chap Ben Macintyre.

Harriet remembered with a pang that Macintyre was a serious author and journalist, not the kind who lived hand-to-mouth by writing lifestyle features.

Now Dan was struggling in the kitchen with coffee cups. Harriet got up to give him a hand.

"Thanks." He passed her a tray. "You know what else you could help me with? I need a new word."

"A new word?"

"Yep. Every day I have a word of the day." He dropped a clutch of spoons on the tray. "Thought you'd be able to suggest one. Seeing as you're a writer and all."

"*Every* day?" This was bizarre.

"Yeah. I usually get one out of a dictionary. Helps me speak better."

"I don't think I use that many new words," reflected Harriet. "I just look for new ways of putting old words together and turning them into cash."

"I get you," said Dan. "We all need recipes for money."

She leaned against the doorframe with the tray. "Well, I do have a word for you. *Harbinger*." It was the first word that came to mind, without a thought for its significance.

He tried it out. "*Harbinger*. What does it mean?"

"It's kind of a warning. A signal that tells you something is on its way."

"Right. I'll use that one. If I remember it."

"*Harbinger*," Harriet repeated as she took in the tray. "Begins with an H, like *Harriet*. You'll remember it."

This time Laure got up to breastfeed in the armchair. It must have been a whole thirty minutes since Jack's last feed. Sanjay swivelled round to watch, his eyes on stalks.

SANJAY

Hell, he didn't recall Laure's boobs ever being like this. She used to go from shop to shop to find a bra delicate enough and small enough. Now they had obviously escaped and found a life of their own.

"You can climb up over the 02," Dan was saying. He removed the tea towel from his shoulder and draped it over the back of the chair as he set himself down the other side of Daisy.

"I believe so," said Daisy. "But I've not done it yet. Have you?"

"Nope," said Sanjay.

"You can also get a cable car from Royal Victoria Docks." Dan wiped his brow with his sleeve. "I'd like to do that, but there's never enough time."

Eliot wanted to go up the Shard building soon, and Daisy said she too spent so much time working that she never got around to doing half the things she wanted.

Sanjay nodded. When he'd got healthy again, he figured he'd get around to doing loads of stuff, including visiting bits of London he'd never seen before. Somehow he'd never done half those things.

Now Daisy was on her way outside to vape again.

"Why don't you stay here? It's only an e-cig," Sanjay said.

"I need some air," said Daisy.

HARRIET

Those wine glasses were huge. And the pictures on the wall were crooked. They were also moving diagonally every time she blinked.

"Sanjay," she said experimentally. Her tongue had grown too big for her mouth.

Sanjay ignored her, and she didn't dare try any louder. A thin breeze came through the open window, but it did little to cool her down, improve her vision, or help her speech.

Dan had gone to the kitchen for liqueurs, leaving Sanjay talking to the actress woman again, hanging onto her every word. Did he realize how stupid it made him look?

"Food bank use has risen nearly three-fold in a year," Daisy was saying. Even at this stage of the evening she looked amazing, in a way that Harriet never did. Her halo of hair, her perfume, her ivory silk shirt nonchalantly unbuttoned just so. Whenever Harriet wore a shirt like that, she had to check constantly to make sure her bra wasn't showing.

"It's a disgrace," replied Sanjay. "So many kids below the poverty line." He would say that, seeing as he worked with a children's charity, but it didn't half make him sound saintly.

Eliot contorted his lips in agreement while Harriet kept quiet. She knew nothing about food banks, and, even if she did, she doubted she could have voiced it without her tongue misbehaving.

"They barely existed in this country until the recession in 2008," said Daisy, waving one hand in a perfectly thespian style.

Sanjay nodded, practically drooling.

Harriet had to get a message to him. He'd ignored her semaphoring with her eyebrows. This left her with no other choice.

She grabbed her bag and picked her way to the bathroom across the undulating floor, using the wall to steady herself. She hadn't had that much to drink, surely. It was just that it was late. And she didn't know the way.

She suppressed a hiccup and located the bathroom.

Its shelves were laden with potions. The only time Harriet ever had nice toiletries was when she'd got a load of freebies for a feature on Christmas presents. Actually, Rudolf bubble bath wasn't that nice.

She sat down and texted Sanjay. *Youre being a prat.*

He was probably going to be even more of a prat and read it out loud as he usually did, but she risked it anyway.

Her handbag responded with a familiar ping. Oh, crap. She'd forgotten he'd put his iPhone in there earlier.

Looking in the mirror, she saw that she was shiny with sweat and had red wine mouth.

What were you supposed to do for red wine mouth? She cast her mind back to a feature she'd written on exactly that. Drink white instead. Use a straw. Prep your lips with gloss. All things to prevent this gruesome look, not cure it.

She grabbed a make-up wipe from the shelf and rubbed until the purple colour began to fade from her lips. It made her mouth bloody sore, though.

Back in the dining room, the conversation had moved on, to what topic Harriet had no idea. Laure must have got the baby to bed, because there she was at the table, joining in for a change.

Eliot had become animated. "Let me just finish my sentence first."

"Well, I think you just need to decide which is most important," said Laure. "Economic stability, or welfare."

Daisy stuck out her chin. "But you said right at the start—"

It was getting bad-tempered. The booze, thought Harriet. Or else the other problem. Whenever there were six or more people gathered around a dinner table, it was a dead cert that at least one of them didn't want to be there.

Harriet very much wanted to be there. She just wished she felt less out of place.

CHAPTER FOUR

DAN

Dan peeled off a sock. "How do you think that went?"

Jack had woken up so there was Laure, feeding him again. She didn't answer right away because she had to rearrange Jack's mouth. Although by now the lad should have got the hang of nipples. In fact he should have progressed to drinking out of a pint glass, in Dan's opinion.

"It was excellent," she said finally. "And that's an understatement."

Dan dumped his socks in the basket. "What about the sweet potatoes with harissa? They weren't too spicy for a hot night?"

"They were perfect. Can you pass me a nappy?" She hadn't bothered to tuck the discarded tit back into her blouse.

He wondered fleetingly what she would do if he lunged at her with a hungry mouth. "And the timbale? You didn't think it was a little too much having beef with it?"

She looked up briefly. "Dan, if I didn't know any better, I'd suspect you of being gay."

"Thought you'd be relieved if I went over to the other side." As soon as the words were out, he regretted it. Him and his big mouth.

"Don't be silly. I love it that you love me, even looking like this."

Yeah, he still loved her. And she still had it. Tonight she was looking better than she had for ages. She'd done her hair all smooth, the only way she was happy with it, though now it had gone frizzy again. Probably the heat. She moaned that her highlights needed doing, but said that took over two hours at the hairdresser's and she didn't like leaving Jack that long with anyone.

Dan must have paused a tad too long before saying, "Of course," because she then asked, "You do love me, don't you?"

By way of response he kissed the top of her head. "What do you think?"

"You did look down Daisy's front quite a lot tonight."

"I did not look down her front. I have no interest in her. Not at all." How could it hurt just to look?

"That's not what it looked like from where I was sitting," she pointed out.

Now she was changing Jack's whiffy nappy on the bed. Jack wriggled and threatened to crawl away. Dan couldn't help noticing that her boobs had popped out again of their own accord. One nipple brushed against the baby's shoulder when she bent over him.

She used to do that to him. Back in the day.

"Well, you're wrong," he said. "Besides, you've got much nicer boobs." Fuck. That was stupid. As he realized immediately.

Predictably, Laure said right away, "So you did notice her boobs then?" She dumped the stink-bomb into one of those scented nappy sacks and knotted it with a triumphant flourish.

The issue of Daisy's cleavage apart, the evening had gone well. Everyone liked the food. He didn't remember Harriet from speed-dating two years ago, but he must have met her. She seemed nice, a bit ditzy. As usual, Eliot was strange, but Sanjay seemed a good guy. Dan could see himself liking him, despite every intention not to. He reminded Dan of someone decent from his time in prison. It was the screw who'd helped sort out the injury to his hand. And the only screw who actually believed Dan was innocent. You didn't forget the good things that happened inside. Those were few and far between.

"Let me put Jack to bed," said Dan. "I've hardly spent any time with him today."

He loved holding Jack like this, especially when the little lad was sleepy and happy. Best feeling in the world.

HARRIET

Shelley made a fuss over Sanjay, twisting herself round his legs as soon as they were through the door of his flat. Harriet loved Shelley, but she was basically a one-man cat.

Her welcome ritual was unchanging. Shelley meowed when Sanjay appeared, wound herself round him leaving copious amounts of black, ginger, and white fur, then showed how long she was by standing on her back legs and pawing the edge of the counter until she got a full bowl of whatever her latest favourite food was.

"Eliot was cute," said Harriet as she scooped a string of new lumps out of the cat tray and flushed them away. It was neither her flat nor her cat, but that didn't matter. A little unsteady, Harriet stood up and made for the kitchen. When she'd downed an ibuprofen and two glasses of water, she said again, "Eliot was cute."

Sanjay flopped onto the sofa and removed his shoes. "Not my type. Or yours, obviously."

"What do you mean, 'not my type'?" She installed herself next to him and let her body sag. "He's a very good-looking man."

"He's gay."

Her eyes widened. "He is not!" Although that might have explained why he barely batted an eyelid when she fed him fruit salad, or when she let her hand rest on his knee while she told a joke.

"Harriet, he was wearing make-up. Case closed."

"Hasn't he just got very dark lashes?"

Sanjay gave a snort. "He's as gay as the gayest waiter in the gayest bar we went to in Barcelona."

Barcelona. Just over two years ago, and the most incredible weekend of Harriet's life. She'd escaped with Sanjay, even though they'd only just met. It had been the best and most significant sex of all. If she shut her eyes, she could be there again any time she wanted. The trouble was that she had to open her eyes again eventually.

"I'm sure there was cauliflower in the timbale," said Sanjay, stroking Shelley who had just landed on his lap with a chirrup.

"Do you think so?" said Harriet as she removed a sandal.

"It was disgusting. I've always hated cauliflower," he said. "Even in my mum's bhaji."

"I thought the food was amazing. I've never had carpaccio like that. He'd made the bread himself too."

"How hard can that be? You don't exactly need a degree to make bread."

This wasn't going the way she'd hoped. "So you only value things that require a degree?" Sanjay was just a snob after all, like every other Oxford graduate who made her feel inadequate.

"I don't mean it like that. Just saying he's not exactly Hampstead's answer to Jamie Oliver."

"Well. Daisy seemed nice," said Harriet, thinking the exact opposite.

"Did she? I hadn't noticed."

"Yes, you did. You barely took your eyes off her all evening. I've never seen anyone so enthralled."

"She's very interesting as a person," he protested.

"I didn't really get a chance to talk to her. What makes her so interesting?" Apart from the luscious lips, doe eyes, and pert bosoms.

"She helps train doctors," Sanjay said.

Probably in mouth-to-mouth, thought Harriet. "Oh yes? What does she do?"

"She does role play."

Harriet sipped more water. "Doesn't every actor do role play?"

"She does patient role play. Consultation scenarios, they're called. There's a bunch of actors who go round medical schools, and they play at being patients. The students do a simulated consultation."

"Right. So they practise on her." Did they undress her as well?

"It's better than practising on real patients, isn't it?" A vein stood up on Sanjay's forehead. "If the doctors who'd looked after me had had better training, maybe they'd have got it right a lot sooner."

Safer to change the subject. "Laure wasn't really what I expected."

"God, this is wringing wet," said Sanjay, taking his shirt off. "I can't believe how hot that flat was."

"Let it dry out before putting it in the linen basket then." She paused. "Laure wasn't very talkative." Harriet had expected to be in awe of her, but Laure wasn't like a high-flying lawyer at all. Just a mum who couldn't get her baby to bed.

"She was probably tired. Don't read too much into things, Harriet. You have a very active imagination. But then of course you *are* a writer," he finished with a grin.

That was exactly what she wanted to be. A writer. A successful one. "You're right." Harriet smiled back and decided not to stir up trouble. She was a writer, and one day she'd be a published author. Of actual books, not forgettable features on keeping that holiday feeling alive.

She loved sex in the heat, and it was she, not Daisy or anyone else, who was about to get into bed with her gorgeous man on a sweltering summer night.

Harriet closed her eyes and grabbed Sanjay's neck to give him a long passionate kiss, complete with Merlot, carpaccio, and even cauliflower, for all her tongue was worth.

CHAPTER FIVE

KAREN

"They've all gone," said Footie Dad. "Want to feel my dick?"

Her hand was there already through his flimsy shorts. Damp nylon kit was hardly a fashion statement, but so what? In a moment it would be round his ankles.

She swept a stray shin pad onto the floor and pushed him onto the bench.

"Treat me gently," he said. "I've got footballer's groin."

"No you haven't."

"You're so fierce. Like a tigress."

"Mrowr," obliged Karen. She'd never have believed she'd ever say anything that corny, but it seemed to spur him on, which, considering it was four fifty-three, was exactly what was needed.

The front of his shirt was dripping with Brut and sweat, and its logo was peeling. Someone must have ironed it. The bench rocked back and forth, scraping the tiles. From the floor his mobile rang, emitting the theme from *Dr Who*. He ignored it.

Karen's neighbour Rose maintained that women differed from men. They both wanted sex just as much, until there wasn't any. In times of drought, Rose said, women managed just fine without.

Rose's theory was wrong, reckoned Karen, digging her fingernails into Footie Dad's arms. She had to have this, as empty as it was. She just had to, she thought as a wave of flame engulfed her, fiercer than any of her hot flushes. Was there a fire extinguisher in here at all?

"That was some fuck," he remarked as he pulled his shorts up. He didn't need to do his trainers up as he hadn't bothered to take them off. "See you next week?"

"Sure."

Back home, Damon had already let himself in with his newly acquired key, and was at the kitchen table, apparently engrossed in a book. Karen suspected he'd been on his computer game until he heard her at the door.

Charlotte sat on the stairs, a phone glued to her ear. She was twelve, so that was probably how her ear would look from now on. Karen said, "Hi," and Charlotte lazily waved an arm in response. Probably how that was going to be from now on too.

Karen put a large cupful of lentils on to boil. They were nourishing and cheap, unless you got conned into buying those ridiculously over-priced Puy lentils. The bake would be ready by the time Ashley came back from his friend's, where he always went after Sunday football.

Rose was already at the gate with Edward. Through the kitchen window she could see her youngest stumbling up the garden path, complete with Mister Cow under his arm even though he was in Year Two now.

"Mummy!" he shrieked as he crashed into the hall. "Need a wee-wee!"

"Well, go on. You know where the toilet is."

Of course Edward knew. Didn't mean he always used the toilet though. Sometimes he tried to pee on the carpet and had to be reminded that six-year olds didn't do this.

"Thanks so much, Rose. I owe you."

"No problem. It's a madhouse out on the roads today. Got any tomato paste I can borrow?"

Karen located a much battered tube in the depths of a cupboard. "Here you go."

Damon eyed his dinner plate. "What's this?" he said, using his knife to poke at the edge of the crispy potato topping.

"Lentil surprise," Karen lied. Lentils were hardly a surprise anymore. She'd made lentil bake many times before, only this one was minus the tomato paste that she'd lent to Rose.

"Mu-um!" Charlotte looked as if she was about to cry.

Edward was feeding bits of lentil bake to Mister Cow. Ashley was silent, obviously plotting something. The scheming powers of a seven-year old were not to be underestimated.

"I'll make something nice tomorrow night," she promised. She was pretty sure she'd said that last night.

"Can you make *carfoolay*? Belinda's mum makes *carfoolay*."

Damon gave up prodding his dinner. "Who here knows how many teeth a crocodile has?"

Edward looked up. "What's *carfoolay*?"

"I've been thinking," Ashley piped up. "Why don't they build car parks on top of towers? That would save space on the ground."

"Go on. How many teeth? Just guess," said Damon.

"*Carfoolay* is really lovely. Belinda's mum puts vegetarian sausage in it."

"I'm going to guess eighty teeth," Karen offered.

Damon snorted. "Course not."

"WHAT'S *CARFOOLAY*?" yelled Edward as he kicked the table.

The penny dropped. "*Cassoulet*," said Karen. "I made it for you once." As they had barely touched it, it had been a complete waste of five hours, not including soaking the haricot beans.

"It's different when Belinda's mum makes it," said Charlotte.

"It would save a LOT of space on the ground. Then you could build another football pitch."

"Sixty-eight teeth." There was triumph in Damon's voice. "And none of you knew."

Mister Cow had finished and now Edward was busy lining up lentils on the edge of the plate again.

"I could get the recipe from Belinda's mum," said Charlotte.

Something was bothering Ashley. "Who counted all the teeth? Because someone must have had to hold the crocodile's mouth open while another person counted them."

"Duh, door-brain! They probably killed the crocodile first," said Damon.

"That's horrible," said Charlotte. She said that a lot since she'd turned vegetarian.

"How did they kill it? With a spear?" asked Ashley. "Or with a laser gun?"

"Please try to eat up."

"Did they just shoot it? Or maybe they used a poison dart."

Karen asked brightly, "Now, what shall we have tomorrow evening?"

"Chocolate soup!" shouted Edward.

"Cassoulet," said Charlotte. "Belinda's mum can email you the recipe."

Ashley asked, "I wonder what they did after they killed the crocodile and counted its teeth?"

"Probably made a handbag," said Damon.

"Crocodile soup!" shouted Edward.

Damn heat. Another hot flush was on its way, and she wasn't even forty yet. Karen stood at the sink and ran cold water over her arms. It sometimes helped, but it didn't prevent the flushes. She just hoped she wouldn't get them at school next term, when she'd have a whole class of six-year olds to contain.

GEOFF

Today the first patient complained of a cold.

"There's nothing worse than a summer cold," she told Geoff.

Typhoid, polio, and pancreatic cancer all came to mind, as did visions of young life ebbing away while blood spilled out onto remnants of uniform. "Hmm," said Geoff.

The second patient had spots. On his dick, no less.

Geoff sighed. His female colleagues were mostly spared such symptoms. On the other hand, they saw all the patients with vaginal discharge, which was arguably worse because they took longer to undress. Whereas Spotted Dick here could simply whip out the offending member. As indeed he just had.

Geoff appraised the sorry looking todger.

He had chosen medicine to save lives, to be respected and valued, and obviously to get lots of sex as well. Sadly, all that was hardly going to happen to a GP in North West London, especially a GP with erectile dysfunction.

Geoff sighed as he peeled off his disposable gloves and dropped them into the bin. "You need the GUM clinic," he said.

"Eh? Nuffink wrong with me gums."

"I mean the sexual health clinic. GUM is short for geni-to-urinary medicine. Sorry, should have explained."

"Can't you just give me some jollop to dip it in, like?"

Geoff shook his head. "'Fraid not. You've already dipped your wick. Now you've got to pay for the oil."

The patient's blank face morphed into fear. "You won't tell the missus, will ya, doc?"

Geoff looked the patient in the eyes. "I won't, for now. But you must go to the clinic. And until you do, make sure you use condoms."

Spotted Dick pulled a face.

"It's to protect her," said Geoff. He didn't add 'from your

fucking stupidity'. "If you don't, I might have to tell her. Hang on a minute."

Geoff went and got the patient a handful of condoms from the supply in the nurse's room, though it was futile. The man would never use them.

Geoff shoved a few spare condoms in his own pocket. You never knew.

DAN

While walking home from the restaurant, he thought about Laure. Looking forward to seeing her like he'd been alone for a month in the desert. Which was pretty much right after five consecutive days of temperatures over thirty Celsius. Even now, at gone two in the morning, the air was baking and hot blood coursed through his veins. Probably his arteries too. He'd read that in a book.

The bedroom was dark. And quiet. Dan crept in, taking care not to bump into the cot. Or let his belt buckle make a clank as it hit the floor. Or breathe too noisily. Or anything.

On the one hand, he would have liked Jack to be awake, so he could see him. On the other hand, Dan hoped he'd be asleep, so he could catch some much-needed zeds.

Now that he was by the bed, he could see they were both asleep. Deeply asleep. Jack wasn't in the cot, but snuggled up against Laure in the crook of her arm.

He could smell her scent. The scent that always did it for him, even if he couldn't describe it. He caressed her arm lightly.

She pushed him away, muttering about snatching a couple of hours. "Can you put Jack in the cot please?"

"Sure." He picked Jack up gently, arranged him in his cot, and got back to his own bed. Jack hadn't stirred.

Dan lay there for a bit, eyes wide open, thinking. It was nearly three o'clock in the morning.

He got up slowly and tiptoed out of the room.

It was in the kitchen, right where he'd left it the last time he'd used it. High up so Jack couldn't reach it. He installed himself at the kitchen counter, plugged it in, switched it on, and Googled *postnatal lost sex drive*.

Loss of libido, he read as he idly scratched himself, was a widespread problem after having a baby. There was a whole range of reasons including vaginal dryness, tightness, irritation or bleeding, depression, and fear of pregnancy.

Was Laure worried about another pregnancy? She shouldn't be. She was still taking those pills, the ones that were OK if you were breastfeeding.

Here were some stats. Over four-fifths of first-time mothers had sexual issues three months after giving birth.

He paused to rearrange his sac. It had been nearly a year with Laure. That was the same as about half of all women. Lots of them wanted help with this, but didn't ask.

Why not? That was dumb.

Now here was something interesting. He stared at the screen. Mums who breastfed were more likely to have a low sex drive than those who bottle fed.

Fuck! Dan snapped the laptop shut. He couldn't in a million years imagine Laure giving up breastfeeding.

CHAPTER SIX

GEOFF

When it came to Daisy, Geoff's diagnostic skills deserted him. All he knew was that she was a high-end fuck. Those legs. That magnificent arse. The knowing smile that whispered 'silk sheets'.

Not that she'd actually said anything about sheets. The first thing Daisy said directly to him was, "Are you going to offer me a lift?"

This came right at the end of the teaching session while he was perched on a wonky chair, marking his students' attendance sheets and scoring their consultation skills in the workshop.

Geoff enjoyed Wednesdays, teaching medical students at the hospital. He also enjoyed watching Daisy, the newest and most entrancing of the troupe of actors.

Geoff had trouble with names, which was a shame as there was a new crop of students every week. The line-up, however, was pretty much constant. There'd be at least one swot from France, Germany, or Hong Kong, a student in a hijab, a gay man, a babe who fiddled constantly with her iPhone, a stroppy leftie, and a home-grown rugger bugger who kept fidgeting because he was too big for the chair. Sometimes there was also the son or daughter of an eminent consultant. Those often had most to learn.

Geoff was in the corridor marking the last student when Daisy touched his arm and asked, "Are you going to offer me a lift?"

Of course he was.

"It's cold," she said as soon as she got into his Toyota even though his dashboard showed twenty-one Celsius. That alone should have told Geoff she was trouble, but his ears weren't doing the listening.

She rolled down her sleeves and shivered. As Geoff engaged reverse gear, he caught a glimpse of something ornate and provocative beneath her blouse, probably from Victoria's Secret. Pale green looked amazing on her dark skin.

He drove out of the car park and into the main road. "Where are you going?" he asked, somewhat belatedly.

"To see my agent." She didn't actually say where, just that he could drop her off near where he lived. That was the second warning that Geoff didn't hear.

Daisy did other 'bits and pieces', as she called it, but she said she liked medical role play the best.

"What did you think of the students today?" he asked.

She fanned out her toes and studied them before answering. He couldn't resist a glance as he turned left. She was wearing strappy sandals and her toenails were painted light green. He thought of her bra.

"Well," she said. "That Asma should do something about her spots."

Was that all? "What did you think of the group as a whole? I thought the second lot were pretty keen but they were a bit slow to pick up on domestic violence."

She shrugged.

"I mean, the patient practically gifted them the information that her husband went wild every night when he drank."

"They were OK."

"You're not getting it," Geoff said. But she very much was. Or rather she was about to.

Geoff didn't learn where Daisy's agent worked, but it turned out that the agent could wait a little longer. She accepted the offer of a coffee with Geoff first.

As he boiled the kettle and fiddled with the mugs, she leaned in the kitchen doorway, licking her top lip. You didn't have to be a mind-reader to work that one out.

He handed her the coffee. She was already perilously close, her scent musky and dangerous. Fleetingly, Geoff thought of the experimental psychology course he'd done as an undergraduate. This was the classic approach-approach situation. Once the lab rat noticed the food, there was no going back.

She put the mug down on the sideboard. The musky smell intensified as she closed in, her eyes wide, her lips slightly parted. Could he delay her for just one hour without losing her altogether?

"I've got to pop back to my consulting room," he said. "Only an hour, though. What are you doing later?"

She gave a knowing smile, showing perfect teeth. "Have I scared you off?"

He studied the life in those abundant lips, imagining how they would feel around him. Perhaps he wouldn't need those little tablets. But he couldn't take the risk.

"Do I look scared?" he countered. To prove his macho credentials, he could have bragged about having worked in a war zone, dealing with a relentless tide of major trauma, greater than in any other hospital in the world. But the truth was that, like every male, he was petrified of failure.

Once he'd started using sildenafil, there was no knowing if he could manage without. Mr Wibbly Wobbly was an erratic fellow. In Bastion, there'd been more than one occasion when Mr WW had stood to attention on only the slightest provocation.

As he recalled, one time he'd been discussing the merits and demerits of frozen yoghurt with one of the female reserves.

Daisy said it was fine by her if he needed to go back to the office. She'd return in an hour and a half, tops. Off she waltzed, green toenails and all.

It had been nearly three hours and she still hadn't reappeared. He went to the window, looked up and down the road, checked his watch again.

He had taken 100mg, so he now had a headache, sore eyes, a blocked nose, and leg cramps.

He didn't have a hard-on yet. That was the great thing about PDE-5 inhibitors, he reflected as he checked the road again. They only worked if you were turned on. Unlike, say, the intracavernosal injections that some of his patients needed to give themselves.

As Geoff waited, he passed the time imagining himself standing by this window with an absolute lamppost of a hard-on caused not by the prospect of an imminent screw but by a little syringe secreted in the bathroom cabinet. It was a good job he didn't have one, because a gaggle of young mums with pushchairs went by just then.

"Ready to roger," he said to no one in particular. "Now don't let me down, boy," he added for Mr Wibbly Wobbly's benefit.

As Daisy still hadn't showed, he turned his mind to Mrs Thing who'd consulted him the previous day with the most impressive Baker's cyst he had ever seen. She'd had knee trouble for years and just got on with it, till the day this massive balloon appeared behind her knee.

Geoff filled in time by beginning an online module on arthritis of the knee. The work could be saved as soon as Daisy appeared.

Forty-five minutes later he'd reached the end of the module, scored ninety-eight per cent on the post-module quiz, and printed his certificate. His face was flushed, his nose needed a re-bore, and his head was pounding like a steam hammer.

Daisy still hadn't returned.

She turned up at half past four, seemingly stoned. Her first words were, "What have you got to eat?" She could have snorted too, as she was sweaty and making smacking movements. Surprising her pupils were still normal.

Geoff led her into the kitchen where she gorged on stale Ryvita that he had forgotten he had.

"Sorry I was late, by the way," she said through a mouthful. "I was a while with my agent."

"Is your agent a dealer by any chance?"

"What's it to you?" she countered with a stare.

She led him back into the living room, shedding crumbs as she went.

Geoff didn't know what to say or do next, but that didn't matter. She grabbed him by the scrotum and rammed her hot tongue into his mouth. He tasted remnants of Ryvita.

Seconds later she'd ripped his shirt off and pinned him against the sideboard. There was no need to worry about Mr Wibbly Wobbly. He was in pole position, engine throbbing, threatening to overheat.

Seemed she was ready to go too. She undid his trousers and got down on her knees. Mr WW had never had it so good.

She was kneeling in crispbread crumbs but he didn't want her to stop. Now she was making gagging noises. He hoped to God she wasn't going to die. Then, like a woman possessed, she sucked each testicle, almost popping it out of its sac. Only when he thought he would go mad did she finally let go.

"Condoms," he whimpered, afraid he might boil over. They were in his trouser pocket, and the trousers were on the floor.

She waved a finger at him by way of response. When she finally let him go for a moment, he reached for the Mates he'd nicked from the nurse's cupboard. He needn't have worried about fading away while putting on the condom. She studiously helped him roll it on with her mouth.

Two people walked past, as he saw because he hadn't thought to draw the curtains. He inched his way along the sideboard to get out of their line of sight.

Geoff could barely remember the rest of that frantic fuck. Just their bodies seared together, and her writhing pelvis, and the fire and the heat, and his explosion at the end which came just as his neighbour Mrs Whatsit rounded the corner and hove into view.

CHAPTER SEVEN

LAURE

Another stifling evening, and Jack was crying again. Nearly a year old, and she still couldn't read every cry. She sighed, picked him up, and put him to the breast. The left one was nearer her heartbeat. Perhaps that would help.

During pregnancy, there'd been a time when she'd felt calm. A little person was in there, not a test result that could be ignored at will. As he grew, she became aware of his sleep cycle, tuned into his every movement. She felt at one with him and everything he did.

Little Person could hear, and distinguish light from dark through closed eyelids. He, or maybe she, could taste what she ate, because traces of her food passed into the amniotic fluid, to be gulped down when he made swallowing movements. When she ate garlic bread, Little Person ate garlic bread too. Laure knew all of this. Pregnancy and childcare manuals had displaced the shelf-loads of self-help books on moving on from childhood trauma.

Everything was going to be fine. That was the progesterone talking. The books said the hormone had a calming effect. As the books also explained, progesterone levels dropped eventually.

Was that why she was so anxious now?

Jack had finished feeding. She put him in the cot, then went back to bed.

"What happened to you?" asked Dan just after she'd turned out the light. "You used to be so spontaneous."

If by spontaneous he meant leaping into bed with someone you barely knew and spending three days there, then he was right. But she was a grown-up now, and those days were long gone. "How can I be spontaneous when I'm looking after Jack?"

"Jack's spontaneous."

She gave an exasperated sigh. "I'm assuming you don't want me to shit or wee without warning."

"Well. No. That would be a bit of a turn-off. But you could try to relax."

"But there's so much to do." She sat up in bed and reeled off a long list which began with washing, ironing, and cleaning. She left out worrying. That was the main barrier to spontaneity. You couldn't allot two hours for worrying as you could allot two hours to, say, going to the park or doing laundry. Worrying took up increasing amounts of her time. Almost all her waking hours, and some of her sleeping hours too.

At the start of her maternity leave, she assured herself she'd be back very soon. Now she knew she couldn't leave Jack with a nanny and go back to work. Terrible things could happen to a baby.

"Relax," Dan said again.

I am calm. I am serene. All is well, she told herself as she lay down next to him.

DAN

Dan turned on the TV and flicked through the channels. No less than three cookery shows this Saturday morning.

"Please keep it down," said Laure as she went through to the kitchen. "Jack's napping." She nodded her head in the direction of the play mat on the floor where Jack had slumped, exhausted.

"Didn't you say babies could sleep through an earthquake?" Dan said.

"This one can't."

Dan lowered the volume and whizzed through the channels again, finally settling on a programme where a woman was demonstrating how to make choux pastry, following which she promised to take viewers step by step to the perfect zabaglione, a recipe that went back to the sixteenth century yet was still perfect for modern taste buds.

As he watched the zabaglione take shape, Dan picked at a nascent hole in the sofa cover. *Nascent* was a good word when you had a baby in the house. Or a sofa arm that had become threadbare in just two years. All of Laure's things from her old flat in Fulham were here, and some didn't look as smart as they once had. Walls needed a lick of paint too. He couldn't see either Laure or himself finding time for that. Or the money to get someone in.

The nascent zabaglione was coming along nicely now. While she whisked, the presenter bit her lower lip and wondered if she might add a few fresh berries from her garden.

Made no difference what the presenter put in. It was a fact that hardly anyone followed these recipes in their own homes. Takeaways were more popular than ever and restaurant trade was bloody booming. Thankfully, that included Lolo's in Hampstead.

Just how much did these telly chefs make, anyway?

He switched to another channel and watched a sultry woman

talk about her saucy marinades, great bowls of temptation, and the tangy heat that would suffuse into the recipe.

Food porn, they called it. They peddled this stuff to the masses, beaming in dishes to make viewers drool. None of it bore any resemblance to the real thing that punters settled for night after night.

When the saucy bird had finished, a guy with a mallet began bashing a steak to within a centimetre of its life. Pure testosterone, that was. Nothing to do with cooking.

A nascent idea formed in Dan's head.

Fuck it. Make that two nascent ideas.

SANJAY

"That's not the best picture of her. Look, this one is from yesterday morning."

"Aww. She's so pretty, innit," said his sister Sita, as if she'd never seen pictures of Shelley before.

Sanjay's iPhone was bulging with photos of his cat. Just about the first thing he did on getting to thirty-two Cornwall Gardens in Harrow was to show the latest pictures to the family.

"Whoa, cuteness alert!" went Sita. "Is that a toy mouse she's got in her mouth?"

"Yep. She hunts it down, then carries it around the flat. Does that a lot, mostly at night," explained Sanjay.

His mum feigned interest, but cats weren't her thing.

Today Sita wore an understated onesie thing with orange stars all over it. It disguised her spare tyres, but, on the minus side, there was a big star over each of her boobs. It pained Sanjay to see how big they had got. The boobs, not the stars. Although Sita was in her thirties and about a size sixteen, it didn't stop her wearing the least flattering clothes.

Mum was looking her over from her over great height of four feet eleven, finally fixing on the chain around Sita's neck. '*Beti*, why you wear cross when you are Hindu?'

Sita's eyeballs shot up to the ceiling, as if you couldn't expect parents to get fashion.

Mum gave up on her and asked Sanjay, "So tell me, *beta*, how is work?" The Shahs might not have had images of Lakshmi all over their walls, but they still revered wealth, fortune, and prosperity. She and Dad would have preferred Sanjay to be a bit more of a capitalist, or at least to work some place nicer than the tatty Clerkenwell basement occupied by Kids First.

Sanjay nodded. "It's good." Mum didn't need to know about the damage caused by the latest argument between a crack-headed teenager and the charity's front door. She got enough work-related moaning from Dad.

When Dad came in, he collapsed onto the massive leather armchair by the window, holding his head as if words couldn't describe the kind of idiots who worked for him in import-export. He looked properly tired this evening, and his moustache was greyer than Sanjay remembered.

Booze wasn't Dad's thing, but tonight he made an exception. "Day from hell, yar. I am needing drink," he explained as he got up. He located an ancient bottle of tonic water and added the tiniest splash of gin from a bottle normally kept for guests. Every British middle-class family had to have a well-stocked drinks cabinet. It was practically the law.

In point of fact, his parents had excellent and somewhat western taste. Furnished with a large cream sofa that could have been from an Italian showroom, the room had none of the clutter of his friends' parents' homes. The walls were a soothing off-white, there were a couple of tasteful prints as decoration, and the sheesham table was about the only clue to the family's Indian roots.

Sanjay joined Dad in a drink and slumped on the sofa to

listen to his tirade against all bloody fucking numbskulls who made more work for him. It was better than mulling over the situation with Harriet.

As soon as Dad finished, Mum piped up with her equally familiar tale. "Every time I go to GP, he says, 'Mrs Shah, how nice to see you.' What am I supposed to say, har? That it is nice seeing him? It is not nice! Surgery is whole mile away, maybe mile and half from house, and always I have to wait, wait, wait."

Mum paused to let this sink in. "Then he smiles at me. So I must be polite and smile also. But I am not wanting to." At this she did her over-the-top sideways headshake that only Indians could do. "Because my leg is worse. See?"

She rolled up one leg of her salwar. Displaying the evidence was par for the course whenever she told her story, so that all could see for themselves the puffy ankle, the network of little blood vessels, and the scaly red rash which wasn't getting any better. As today, there was invariably an account of the conversation with the GP, even though it was always the same. But the jewel in the crown was how much it hurt, and how it stopped her from walking, sleeping, or doing any of the things that made life worth living.

Probably best not to remind her that his buddy Ben was permanently crippled from an IED.

Dad, who had nearly passed out from his minute dose of alcohol, came to and said, "What did GP give you this time?"

"GP said to me, 'We will try different cream today, shall we?' So I am thinking, my God, maybe my eyes worse than I think! I must look behind me to see who is there, yar. So I look. And there is nobody at all. Who is this 'we'? Nobody else there in consulting room. Just GP and me. Ha!"

They duly laughed.

She pulled down her salwar and rose to go back to the kitchen. "*I* is for one person. *We* is for two or more. Is not rocket salad, ha."

No point telling her.

The pain in her leg notwithstanding, Mum had prepared a traditional dinner that could have fed the whole of Cornwall Gardens. Sanjay forgot all about Harriet as he tucked into his mother's chicken and saag, plus the best daal in town. Mum's cooking was more therapeutic than Nurofen Plus and more addictive than any street drug, which explained why everyone ate till they were as stuffed as a samosa.

Tummy stretched tight, Sanjay helped Sita clear up. Normally it was Dad's job, as befitted the modern male he claimed to be, and actually was. But tonight after dinner, he resumed his place in the armchair and emitted snoring noises.

"So what's up?" asked Sita as Sanjay dried a massive serving dish.

He shrugged by way of response.

"It's Harriet. Am I right, or am I right?"

She was annoyingly right. He resisted the temptation to chuck the tea towel at her and instead picked up a saucepan lid, wiping it with more attention than it needed. Harriet hadn't wanted to move in with him too soon. But now, two years on and in their late thirties, they still lived apart and Sanjay couldn't see how, or if, it was going to progress. Bollocks! He was still as messed up at relationships as a kid. Even though Sita was quizzing him with her eyebrows, he didn't tell her all this. He just shrugged and said, "I don't know. We've just stalled. I'm not even sure we should stay together."

Sita plunged her arms into the sink. "Maybe you need protected time, innit."

"What do you mean?"

She rolled her eyes. "Go away together."

"You're not that stupid after all, are you?"

Sita retaliated with a playful kick to his shin which wasn't really that good-natured.

CHAPTER EIGHT

GEOFF

Geoff beamed at Daisy on the way to the workshop in Room 181. Nothing.

She was preoccupied, he told himself. With actors in short supply today, some of them had several roles. Geoff observed Daisy as she played first a bereaved young mother whose son had been knifed by a gang member, then a woman with schizophrenia.

He smiled at her again after the second role play. She blanked him.

Ah! Maybe she really did have a mental health problem. Bipolar, perhaps. Could explain the sex and drugs.

They'd only done it the once, but he'd replayed that scene in his mind many times over, analyzing it with the same attention to detail he'd given his anatomy dissections for Second MB, though enjoying it far more.

Now he watched her as the bereaved mother again. She switched between roles like a true professional. Which of course she was, but he wasn't planning on saying so for fear of sounding patronizing. All the same, a word of congratulation slipped out at the end of the case.

Daisy's eyes challenged his as she acknowledged him for the first time that morning. "Do you know how deeply patronizing that is?"

Then she took herself off to vape. It was the sign of an addictive personality. Right now, however, Geoff suspected he was the one getting addicted.

He observed her with the next group, playing the schizophrenic woman again. She was flirting with one of the students, crossing and uncrossing her legs with more friction than seemed necessary.

Geoff imagined those long legs around his neck.

The two male students seemed captivated, while the female medics had an air of studied indifference.

"Dr Taylor," said one student, bringing Geoff back into the present. "Do you think I should have asked more questions about her previous history?"

"No, I think prescribing as you did is fine," said Geoff. "Keep the NICE guidelines in mind, of course, but there's no need for further questioning at this stage. You've made your patient another appointment, so you can go into that later."

He watched Daisy as he said all this. She was heading for the door, the scarf she wore over one shoulder trailing behind. He would have winked, if he knew how. Instead he flashed a smile as she brushed past, but she didn't respond. A glimpse suggested she wasn't wearing a bra. Had she gone commando as well?

In the break he touched her elbow. She coolly moved out of the way and continued on her path to the coffee machine.

He went back to his workshop.

"Dr Taylor? I was wondering if..." It was the student who'd spent the first part of the session alternately communing with his mobile and gazing into space.

Geoff responded by taking his own phone out of his pocket and checking his emails.

"Er, Dr Taylor...?"

"What?" Geoff finally looked up. "Did you think I wasn't listening? Well, that is what people tend to assume if you study your phone instead of participating in the discussion."

The student blushed.

Geoff took a moment to drop in on the workshop next door, which a new GP teacher was running. From what he saw in those few minutes, Daisy was pouting rather than grieving. She wasn't playing the bereaved mother at all well now. But then how could she have done? She didn't even have children.

When he got a moment, he found Daisy and said, "If I may pass on some tips for when you next play the battered wife whose child——"

"I never needed such advice in *Holby City.*" There was a petulant cast to her mouth, but at least she'd answered.

"Was it a speaking part?" asked Geoff.

"I had to groan," she replied.

I'll bet, thought Geoff.

"That is not the point," she continued. "You see, Jerry, this is just filling in time for me."

"Filling in time? Is that how you see the job of shaping tomorrow's doctors?" Most irritatingly, she had called him Jerry again. He recalled a particularly sadistic professor from years ago, who habitually misremembered junior doctors' names when she wanted them to feel smaller than they already did.

"I could just as easily be working in Byron Burger, since you ask."

"Then why don't you?"

"There are no vacancies." She gazed at him loftily before swanning off.

He glanced at his watch. Time to go back to the workshop. The fifteen-minute break had gone, yet he hadn't read his emails. There was a message from his ex-wife too, still unreturned: *Tried to call but not urgent. See you on Skype.*

He was just near the lifts, texting Sonya back, when a voice came down the corridor.

"Have you brought your car today, Dr Taylor?" It was Daisy. Of course he had.

She jammed her hand between his legs before they had even left the car park.

LAURE

Laure checked her watch. Was there something wrong with Jack? He never slept for two hours. Perhaps it was the effect of their mammoth outing, she told herself as she willed her breathing to stay slow and steady.

The heat was less oppressive today, so, instead of going to Hampstead Heath, they'd taken the bus to Oxford Street. Jack was enchanted with the ride, the colourful hand rails to grab, and all the people to chatter to. "Kak kak, umm gah?" he'd said to one elderly man whose sour old features instantly transformed into a smile.

In his stripy top and sun hat, Jack drooled at strangers and reached out for their shopping bags, getting plenty of indulgent looks. He also ran his hand along the sides of the seats and then sucked his fingers. Laure got out another baby wipe and gave his hands a clean.

"Dop!" he said when Laure pointed out that they'd reached their stop.

Laure manoeuvred the buggy off the bus, then crossed the street at the lights. "There used to be a pub here," she said, with no expectation of a reply.

"Bub?" went Jack.

The pub had long gone. Now it had as little substance as the pregnancy she had terminated, what, three years ago last Christmas? This was where she'd told Sanjay what she'd done at the horrible clinic in South London. The pub, she saw, had mutated into just another expensive shop on the fringes of New Bond Street.

Laure wondered whether she'd have been less panicky about Jack if she hadn't had that abortion. But she didn't wonder for long. Jack was bashing a toy against the side of the buggy, a clear indication that he was fed up with being stationary on a hot pavement outside a boring building.

"Come on then," she said, turning west.

It was luxuriously cool as soon as they got inside the art deco entrance. She never could resist the lure of Selfridges. Jack, open-mouthed, shared her admiration of its interior.

The fragrance hall was redolent with perfume and filled with shiny products. At the MAC counter, Jack stared at an androgynous assistant posing in front of the lipsticks.

Not so long ago, Laure would have bought whatever she fancied. Today she left without getting anything, not even a new lip gloss, and certainly not magnolia body crème, not at this price. Jo Malone products, however tempting, did not constitute a reason for going back to work. She didn't have much spare cash, but she had something money couldn't buy.

They went to John Lewis where Jack exclaimed at the toys. She bought him another rubbery car. This one gave off a subtle smell of vanilla. Jack clutched the new car all the way home, chewing it appreciatively now and again.

When they got home, he'd had some lunch then fallen asleep on his play mat soon after, his fingers lax, the car on the mat next to him.

Having a baby cut your life in two, she mused over an iced tea. All the years before felt illusory. This was the new normal, as solid and real as the weight of her child. One day she might go back to the law, but right now she couldn't bear being away from Jack. Besides, how could she continue to breastfeed if she went back to work?

He was still asleep. As his chest rose and fell, she counted each breath against her watch. She checked with the new app.

His breathing rate was normal, but why hadn't he woken up yet? He wasn't even clutching his blankie. This wasn't him.

On a TV documentary, there'd been an unconscious child lying just like that.

No sooner had thoughts of sepsis and air ambulances entered her head than her heart began to race, and her breathing grew harsh.

I am calm. I am serene. All is well.

Her limbs were trembling now, and there was something in the pit of her stomach that didn't belong there. The unpleasant sensation would have overwhelmed her had Jack not stirred, whining as he did so.

"Jack, Jack," she said over and over, clutching him to her chest.

He had woken grumpy, sweaty, and full of woe, with a crumpled face, and crying for his toy car.

"There you go," she said, smiling. "Everything's all right now."

She was exhausted.

She wiped his face, then hers, with cool water. He seemed all right as she read him *Each Peach, Pear, Plum*. These times were the best, when Jack was alert and content. Her heart rate had slowed down. Sitting together on the sofa with the book, she could feel the love between them just as she could feel his warm body tucked beside her. From time to time, he poked a finger at the pictures, trying to find the concealed images.

"Pear?"

"That's Little Jack Horner."

"Mf," replied Jack.

After supper, she gave him a bath. Jack loved bathtime. He brought his new car into the water, held tight in his hand. He splashed, getting her face and hair wet. Water always made her hair ridiculously curly, but she was past caring now. The little car went *brm, brm* over the wall, around the edge of the bath, and around the taps that Laure had carefully wrapped in a towel so that Jack wouldn't burn himself.

Predictably, Jack didn't want to sleep that night. It took ages to get him down, another tiring procedure she had to do alone. Afterwards, Laure lay drained on top on her bed, too weary even to get up and brush her teeth.

The next thing she heard was Dan's key in the lock. Her heart sank.

She quickly got under the sheet and feigned sleep.

"Hey, gorgeous," he said, kissing her.

"Hey." At least she could pretend to be too drowsy.

"I've got you something. Well, it's for us, really. Here."

Curiosity won. She sat up to open the little carrier bag.

It was a DVD with a lurid cover and a clichéd title. "I don't want to watch porn! Especially not with Jack in the room. What do you take me for?"

"We don't have to do all those things. I mean, I'm not sure exactly what things, but just to get you in the mood, I thought you might like—"

"You didn't think at all," she yelled as she hurled the bag and its contents against the wall.

CHAPTER NINE

KAREN

The flowering currant bush smelled exactly like cat pee, as Karen discovered while waiting near the pavilion. Ashley had gone off to play at his friend's. There were only a few others yet to be collected, but Karen judged it best to wait till everyone had gone, including the mum of the week who had to hang around to take a hold-all full of dirty kit home to launder. There was a well-planned mothers' rota, and everyone whose kid did Sunday football considered the arrangement perfectly fair.

Everyone but Karen. Why was it a mums' rota, she thought as she finally went into the pavilion and locked the door behind them. Couldn't it have been, say, a parents' rota?

"Come here." Footie Dad grinned as he hobbled towards her. It was probably quite difficult to walk with his member waving proudly and his shorts round his ankles.

She tossed her T-shirt into the corner and her knickers followed. Then she straddled him and the bench, riding high, albeit more like a gym horse than a stallion.

Too caught up in the moment, he ignored *Dr Who* playing out from his mobile phone. She barely heard it herself as he screamed in ecstasy. Or was it because he was sliding off the bench?

"See you next week, yeah?" he said about five minutes later.

That was the sum total of their pillow talk. Maybe one day they'd even dispense with that, thought Karen. But she'd got what she came for, a little uncomplicated sex. Where else could a single mum and infant school teacher find that?

She tugged open the door of her ancient Toyota. "Yeah, sure."

Finally it was the day of her appointment. Although she hadn't brought him along, today's appointment was about Edward. The summer would be gone and term would start before you knew it, and there she was, a teacher herself, unable to control her own kid.

He was disruptive in class, and not much better at home. Karen always prayed he'd use up his energy during the school day, but once through the door he got a second wind, followed by a third wind around bedtime.

Just before the end of term, he'd thumped two of his class-mates. They deserved it. They'd taken the yellow pencils he wanted.

Their parents didn't exactly agree. The mother of one of the victims reckoned Edward should have a damn good hiding. The other one was kinder and recommended cranial osteopathy.

Karen knew Edward was a problem child. According to Google, he had symptoms of ADHD, as well as some features of autism and obsessive-compulsive disorder. He was clumsy enough for dyspraxia and naughty enough for oppositional-defiant behaviour. Could he possibly have all these things?

"What can I do for you?" began the doctor. Doctors always said that, though Karen doubted he would actually do anything.

"I'd like to know what's wrong with my son." Karen sum-marized the problem. Edward did manage to concentrate when playing. The snag was that he didn't play like the others. He loved Lego as much as his brothers did, but mostly he mixed it up in a big bowl and called it soup. He talked about soup a lot, which was odd because he didn't actually like the stuff. And he screamed when there were no yellow bricks left, or yellow crayons. Was all that because he missed his father, or perhaps because, as yet another mother had suggested at the school gates, he had a neurodevelopmental disorder?

The GP twiddled his biro and said, "I expect he's just a bit naughty."

"More than just a bit," Karen said. "What do you think is the reason?"

The doctor clicked his biro repeatedly and asked if there had been any changes in the household lately. "New arrival, maybe?"

"Departures," Karen replied. "Their father—my husband—left us two and a half years ago. He pops by from time to time, but that's about it." She could have said a lot more about Thomas and his appalling lack of parental responsibility, had appointments been thirty minutes long.

The GP was peering down the barrel of the biro as if his life depended on it.

"And Edward's very fussy about his food," Karen added, aware even as she said it that this didn't sound very pathological.

"All children are fussy about food," the doctor replied with authority. "As are many adults. I, for instance, dislike tomatoes."

She refrained from telling him tomatoes were very healthy and might even prevent prostate cancer. Eyeing him steadily, she asked if he had any children.

The biro was in pieces on the desk. Now he was exercising the little spring from its innards, seeing how small he could make it, then how long he could stretch it. "Yes, I have two children. Sorry, I mean three. A boy and two girls."

"You just said two."

"It's three. Sorry. Long week."

Karen chose to overlook his little miscalculation. "How often do you, in fact, prepare their meals?"

He paused to replace the spring in the barrel. "Maybe once a week."

Karen suspected he'd got that wrong too. "And do your children pick out every single kernel of corn out of the casserole before they eat it? Or arrange lentils around the rim of the plate in a perfectly symmetrical pattern?"

"They don't, no. But we never have sweetcorn. Or lentils. I hate them." For a moment there was pure disgust in his face. Then he went back to inspecting the spring from the biro, squeezing it up again then stretching it out. "Why, do you think it's a strange thing to do?"

"Maybe it's not that odd," she said, thinking all the while how weird males could be.

HARRIET

Harriet smiled down the phone to sound more confident, but it made no difference.

"Come back to me with something better," said the editor who'd just published a feature called *Can Doing the Dishes Give You an Orgasm?*

Another put-down. Harriet made a face at the phone and poured the rest of her undrinkable coffee down the sink. Until she got paid, it was the dirt cheap stuff that looked like dust and smelled of old ashtrays.

Years ago, she'd wanted to be a celebrated journalist. Now she was a freelancer and rarely made ends meet.

She checked her bank balance online. Today a payment had come through, but it wasn't enough to solve her problems. She wouldn't even be able to pay the rent, let alone contribute to a weekend away with Sanjay.

She urgently needed ideas the editor would like. The crotchless knickers sat on her shelf in reproach. *Can You Guess the Bottom Line?* had been a great concept. Readers would be invited to guess which of the women pictured preferred which type of underwear: the Bridget Jones grandma-type pants, the lacy thong, the more modest bikini, or the crotchless knickers.

In the reveal, the plump carer would turn out to be a thong-wearer, the model would have the passion-killers, and the librarian would favour the little crotchless number, while the fashion stylist would prefer a plain M&S bikini.

To balance things a bit, Harriet wanted to include a doctor, vet, or nuclear physicist, but had failed to track down a single one. As it turned out after Harriet had bought the knickers, none of the other case studies she'd sourced wanted to play ball anymore either.

Worse, she'd had to explain it all to the new editor of *RightHere!*, an Oxbridge-educated bitch who had the disconcerting habit of shouting 'Next!' as soon as she lost interest. Harriet described the fix she was in, and her idea for salvaging the feature, but the editor was unimpressed.

"Harry," said the editor, even though nobody else ever shortened Harriet's name. "I get that you needed to buy the knickers, but I don't think I can include a large bribe, times four, as expenses for this piece. It just won't wash. Next!"

Now Harriet (aka Harry) was left with no commission, though she did have several pairs of knickers, including a scratchy crotchless number, size twenty.

Phoning Sanjay used to make her feel better when others made her feel small. They would speak several times a day. Sometimes he'd give her ideas for her writing, or just make her laugh. She'd phoned him this afternoon and all she got was the whispered, "Trustees' meeting. Sorry."

Harriet made a cup of tea and resisted the temptation to find solace in a kitten video.

"Think, Harriet, think," she told herself, and promptly watched the kitten video anyway.

Animals. People loved reading about animals.

Say she visited the local vet surgery, got advice from the receptionist and the nurse as to what kind of dog or cat to consider. Even better, what was the most unusual household pet? There was surely a feature in that.

The editor listened to Harriet's pitch for a full five seconds before slapping her down with, "And what is so special to *RightHere!* about that?"

"Well." Harriet knew she was prattling, but she couldn't stop now. "What about a piece on pets that go missing? Some of them end up living with a neighbour, while others get run over or end up in a vivisection lab—"

The snort was audible. "We're not the newsletter of Battersea Dogs' Home, Harry."

CHAPTER TEN

DAN

The presenter sounded a complete knob. Still, Dan was lucky to get the gig. Only two weeks ago it had just been Dan's nascent idea, then some random producer had called Lolo's asking for a cook for a radio show. Proved that good things happened as unpredictably as a roll of the dice.

Dan had never been on radio before. And this was live. Even though he was only in the reception area, his heart was already leaping around in his chest.

The building had a massive atrium. All shiny marble and glass, courtesy of the licence fee. No wonder they weren't paying guests anything. Still. It might lead to TV, where the money was. That was exactly what their bank account needed, seeing as Laure wanted to stay at home as long as she could.

Dan had a tray of his new monkfish parcels. He'd made them roughly bite-sized, a toothpick holding each one together. Took him forever, but they'd be great cold, and they looked the business with a light garnish of red amaranth.

The woman in the lobby barely looked up from her desk to tell him to take a seat. It was the kind of seat designed to make you uncomfortable. So there he perched, balancing the foil-covered tray on his knees, staring at a bank of silent TV screens for what seemed like ages. Lucky old people on TV.

Or maybe not that lucky, because one of the programmes was this hilarious reality show in which children competed to humiliate their parents. Dan supposed Jack would do much the same when he stopped being a cute little baby and grew into an egregious adolescent.

Egregious. Dan's word today. He rolled it around his mouth, still not sure if he dared use it on air.

People came and went through the lobby. Dan's expectations soared when someone came to talk to him, but the man only wanted to know if he was waiting for a car. "No. I'm waiting to go into the studio," Dan said, but the man had already lost interest and wandered off.

A tall bloke who looked like an older version of Jeremy Paxman strode through. Dan stared. Maybe it really was Jeremy Paxman.

Then nothing happened for ages. Dan sat with the tray on his lap, making sure he kept it steady. Two of the toothpicks had poked through the foil and there was a smell of fish.

Finally a girl in trainers came out to get him. She beamed at him then led the way through security and up some stairs and round the houses. The clock said ten to midnight when they reached the studio.

The presenter, Big Zach, was in full flow, and the other guests all looked at home. Zach waved at him and gestured to a chair. Dan put his tray on a table against the wall and took his seat as quietly as he could.

The guests included a doctor who was talking about some new research, a pole dancer with ambitions to be a ballerina, and a woman campaigning against basement developments.

Plus himself. And his fish.

The show kicked off with basement developments. Turned

out the woman was against rooftop developments too, especially the ones in her street.

Big Zach wanted to know where the hell she expected Londoners to live, given that the population had grown exponentially and was likely to continue doing so for the foreseeable if not beyond. What answers did she have to that?

She went pretty quiet, while around the studio the other guests nodded like wobbly dogs. Dan did the same.

"They've got to live somewhere," Big Zach pointed out. "Or would you tell them all to go back to their own countries?"

The woman didn't get a chance to respond before Big Zach continued, waving a sausage of a finger. "I know what you Nimbies are like."

The population of London could bloody well live right here, thought Dan. In this humungous building full of offices where nobody seemed to do anything.

After midnight a woman came in to read the traffic news. There wasn't any, so the woman mentioned some earlier incidents that had now cleared, and added that the Blackwall Tunnel was flowing nicely.

The fish parcels were ponging the studio out. Next up was the doctor. He talked about how many thousands of people had arthritis and could benefit from the latest developments in artificial hand joints.

"Wow," said Zach.

The other guests echoed this. Turned out Zach had got his facts twisted. It was just the joint replacements that were artificial, not the whole hand.

"The research in our department is a team effort," explained the medic. "We've got physios, occupational therapists, and of course a top-notch engineer. Can I give a shout-out to our engineer Conrad? We'd be at square one without him."

Turned out the doc was planning to abseil down some building, wearing a contraption that mimicked having arthritis, to raise funds for research.

"Wow," said Zach again. "Did you abseil at medical school?"

"Um, no. This is my first time so if anyone wants to check out my Just Giving page..."

Dan nodded a lot, to show he was still there. He butted his tongue against his plate again to make sure it would last the course, and wondered all the while when he'd get a chance to say anything.

"And are Conrad and the team abseiling with you?" asked the basement woman.

"Just me."

The pole dancer wriggled sweetly in her seat until it was her turn. Then she explained she'd always wanted to be a, you know, *serious* dancer, but when she was eighteen she had to give up her dreams and make ends meet. She had a kid. What choice was there?

Big Zach immediately asked if she could do something for them. "Why don't you take your cans off and give us a little demonstration?"

It was an idiotic thing to do on radio and there wasn't even a pole, but she managed to wiggle her egregious buttocks in their faces. Everyone found it hilarious apart from the po-faced basement woman. Big Zach laughed so much that his belly developed a life of its own.

That dancer was a tough act to follow.

"So, Daniel, you're a chef at Lolo's. I know it's a new restaurant in Hampstead Village. But there are lots of restaurants in that particular part of North London. Tell us what's different about Lolo's?"

Dan's mouth went dry. "Well, its basic ethos is that we don't mess with your food. Apart from the Eton Mess, obviously." He grinned and paused.

Dead silence.

Swallowing, Dan continued. "And all the ingredients are really fresh. We insist on that. It's good honest food with fresh local ingredients. Not pretentious. Not weird. Basically, it's food just as it should be, and it's always served at the right temperature." As he spoke, he remembered that he'd brought a dish usually served warm. It would be cold when they got to it. And monkfish wasn't exactly local.

"Wow," said the dancer.

"And we use plates." That sounded fucking idiotic as soon as he said it. "Proper plates. Lots of restaurants use, um, little baskets, and wooden boards and such like."

The basement woman knew what he meant. "I went to a seafood place recently and they served my scallops on driftwood. Driftwood! I ask you."

Luckily Big Zach also lobbed him some easy ones, like how long Dan had worked there, and how many covers there were each evening. Then he asked, "And what's your signature dish?"

"Well, Lolo's does lots of things brilliantly, like—"

"Never mind that. What's your personal signature dish?"

"Chicken arrabiata," Dan replied without hesitation. This was the recipe he'd learned when he worked at the garden centre, the first job he'd got after prison. He'd made the dish for Laure after they'd got up some two days after first going to bed together. He'd rearranged her furniture and she'd totally rearranged his head. That was always going to stick in his mind especially as it was also the first time he'd persuaded her to—

"Any other good chicken dishes?"

"Well," began Dan, aware that he had started almost every answer with the word 'well'. "I do harissa chicken. Cuban arroz con pollo. Barbecue tenders. Cajun chicken. Coq au vin, of course. I don't think the world will ever get bored of chicken recipes," Dan added, warming to his theme.

Big Zach nodded and agreed with that. Then the basement woman chimed in with an anecdote about a chicken restaurant she'd been to.

"So," continued Zach. "What have you got for us tonight,

Dan? Would it be chicken, by any chance?"

"It's monkfish."

"You're just dazzling us with your repertoire," said the joint replacement medic. He had to be the nicest doc ever, but then Dan mostly knew crap prison doctors.

"Bring it over here," said Big Zach.

"Ooh, can I see?" The dancer lifted a corner of the foil.

The foil came off and everyone helped themselves. "This is simply divine," declared Big Zach. The listeners weren't to know he began smacking his lips before he'd even tasted it.

Dan took a parcel after everyone else. It was pretty good, even if he said so himself. The lemon zest worked. Not so much the amaranth, which was dropping all over the desk.

Everyone was making *mm mm mm* noises as Big Zach gave a running commentary to the listeners. "Here we all are enjoying a lovely plate of – what is it called? Yes, monkfish parcels, thanks to the generosity of Lolo's Restaurant in Hampstead Village and their brilliant new cook Daniel."

Dan was just thinking that hadn't been the worst interview in the world. Then the basement woman began coughing. As soon as she clutched at her throat, the doctor was up, bashing her on the back. "Not to worry," he said. "It's only a partial blockage."

Partial blockage or not, the woman looked terrible. Big Zach intervened in the only way he knew how. "Now we'll just play you some music while we clear the place up after that wonderful dish. So sit back and enjoy the latest mellow track from the fabulous Emili Sandé," he oozed as he flicked a switch.

"She's still breathing," said the doctor. "It's not like she's gone blue."

The woman had calmed down a bit. Now she was fanning her face with a hand. "I think there's something stuck."

"Possibly a fishbone," the doctor said.

"I filleted them very carefully," said Dan. There weren't

normally many small bones in monkfish.

"And that wraps it up for another evening with Big Zach. Who says things don't happen on radio, eh? If it's great conversation you want, and a touch of excitement when you least expect it, tune in tomorrow night at the same time."

The choking woman was fine in the end. The runner got her more water, and the dancer produced a sandwich from her handbag, swearing bread was the best thing ever when you had something stuck in your throat. Everyone congratulated the pole dancer like she'd invented a cure for Ebola. Dan just wanted to smack himself on the forehead for not having taken out every single bloody bone.

As he went out into the street with his tray, the truth hit him. Making a name for himself was going to be a lot harder than he imagined.

He still had a few monkfish parcels left. Shame to let them go to waste. Egregious waste.

In Oxford Street, the first tramp turned his nose up at the offer and asked for two quid instead.

The second one was more eager and took all four. Two for himself, two for his dog.

"Better watch out for bones," Dan said. "There's not meant to be any bones at all in it, but you never know. Wouldn't want you or your dog to choke or anything."

Dan rinsed the tray at the nearest McDonald's. Bit of an ask since the sinks were tiny. But he managed, all the while adding to the list of things he'd forgotten to say on air. Plus the other list, the things he should have kept to himself, starting with chicken dishes.

So many different ways of making an arse of yourself. Only one way to get things right. That stupid DVD as well. He hadn't meant to insult Laure with porn, but now he could see how wrong it had been. It was tough, being out of jail and in the real world. Even tougher now he had a family.

The tray still smelled when he got home. So did he. After a shower, he did his denture and crept into bed. He'd have liked to talk, but nothing doing. Laure was fast asleep. Elated and disappointed at the same time, Dan lay down next to her and tried not to move.

CHAPTER ELEVEN

LAURE

"*Comment vas-tu, chérie?*" shrieked Tante Lina before she and her sister had even got through Laure's front door.

"And how is your darling little boy?" Tante Victorine's voice would have been useful had telephones not existed.

An opening round of kissing. An avalanche of lipstick. A haze of Diorissimo, as always.

Despite being tired, Laure had made an effort for Tante Lina and Tante Victorine. One had to, after all. That meant tinted moisturizer, a slick of lip gloss, a little mascara, and a whole lot of blusher.

Laure put the kettle on. To Laure, Earl Grey tea was like drinking cologne, but her aunts loved it. They were from the Lebanese side of the family and they worshipped everything British, especially *The Times* newspaper, Harrogate toffee, Marmite, the Houses of Parliament (though they understood little of its workings), and cricket (which they understood even less).

They were eager to see Jack, for whom they had brought a present, a pale blue all-in-one thing from Harrods, no less.

"*Une barboteuse, chérie*," explained Tante Lina.

Laure thanked them profusely, although a dry-clean-only garment in merino wool was a bit impractical, especially this August.

"Now let me see him!"

Laure led the way to Jack's cot. "He cries a lot. He's a terror at night."

The two widowed aunts elbowed each other out of the way to admire him.

Lying in his cot clutching a corner of his favourite blanket, Jack didn't look much of a terror. His lashes rested on his golden skin and his fair hair had curled in the sweat of his slumber. Then, just as Laure thought he might stay quiet all afternoon, he stirred and started up with a whimper that changed to 'Uh, uh, uh' before threatening to develop into a full-blown cry.

After a quick sip of tea, Laure picked him up and jiggled him up and down. Jack remained tetchy.

"He's a real challenge today," said Laure. When he cried, it wasn't just exhausting. It was worrying. If she couldn't console him right away, wasn't there always the chance that he might be ill?

"Let me take him," said Tante Victorine, gold bracelets jangling.

"I'll hold him," said Lina. "I hardly had him at all last time."

"*Vraiment chérie*, your memory is getting very poor. You played with him all afternoon and I didn't get a chance. I don't know what I've done to annoy you, I'm sure."

"Well, OK. But if your arms get tired..."

Laure handed him to Tante Victorine. Jack was heavy, but Victorine showed no signs of dropping him. She clasped him to her chest and held him close.

"Gimp," went Jack.

Laure thought his language skills were average for his age, but the aunts looked at each other as if Jack was a genius.

Neither had raised a child. Victorine's baby died an hour after birth, the same year Laure was born.

Miraculously, Jack fell asleep again, loosening his grip on the blanket. His hand now hung on the side of Victorine's dress. Laure smiled at her aunt and noticed her eyes were glistening.

"Well," Laure said. "Anyone for another cup of tea?"

"*S'il te plaît, ya ma chère,*" replied Victorine as she stroked the nape of Jack's neck and smiled. "He is very beautiful. *Helou awi.*" So beautiful was he that Victorine had to break into a uniquely Lebanese mix of French and Arabic. Being Christian Lebanese, they mostly spoke French, but, when in the presence of great beauty like a pretty child or perfectly stuffed vine leaves, only Arabic would do.

Victorine was right, thought Laure as she boiled the kettle. Jack was gorgeous, only not at three in the morning when you'd just managed to get him to doze off.

Lina took her cup. "*Merci, chérie.*"

"*Yiy,*" said Victorine as soon as Jack surfaced again. "His eyes are exactly like yours."

She had said exactly the same thing last time, right down to the very Arab expression *yiy*. "True," Laure agreed. "Dan's eyes are completely different."

"And he has your hair, not Dan's," Victorine pointed out.

That was true too. Laure knew Dan had gone bald in his twenties. The half dozen hairs left on his head got shaved on a regular basis. It suited him.

Lina gave a sideways glance. "How is Dan?"

"He's well," said Laure. She told them about his recent radio interview.

"*La radio!*" said Victorine. "Wonderful!"

Lina appeared to reflect as she drank her tea, her little finger crooked. "*Quand est-ce que vous allez vous marier?*" She gazed over the rim of the cup, waiting for a reply. She hadn't asked Laure about getting married for a long while now, maybe almost a week. In the aunts' opinion, cohabiting was for lesser people, like the kind on Big Brother. Clearly their niece ought to aspire to better, especially at the age of forty.

Laure shrugged. That was the same answer she always gave people who talked about marriage. Jack bonded them together for life and there was no reason to get hitched, unless you worried about inheritance tax.

The aunts were assessing her response. Laure finally got off the hook with, "Maybe one day. We'll see."

Jack finally became too much for Tante Victorine, who handed him over to Tante Lina's waiting arms.

"*Ism' Allah*," said Lina when she took his full weight.

Laure congratulated herself for having persevered with breastfeeding. Over a year now. Her friends said she should have stopped long ago, but what did they know of all its benefits, or the satisfaction it gave her?

Tante Lina made Jack comfortable on her lap. He was quietly awake now. Laure half-hoped Jack would give just a sampler of his howls, but he seemed content in his great-aunt's arms.

"He's such a good baby," remarked Tante Lina. "Smells beautiful too," she added, inhaling the top of his head. It was a wonder Lina could smell anything when she had drowned herself in Diorissimo.

"Yes, he's very good," Victorine agreed.

Laure refrained from inviting them to pop round in the small hours of the morning.

The aunts took the customary pictures on their phones, with each of them holding Jack in turn, while saying repeatedly how stupid they were with technology, and how all the photos would be nothing more than close-ups of their thumbs.

"I have no idea how it came out so well, Laure *chérie*, but I have a nice one of you here," said Victorine.

It wasn't bad at all, thought Laure. Her aunts were a lot more capable than they pretended.

Lina grabbed the phone and studied it carefully. "*Chérie*, you look really lovely. And what a figure you've kept!"

Victorine chimed in approvingly. "It's good to look after your looks. Men stray when you let yourself go. Not that your Dan would do such a thing, of course," she added. "But, you know."

Laure didn't bother chiding her. The aunts had such dated views of the sexes.

Lina and Victorine left some time later, bound for Oxford Street to check out some boring middle-aged fashions. Laure then remembered that she could already be classed as middle-aged herself, though she didn't feel it.

She'd hardly put the cups in the dishwasher when Jack started up again.

"Aww. What's the matter, little man?" She beamed at him, hoping to put him in a better mood. He stopped wailing momentarily to make a boot-face accompanied by rapid breaths that suggested the sound effects would soon be at full volume again.

In the next hour, Laure worked out that he wasn't hungry or thirsty. He refused the breast, and he didn't have a dirty nappy. Further checking showed that he had a normal temperature, pulse, and respiratory rate (except when crying), and didn't have cold extremities or anything else to suggest a dread disease. Every parent feared meningitis, but it was really sepsis or blood poisoning that made it so deadly. Laure had studied the child care manuals well.

"Come on then, little man. We're going out."

Taking your infant out in a buggy, said one of her books, *may not always stop the crying but the sound won't seem as loud once you're out of doors.*

"Ah-goo," replied Jack, approving of the plan. He did not protest as she bundled him up, strapped him into his buggy, and took out him into blazing sunshine, protected by a sun hat and factor thirty sunscreen.

They went to the park. People stopped to remark on what a lovely child he was and how cute he looked in his hat. His mood improved when Laure put him in one of the baby swings.

Once he tired of the swing and she'd got him back in the buggy, Laure spent a little time watching daredevils on the climbing frame, and children elbowing each other out of the way on the slide. Grown-ups sat on the benches nearby for a breather, but Laure couldn't relax. It was difficult enough as it was. How was she going to cope when Jack got bigger and ran amok, with all the dangers that entailed?

A skinny woman with a pram approached and admired Jack's blond locks. "Is he a good baby?" she asked. Laure noticed the dark rim around her eyes.

Laure laughed ruefully. "Not really."

The woman said she knew that feeling.

"Kat kat kat!" went Jack. Next to *ah-goo*, it was his favourite word.

"Maybe see you tomorrow?" said the woman as she got ready to go.

"More than likely." Going to the park was the highlight of a stay-at-home mother's day. She came here almost as often as she used to go to the office.

No sooner had they reached the street than Jack's mood changed. First he did his impression of a crumpled sock, then his lower lip wobbled as he threatened to yell. Laure could see why so many parents gave children sweets to shut them up.

To avoid a tantrum at the grocer's, she hurried home without the potatoes she wanted. Jack limited his complaining to, "Uhh, uhh uhh" till they reached the front door. He began wailing, arching his back in his buggy and fighting against the strap and harness even before Laure turned off the intruder alarm. Maybe she should have let it go off instead. No alarm, however shrill, could get to her the way her child's crying did. She loved him to pieces, as she knew she always would, but times like these made her feel so out of her depth. If only she'd stayed at work instead of becoming a full-time parent. No, that was unthinkable. She could do this.

I am calm. I am serene. All is well.

"Come along, Jack," she said, undoing the buckle and picking him up. His body eventually softened into hers but he was a long way off smiling. "Do you want a little nap? Or maybe a little play-play? Or perhaps I can read you a story? Ooh, who's that at the door?"

Through the glass in the front door she could see Daisy's multi-coloured sun-dress.

"Hello, my darlings," trilled Daisy as she wafted in, tossing the silky shawl off her shoulders and onto the sofa along with her e-cig. "Where have you been today?"

"The park."

"Lovely weather for it. I've just had the day off myself," she added. "Today has been a Daisy day."

There seemed to be a lot of these. Laure had never figured out what she did on them, and questions usually led nowhere. "Pretty dress," remarked Laure.

"Primark. You should get one. It's got no shoulders, as you see, so you wouldn't get baby sick on it. Now why is lovely Jack crying?" Daisy continued. She held her arms out and Laure willingly transferred Jack. Daisy cooed at him then made a face with wild eyes. He loved it.

Something caught in Laure's throat. Was everyone in the whole world better than her at parenting?

CHAPTER TWELVE

HARRIET

The mini-break was Sanjay's suggestion, though Harriet had once written a feature on exactly this.

If love is on the wane, try packing your bags. No, we're not suggesting a trial separation. We're talking a sensual mini-break to invigorate your passion and rekindle your lust. Here are six sexy destinations to break the monotony without breaking the bank.

As Harriet recalled, the destinations she had reeled off in her piece were Barcelona, Suffolk, Bath, Lyon, Bruges, and some boutique hideaway in the Cotswolds.

When had she and Sanjay last been away? Ages.

With a little Googling, Harriet discovered that Bath was horribly expensive, and the place in Suffolk that she'd described in breathy tones was full up. Luckily she sourced an alternative not far away. Sanjay said it sounded OK.

By all accounts, Bury St Edmund's was a magical place. A unique and dazzling historic gem, no less. According to the website, it was an important market town with a richly fascinating heritage. She couldn't wait to visit its elegant Georgian squares and glorious abbey, all places bound to revitalize a relationship, if you believed the media.

That was where they went. Their affordably comfortable inn was just past the Pull-Up Café and a used car dealer.

They parked round the back of The Horse & Carriage and carried their bags up a narrow staircase to their room at the very top.

"What are you doing?" said Sanjay.

"Trying to air the room," said Harriet. Although they were miles from the coast, the room still had that musty aroma of seaside B&Bs.

Sanjay pointed out that the air wasn't that fresh.

They had driven in Sanjay's car and a deep silence. Harriet wasn't good at silence. She fiddled with the radio. Nothing but crackles.

"It works some of the time," said Sanjay.

"Can't it be fixed?"

Dimples appeared. "Not by me."

They drove the whole journey without being able to play any of the music he'd brought.

"So what do you think grows in that field?" she asked as they cruised up the A14.

"Sugar beet," said Sanjay, his eyes fixed on carriageway.

"You didn't even look! The countryside's quite interesting," she added, though in truth what she'd had in mind was more Woodbridge, Aldeburgh, or Southwold than the kebab van tucked into a lay-by. Where were the breathtaking heathlands and the endless fields of lavender, as per the guide books?

"So do you miss Shelley yet?" she asked.

"Don't be silly. We've only been gone an hour."

In point of fact, it was over an hour and a half. It was a shame about the radio.

Sanjay gripped the steering wheel as if his life depended on it. She supposed it did. He claimed to enjoy driving, but he leaned forward at the wheel like an old person trying to concentrate. Serious conversation had to wait.

"Oh, look. Piggy houses," she said.

"Where?"

"We just passed them."

They were caught in traffic on the outskirts of Bury St Edmund's, trapped behind the container lorry. If there were any breathtaking vistas, that massive vehicle would have hidden them from view.

"Do you suppose it's going to Harwich?" asked Harriet.

Sanjay shrugged. "Where is Harwich, anyway?"

Harriet didn't know either.

"What's that?" she asked. It was a row of huge concrete silos with a horizontal thing over the top.

"Sugar beet factory," said Sanjay.

Harriet had never thought about where her sugar came from, or rather Sanjay's sugar, since he was apt to take three spoons of the stuff in tea or coffee. She'd assumed it was all from cane.

"They say the Abbey is lovely," said Harriet after a while. She craned her neck hopefully.

They ate somewhere nondescript that evening. It looked like a gastro-pub from the outside, but the inside was chintzy and the chicken and chips were a disappointment.

"How's your steak and ale pie?" she asked.

"Definitely fling and ping."

They were back at the inn with its affordable comfort. Never mind the ageing furnishings. A bed was a bed. You couldn't actually be in a hotel room with a person of the opposite sex and not think of bonking, especially when that person was Sanjay and she still fancied his socks off.

He fooled around for ages with his new iPhone, picking up mail, messing about on Facebook or whatever.

Harriet drew the curtains, coaxing them into meeting in the middle. She undressed as seductively as she knew how. While it had been warm in London, here it was cool. Had she been alone, she'd have gone to bed fully clothed, including a thermal vest and a pair of Ugg boots.

Harriet did her best to feel romantic despite a vicious bed-spring digging into her ribs. Afterwards, he put his arm round her and they fell asleep, heads touching on two stingy pillows.

When he was brushing his teeth the next morning, she crept up behind him, ran a finger down his back, and said, "Sanjay, do we know where we're heading?"

She'd been hoping to find the right moment. Which this probably wasn't, but the question had built up inside till it erupted like Coke from a bottle.

"Sure." He inspected his teeth in the mirror and gave his trademark grin. "I've got sat nav."

"Very droll," she said.

"Although that doesn't stop me from being confused," he added.

This sounded significant. "Confused how?"

"I'm not sure." He concentrated on an imaginary pimple on his chin.

"Can you give me a clue?"

"The same things as usual, I guess. I got a new lease of life, but that doesn't mean I know how to live my life. Or even how to talk about it."

"OK. Let's try again later."

He nodded and put his toothbrush away.

He ruffled her hair affectionately when they got into the car after breakfast. She stroked the side of his chin before they drove off.

They motored past the Ten Pin Bowling, the Pot Black Sports Bar, lay-bys full of lorries, and a showroom called Get Away Cars.

"If I lived here, I'd want to get away too," said Sanjay. "Oh, and what the fuck is the Suffolk Chair Centre? Is that the excitement around here? Sitting down?"

"Looks like it," said Harriet.

"Are there any fun bars around here, do you think? Maybe like the ones we went to in Barcelona?"

"If there's a single fun bar here, they keep it well-hidden," said Harriet.

The Abbey was worth a visit, but Bury St Edmund's, she concluded, wasn't exactly Barcelona. No tapas. No cable car. No night-life. And now it was raining. Little wonder Constable and his wife had decamped to North London.

Sanjay didn't slow down before the yellow box came into view. Sure enough there was a flash, followed swiftly by another one.

"Fuck it." He hit the steering wheel. "Three bloody penalty points. All I fucking need."

"It's not exactly the camera's fault," Harriet pointed out, but Sanjay's face seemed to say that was exactly what it was.

"It's just a ploy," he spat. "To make more fucking money out of motorists."

Not on the ones that stuck to the speed limit, thought Harriet.

"I'd like to give this place a Suffolk punch," Sanjay added, gripping the steering wheel tight.

"Well, you can't."

"Why the fuck not?"

"Because it's a horse. A Suffolk Punch is a horse."

He shot her a glance. "You're kidding me, right?"

"No, I'm not. It's a heavy horse. Like the Percheron, the Shire, and... well, others."

"How do you know all these things?"

"I'm a journalist."

Sanjay considered this before concluding flatly, "All horses are heavy. A horse trod on my foot once, when I was ten."

Harriet sighed. It was pointless trying to explain.

She had hoped the second night would be better, but it wasn't much different, except for a dog barking most of the night in the alley by their B&B. They'd seen him on the way in, an Alsatian tied up to a post for most of the day by the looks of it. When she'd tried to approach, he sprung at her with bared teeth, tensing his chain as far as it could go. You didn't have to be a dog person to know it wasn't right, or to see there was only one reason for keeping a dog like that. She wondered what they had to guard. Maybe it wasn't just sugar beet and turnips they grew around here.

Over breakfast, Sanjay smiled back at her through weary eyes. He reached out and held her hand. There had been a time when the tiniest contact would have sent a high voltage current ripping through her, usually straight to her pelvis.

That didn't happen today, no matter how much she willed it to. Was this the way every relationship panned out, or just theirs?

The route was clear on their way home.

He took his eyes off the road for a moment. "What are you thinking about?" he asked. So he did care.

She should have said she wanted to talk about whether they were going to stay as they were, living apart and meeting up once or twice a week as well as having weekends together, or whether things should change. Instead she said, "Chocolate cake."

It was easier. Besides, Sanjay did remind her of a chocolate cake that had been in the patisserie window too long. Not necessarily his colour, more the fact that you knew it had been there a while, but you still wanted it. It didn't taste as good as you hoped it would. Maybe you couldn't even finish the slice, but you still had to have it.

"Then we'll get you some."

She wasn't actually hungry, but, before she knew it, he had stopped at a café-cum-souvenir place and bought her a huge slice of chocolate brownie cake as well as a fridge magnet.

"Aww, thank you. I'll keep the cake for later."

A fridge magnet might have been less romantic than the dangly silver earrings he'd got her in Barcelona, but it was a nice touch. She turned it over and over in her hand. *Pride of Suffolk*, it said just underneath the county flag.

"Didn't you once mention fridge magnets in an article?" he asked as he started up the engine.

Indeed she had. The feature had never got off the ground, but the standfirst was still in her head.

What can you tell from fridge magnets? They're there to hold your memos, to remind you of a Greek Island holiday or your trip up the Eiffel Tower. There are cute mottos, kooky hearts, the plumber's logo, and of course masses of alphabet letters.

They're small and affordable. No wonder they're popular all over the world.

Unless people had fitted kitchens with integrated fridges.

Now there are collectors around the globe, along with whole communities and discussion groups dedicated to these little ornaments.

The humble fridge magnet holds notes and photos in place, and keeps children's masterpieces on show in the kitchen.

Sanjay took his hand off the gear stick for a moment to grip her hand. She beamed back, but he didn't notice. Once again both hands were back on the wheel, and his eyes were fixed on the road ahead.

Fridge magnets, in short, keep things together.

CHAPTER THIRTEEN

KAREN

On the sidelines where the white paint was still visible, a little boy in red was trying to murder a boy in blue.

"Ow!" screamed the blue one. "Joel bit me!"

"You kicked me. It was a foul," went the red one.

Footie Dad's whistle had barely left his lips the entire match. He blew on it again.

Karen continued to watch as a flush rose up her neck. There was little point getting involved in fights when they weren't your children. Already two grown men had dived into the fray.

"There's blood on my shin pad!" howled the victim.

A dad in a Chelsea shirt scooped up one of the boys. With the lad in his arms, he stomped towards Footie Dad. "Oy! What kind of fucking shambles do you run here, sunshine?"

The shambles was ongoing, with the ball still in play, even though the goalie lay spread-eagled on the grass. "Seven-nil," someone yelled. Several others promptly joined in the chant. Karen was pleased to note that Ashley didn't.

One of the chanting boys was actually a girl, complete with pigtails, freckles, and missing front teeth. She was half the size of the boys, but that didn't stop her trying to throttle the other team's captain. Eventually she let go, but only so she could punch him on the nose.

The game was finally over, injury time included. Footie Dad trudged round to Karen, wiping his face with the hem of his shirt. "I've got to be back early today."

"Not a problem," said Karen.

"Another time, yeah?"

"Sure." She would be home forty minutes early. Perhaps a bit of a bonus.

The game might have been over, but, as the players left the field to change out of their kit, little Miss Pigtails swung in again with her left fist, sending a boy tumbling to the ground.

"Now, now. This is football," Footie Dad pointed out. "Not boxing."

"Says who?" retorted the girl, giving a gummy snarl. It sounded more like *theth who*.

Ashley waved to Karen and disappeared when his friend Paul's mum arrived. A few minutes later, Karen heaved the bag of kit into her car. The shirts themselves were light. It was mud weighing the bag down.

Her turn to wash all the shirts. Having four kids had taught her a lot about football, but this was one bit she couldn't grasp.

It was a fact that males could be trained to operate a washing machine and then hang laundry out to dry, though obviously they'd expect proper recognition for it.

If she took the kit back and laundered it as per usual, it would be taken for granted. And what message would that give her children?

She ruled out leaving the kit as it was. Next week, some child would be in tears because he wanted a clean shirt, not one with someone else's blood on it. That would be unfair. And yet...

She stood by the mahonia bush and pondered her dilemma.

Everyone had gone. As she considered dumping the whole bag by the shrubs at the side of the pavilion, she noticed one of the fathers getting out of his Porsche Cayenne. He had been one of the first to leave, and now he was back. He stopped by the side of the car to adjust the strap on his flashy gold watch, then turned towards the pitch, apparently in search of something.

He hadn't locked the car.

The moment he disappeared round the corner of the pavilion, she sprinted to his Porsche, opened the back door, and flung the bag into it. Then she got into her own car and made her getaway just as another surge of heat engulfed her neck and face.

Today Karen was going to do something about all this. She hoped the doctor wouldn't push antidepressants. Everyone who read the papers knew how GPs loved those drugs. It was only a matter of time before they started dishing out Prozac for sore throats and sprained ankles.

Karen beamed as she entered the consulting room, just to make sure the new doctor got the message that she wasn't about to slit her wrists. "I've got a bit of a list, Dr Cook."

"You can call me Lucy," said the doctor. "Everyone does."

"OK," Karen said. This Lucy was probably about the same age as her, or maybe a couple of years younger. "I think I mentioned the hot flushes last time." She hesitated. "Do you like being called Lucy?"

"I'm used to it."

"Are all the doctors here called by their first names?" Karen persisted, even though she knew the answer.

Lucy tapped into the keyboard before looking up. "No. But Claire—that's Dr Buckler—and myself are. And the nurse, of course."

"Of course." Karen looked at the photos on the GP's desk. Two happy, shiny children, grinning like little chimpanzees. On the wall above the desk hung three framed certificates. "The ones that get called 'doctor'—would they be men?"

"Mmm," she agreed. "Now, what can I do for you?"

Karen told Lucy about the night sweats, hot flushes, and the occasional trouble remembering things. "The hot flushes happen at the least convenient times. It's actually quite embarrassing."

Lucy nodded. "Vaginal dryness? Or peeing more often?"

"Not really. Just the things on the list. It's the menopause, isn't it?"

"What's your weight doing?"

Weekly exercise sessions in the pavilion clearly weren't enough. "Well..."

"Even though you're only forty," Lucy reflected, "I'm pretty sure it *is* the menopause."

"I'm not quite forty," Karen clarified.

Lucy squinted at her computer. "Indeed. May I just check your blood pressure? It hasn't been taken for a while. And you should have a blood test for hormone levels and glucose. Is that all right?"

"Of course it's all right."

The doctor's forced smile suggested bad news was on the way. "You know, if it is the menopause, it will mean you can't have more children."

"I have four kids already." What planet did medics live on?

Karen had to wait to have blood taken.

"Over there, dear," said the receptionist. "Nurse shouldn't be too long now."

Karen hadn't even sat down before she heard the same receptionist call a male patient 'sir'. Karen was about to say something, then decided she would look bloody stupid if the man turned out to have a knighthood.

So she installed herself and waited, leafing through a magazine and watching the receptionist. There seemed to be a lot of men with knighthoods around.

Best not upset her, thought Karen.

The magazine was a lame collection of recipes and tips on pleasing your man, though there was a good piece on ways to upcycle old crates. Might come in useful if days ever became forty-eight hours long.

The nurse took her blood and said the results would be back in a week, dear.

Karen's pocket vibrated as soon as she was out of the surgery. It was only a message from her ex-husband.

Karen was under the impression Thomas had already taken all his suits, but apparently he wanted to pick up a suit he'd left behind. His text also said he planned to pop round sometime for a spooky.

Whatever a spooky turned out to be, she knew it would irritate the shit out of her. The man was an idiot.

CHAPTER FOURTEEN

GEOFF

It was 4 p.m. in Perth, the time Sonya had grudgingly agreed it might be acceptable to call. Geoff got up quietly, pulled on a T-shirt, and crept downstairs to his laptop. He felt his heart race as Skype opened with its familiar yawn.

At six, Davey was too young for his own account, but Sonya was already online. Her Skype profile showed her forced smile and too much make-up. Geoff told himself to have charitable thoughts. She needed to be kept onside.

There he was! Had Geoff not known better, he'd have guessed his heart had taken a leap out of his chest.

"Hiya, Dad," said Davey. He was wearing a baseball cap that hid his eyes, but not his smile.

Geoff waved. "Hiya to you too, Davey."

"I'd rather be Dave? If you don't mind?" He sounded more Aussie every week.

"Dave it is then." Geoff then asked what he'd been doing.

Dave had been hiking and stuff. "And we went to King's Park and played cricket." These days he cropped his syllables a lot shorter. He even made *cricket* end in a D.

"Sounds like fun. Hey, what's that noise?"

"Just a kookaburra." Even with Dave's pixelated features, Geoff thought he could detect a sneer.

"A kookaburra. Right. How's school?" It was term time in Australia.

Dave pulled his cap further down over his eyes. "S'all right. We're going to Freo next week."

"With the school?"

"Nah. Going with Mum and Drew."

So he didn't call Drew his dad. Small mercies. "Freo, eh?" From his gap year, Geoff remembered Fremantle as Western Australia's pretend hippie town, with a dinky harbour and its Cappuccino Strip selling craft beer as well as coffees. "Pretty sophisticated place for a six-year old."

"I'm nearly seven."

"Right," said Geoff again. "Are you going to visit the prison in Fremantle?"

"I don't know."

All too soon, the conversation was over. Geoff spent a minute or so sitting at the desk, gazing at the framed pictures of Davey—sorry, Dave—in which he looked so much younger. It was a well-known fact that all children got bigger, unless they had a profound deficiency of somatotropin, but even so Geoff was taken aback every time they Skyped.

He brewed two cups of tea and took them upstairs, making a mental note to ask Sonya for a more recent photo.

Morning was just forcing its way around the blackout curtains in the bedroom. Daisy lay on her side, breathing slowly, eyes closed in apparent ecstasy.

Geoff had been a doctor long enough to know there was no such thing as karma, but, when things were this good, he could see why people believed in it.

He and Daisy had the whole day together, and Mr Wibbly Wobbly was behaving just as he ought. The little blue pills would remain his secret. He didn't trust Daisy not to try them herself if she found them.

One of her arms hung over the edge of the bed. A lacy navy and cream bra lay on the floor where she'd dropped it last night.

Geoff celebrated his good fortune by going to the bathroom, shutting the door quietly, and telling the mirror, "Yeah, baby. I'm back!" He beat his hairy chest and grinned at himself for added effect. Then, after brushing his teeth, he returned to bed.

She stirred when he kissed her, and gave him a wicked smile.

He kissed her again. "You are so very more-ish," he said without thinking it through.

Her beautiful lips changed to pure disgust. "Moorish? I am not a Moor."

"That's not what I meant."

"It's not what you mean that matters. It's what comes out." The way she said it left no room for argument.

"If you'd just let me explain. I meant *more*. M-O-R-E. The opposite of *less*."

"It didn't come out like that." She sighed impatiently and covered herself with the sheet.

Geoff looked at Mr Wibbly Wobbly and assessed his chances. They were smaller now, just like him.

"I'm not a Moor," she continued. "For your information, no person is a Moor these days."

That was confusing. She was still black. Not that he planned ever to mention it. There'd been a patient in the dermatology clinic when he was a student. He'd told the woman with keloid on her elbow that unfortunately that type of scar was sometimes a problem with black skin. She then informed him in no uncertain terms that she was not black, she was African.

Geoff mulled all this over, coming to the conclusion, not for the first time, that a white man, especially a privileged white man, had to be extra careful.

"I meant that you're habit-forming," he told Daisy. "Addictive."

She had sat up. Arms crossed, she continued with her lecture. "The Moors were Muslims."

"Not all of them." He allowed himself a sip of tea. "Besides, there's no need to be Islamophobic."

She straightened her back and shook out her curls. "I, Daisy Isabella Long, am not Islamophobic, as you put it."

"But that's how it came out." He permitted himself a tiny smile.

She flounced off to the bathroom in silence, which was probably the nearest she ever came to apologizing.

Oh, yes. He could handle Daisy. He'd been dealing with challenging people for over fifteen years.

DAN

On the forum, the woman had said she grew special vegetables. Dan hoped it wasn't code for some psychedelic drug, because now, standing here in front of Vaughan Road allotments in West London, he wasn't sure what he was going to get.

He rang the woman's mobile. She told him how to prise open the gates at the front. Said she couldn't possibly walk all the way down, her hip was that bad today.

Dan did as instructed. There was a railway line right there, the Metropolitan line out into Hertfordshire. He walked alongside it, following a grassy path to the apex of a long triangle. The place smelled of wood chippings, tomato leaves, and smoke. Regular smoke. Nothing wacky.

People had planted rows and rows of veg. Plus compost heaps. Sheds. Heaps of corrugated iron. England flags.

They also had, so the woman had posted online, some very

special baby carrots. Dan reckoned they would be just the thing for Lolo's, maybe with a touch of truffle oil. Great with their rack of lamb. One thing he'd learned from working in a top restaurant was that you had to stay ahead of the game. And that fresh was king. The key to great dishes was fresh ingredients.

OK. So that was two things. Anyway, he'd volunteered to check out these baby carrots.

When he cooked them, he'd probably leave vestiges of carrot top on. *Vestiges.* Dan experimented with the word. It sounded right in his head.

Allotment folks probably weren't meant to sell the stuff they grew. Then again, who was to know? Dan trod on a corner of chamomile lawn. Scent of crushed chamomile. Total class.

The place was pretty empty, but, as Dan rounded the corner, he saw someone digging like a maniac behind a row of runner beans. As he got closer, he could see it was two people. A man and a woman. On the ground between the beans and a row of courgettes. They'd got a frantic rhythm going. And they weren't digging.

The couple were middle-aged at least, and they were down to their shirts. He was thrusting for all he was worth. She was clutching his buttocks with both hands like he was harvest abundance. The bean poles quivered and shook. The couple gasped and moaned. A train went by. They weren't bothered.

Laure would never find herself here, let alone kick off her clothes and her Prada shoes. But Dan could imagine.

"Are you the bloke who's come for my carrots?" said a voice next to him. It was a short round woman with a walking stick and frizzy hair that couldn't decide if it was white or blonde. She chuckled.

"I am he." Dan knew this was correct. Still, it sounded bloody odd.

"Then follow me."

She hobbled to her shed a couple of yards away. On a sack

inside were the carrots, the sweetest smelling ones ever. She told him the name which he immediately forgot. "Aren't they perfect?" she said.

They were, too. She invited him to crunch on one.

There was earth on it. Even so, it tasted even sweeter than it looked. Made Dan forget he didn't much care for raw carrot.

"Why don't you take a few to try? You don't have to pay for these ones, and if you like them then we'll talk about my supplying some more. Broccoli raab?"

"Excuse me?"

"I've got some fabulous broccoli raab, or will have a bit later on." Its other name was *rapini*, she informed him. An Italian veg which wasn't a real broccoli at all. It was so much nicer than that. "Are you interested?"

"Might be. Certainly want some of that," he said, pointing to the carrots. He thought of the couple by the runner beans. He wanted some of that, too.

She went to wrap the carrots. Dan stared up at the railway line, then across at Harrow Hill with its wonky church spire. He filled his lungs. Out over two years now, but he never got tired of breathing real air.

He glanced again towards the runner beans. In his experience, there was nothing like sex to forget your worries. Too bad that was in short supply lately.

She returned with a package neatly wrapped in newspaper for him.

"Thanks very much." He gestured with his head towards the runner beans and raised an eyebrow.

She leaned on her stick and lowered her voice. "She's got a new feller in almost every week. But you know what? What people do on their patch ain't my business. Unless they've got Japanese knotweed."

No wonder there were waiting lists for allotments. Dan picked his way back to the gate, realizing he'd collected more than vestiges of mud on his shoes.

The man had gone. He caught sight of the woman wearing a shirt. Just her back visible. She was sitting on a broken plastic chair, puffing on a ciggie.

He continued down the grassy path, new carrots under his arm and lots of thoughts in his head.

CHAPTER FIFTEEN

HARRIET

"I've been thinking," said Sanjay.

Another bad sign. Harriet already knew something was wrong before he came up to the flat. He normally looked full-on at the camera in the entryphone and gave a cheery wave or said, 'I'm here with a friend. Can we interest you in a copy of *The Watchtower*?'

Today he'd ducked. He never ducked.

She buzzed him in. Then he sat next to her on the sofa, had the cup of tea she'd made him, and told her he'd been thinking. All the while, *Be Here Now* was playing. It had been one of her favourite albums for over fifteen years, but from now on she would always hate the Gallagher brothers and their grating Mancunian accents.

"Why, Sanjay?" It was the only thing she could think of.

At first he stared at his feet. "Look. When we met, I thought I was a goner. Now I've got my life back, and... Well, I guess I want to be single for a bit."

"I knew it!" She'd even told him so about two years ago, as she reminded him. "We should have talked."

He had the decency to look upset. "Yes, we should have. But we can't seem to talk the way we used to."

"Have we even tried?"

"I don't know."

Of course that made no difference. No, he didn't want a break. He wanted a break-up. And no, there wasn't anyone else.

She didn't know whether to believe that or not, but she was as dignified as possible, doing her best to save the tears for later.

Sanjay seemed to agonize. He said he was so sorry, and he didn't want her to blame herself for anything. Over the next hour or so, he even held her hand (which she pulled away) and said he thought he still loved her but needed to do this. It made no difference what he said because at the end of it he still fancied being single more than he fancied her.

He packed up his stuff. He'd never moved in, so there were just a few T-shirts, underwear, and a phone charger.

Then he was gone, leaving nothing behind except the hint of a dent in a sofa cushion. She touched it experimentally. Wanted to rest her cheek on it. Hadn't realized how much she loved him, the fucking bastard.

The air was close. Maybe she should go out. She shoved a wad of tissues into her bag and grabbed her keys.

The first person she encountered on Parliament Hill Fields was actually a dog, a dripping wet Labrador with a ball in his mouth, with a woman in wheezy pursuit, probably all the way from one of the ponds. It was cooler than it had been and the paddling pool was shut, but it was a fine September day, and children down by the swings were screaming their heads off.

Harriet passed the pong of greasy chips from the café and headed up the hill. A couple sat on the grass at the top, drinking champagne. She quickly looked away, eyes filling, and nearly bumped into a jogger.

A man approached her, camera in hand. "Please?"

"OK." Harriet took the required photo of the tourist and

his friend, with the London skyline in the background, just as he wanted.

"Thank you, thank you. I love you," said the man.

Another guy who had no idea what love meant, thought Harriet.

On the path, a white-haired woman warned a little girl not to get too close to the squirrel. Harriet let them pass and found herself by a bench where another couple sat as one, folded in each other's arms.

Tears welled up again despite herself.

The little girl had lost interest in the squirrel. "Nan-nan, why is the lady crying?" Nan-nan tried to shush her, but the girl went on, "Has she lost her dolly?"

Harriet rummaged in her bag for a tissue. She most certainly had lost her dolly.

She took the path downhill as tears clouded her vision. Before she could stop herself, she'd taken a tumble. Her knee hurt right away. It was grazed beneath a hole in her tights.

"Are you OK?" asked a passer-by.

"Fine." Harriet got up, trying not to look him in the eye. "Only hurt my dignity." She picked a few pieces of gravel out of her palm and rubbed her grazed knee, to little effect. The man was still there, observing her with a tilted head, so she laughed nervously and said, "I should put more water in it."

"What is?" he replied, baffled. "I get you water?"

Of course. He was from Poland or somewhere. That was the thing with foreigners. They often spoke English pretty well, but didn't get jokes.

"Oh, no thanks. I'm fine. Really."

Eventually convinced, he wandered off.

If Sanjay had been here, he'd have kissed her knee better. Made her laugh. Rubbed her hands. Bought her new tights. And made her laugh some more.

Well, sod him. She could buy her own fricking tights. She could even kiss her own knee if she really wanted.

Down the hill, she found a charity shop where she got a pair of opaque tights. She put them on in the fitting room, bundled up the bloodied ones, and dumped them in a bin on the pavement. Too bad the shop didn't sell sunglasses too.

SANJAY

Mum came out of the kitchen with more dishes than he'd thought anyone could lift, let alone someone who was less than five feet fall. She set them on the table and gazed up at Sanjay. "How is Harriet?"

Sanjay shrugged and made a non-committal noise. What was there to say? Once, he'd thought he and Harriet would be together forever. Till their teeth fell out and their hair disappeared down the plughole. Till they used the loo in front of each other not because it felt natural but because they needed help. Well, that wasn't going to happen.

"Ha?" Mum persisted.

Sanjay shrugged again. Her interrogation catapulted him back more than two decades. Then, every question your parents asked was loaded, and the only possible answer was a half-hearted movement of one shoulder. To show you didn't give a stuff, you had to use as few muscles as possible.

He studied the polished wooden table while Mum moved a few plates about unnecessarily delicately. She was freaking him out. Normally she banged things about as if she was trying to wake up Uncle Sanjeev who was congenitally deaf.

"She is very nice person," Mum went on. "Why you not bring her for dinner anymore? She has not been here since before Easter."

Harriet had loved Mum's cooking, of course. Everyone did. She hadn't been since—well, Sanjay wasn't sure. Why should he remember? He wasn't the anal type, with perfect recall of every pointless detail of every single conversation going back to prehistoric times, just in case it was needed to throw back at someone later.

"Oh, God! You have had quarrel, yar? You silly young people," she said, ignoring the fact that he was nearly forty. "Your father and I used to quarrel, but then we found it was all about nothing. Let her win, *beta*. It's not rocket salad."

It was amazing how often she invoked rocket salad. Fact: she had never once served it.

She held out more cutlery. "Take, *beta*. Lay the table. Your father taught you, didn't he?"

He gave another adolescent shrug, but yeah, it was true. Dad could be as traditional as anyone, with his little tache, his import-export business, and a stay-at-home wife, but for all that he was totally a new man, exactly as he claimed to be.

Sanjay positioned the cutlery carefully, as if each location required measuring to the nearest millimetre. When he'd finished, Mum was still there, wearing an expectant look. Fuck it! Did someone his age really owe his parents an explanation? On the other hand, they'd taken to Harriet. "Thing is, Mum," he said. "Harriet and I, we're not seeing each other anymore."

After the briefest pause to absorb this, Mum began shaking her head in a restrained English way. He'd have felt more comfortable had she started screaming, or done those over-the-top head movements that the family did when getting emotional.

"So you are not seeing each other." More sad shaking. "*Beta*, I worry about you. You'll see, your father will agree with me."

When his father came in, he didn't agree right away because first he had to bring them up to date about bloody fucking nincompoops he worked with. He shoved a chapatti in his mouth, most of which sprayed out as he explained about damn numbskulls he had to deal with, and flaming delivery office didn't bear thinking about, yar. "I call them five times before bollocking shipment collected!" He held up fingers to reinforce his point.

Sita came in late. "I'm famished, innit," she announced as she raced upstairs to change out of her charcoal grey work suit and into something more appropriate.

When she emerged from her room a minute later, she was an apparition in a purple leopard-print skirt and a skin-tight vest in a clashing shade of puce. Sita regularly changed her looks but, whatever she wore, it had the class of a trailer park. Sanjay stared at an inflamed tattoo on her shoulder. It was a unicorn or maybe a deformed goat.

Mum announced, "Your brother has argued with Harriet."

Dad looked shocked and Sita went, "Whaaat?" losing a chunk of chapatti down her cleavage in the process.

"They are broken up," Mum continued. "And now I will not say anything. They must sort it out." She gave Sanjay a defiant look and added, "It's not rocket salad, is it?"

Dad shook his head in the same worrying English way as Mum. It was giving Sanjay the creeps.

Sita reached across for the brinjal. That was when the folks spotted her shoulder.

"What is that?" Mum pointed as if her finger might get poisoned in the process.

"It's a unicorn." Like it was the most natural thing to make an appearance on an accountant's shoulder.

"Oh, God. Not another tattoo!" went Dad. "And this one is fucking ugly, ha."

That triggered a huge row about tats, especially bad tats, bad language, and lots of other things that didn't seem very relevant to Sanjay. Still, it made it easier for him to slope off early and avoid further interrogations about his love life. He finished his brinjal and made a dash for it.

Shelley greeted him as if her bowl had lain empty for days, although it was, as usual, about a third full. She continued to purr and wind herself round his legs while he topped it up with special new food, the best money could buy because he wanted her to have a long healthy life and silky fur, as per all the adverts.

Sanjay watched her purr and guzzle simultaneously. Cats were easy to love.

Women, now. Far more tricky. He recalled that incredible first weekend away with Harriet. The cable car at Montjuic. The king-size bed. The morning he had told her his cancer was closing in for the kill.

She'd wanted him all the same. Three days later, he thought they'd made a connection that would last forever.

"How wrong can one be, eh, Shell?" He bent down to scratch her between the ears. She assumed he was after her food and growled ominously.

Was it easier to love someone completely when you were going to die? In the bathroom, he scooped a lump of fossilized cat poo out of the tray and made a mental note to give Shelley some oily fish before she got completely bunged up.

Another tough one: why was he so fucking dissatisfied with life now that it looked like there'd be plenty of it ahead? They'd stolen the cancer from Sanjay, and given him TB instead. Being terminally ill was terrifying enough, but surviving could totally unhinge a person. Bollocks! It made no fucking sense.

He flushed the loo and sprayed the room with orange blossom air freshener. Now he knew what he had to do. Make up for lost time.

First he'd call Shofiq. They'd been friends since primary school in West Harrow, he, Ben, and Shofiq, though it had been a while since they'd all been out together.

"Hey, Sanjay, mate," said Shofiq.

"Hey, Shofiq. Long time and all that." He wanted to know what Shofiq had been up to.

Turned out Shofiq had big news. "Me and Shereen are getting married next year, *insh'Allah*."

Sanjay was too shocked to point out that it should have been

'Shereen and I' but he did say, "That's great, mate. What's with the *insh'Allah*?"

The pause was just palpable. "Her family are quite, er..."

Devout? Religious? Radical Muslim? Sanjay waited as the possibilities reeled in his head.

"Traditional," said Shofiq. "Whenever you talk about the future, you have to add *insh'Allah*. I'm trying to get into it, like."

Sanjay absorbed all this. Time was when all Shofiq tried to get into was girls' knickers. "That's wonderful," said Sanjay. "I'm really pleased for you both."

What else was there to say? Now Sanjay couldn't very well ask him if he knew any hot women to introduce him to. They rang off shortly after, promising to see each other soon.

"*Insh'Allah*," added Shofiq.

Sanjay stroked Shelley and put on some music. One day, when he didn't have to live on a charity worker's pay, he might have that room-to-room system, but for now it was a not-too-shabby fifty watts per channel. He decided against The Traveling Wilburys and Michael Jackson. Musicians who were already dead had been his constant companions while he was ill, but new times demanded new tracks. Granted, Ocean Colour Scene were at least twenty years old, but the idea of catching that train they kept mentioning filled him with hope. He let the lyrics wash over him for a few minutes and lift his spirits.

Somewhere he had a number for the stunning woman he'd met at Laure and Dan's dinner party. What the fuck was her name? Daisy. That was it.

He scrolled through his phone.

HARRIET

The next day began with a pounding head and a tongue that was too big for her mouth. She put the empty bottle in the recycling bin downstairs.

The old lady from the ground floor called out, "Hello, dear."

She was outside her flat, clutching a bunch of newspapers and swaying on shapeless feet. She gave Harriet a wide smile, displaying the red lipstick she always applied with complete disregard to the actual contours of her lips. Today she had also tucked a gardenia behind one ear.

Harriet returned the greeting.

Well, she thought, when she got back to her own flat. If that old biddy could be cheerful, then so could she. She gave herself a stern talking to, with the express instruction not to mope about Sanjay.

"Think positive, Harry. I mean Harriet." She now had plenty of time to write her novel. Didn't they say that misery made good writers?

With that, she slung the fridge magnet into the bin. "Take that, fucking *Pride of Suffolk*," she told it as it clanked against the metal.

Her magnum opus would take her mind off her suffering. It was a novel about speed-dating, and loosely based on the information she'd gathered for a series of features called *The Seven Ages of Dating*.

She put on *Jagged Little Pill* and let Alanis Morissette sing her pain for her, though not too loud as there was still a little hammer going inside her head. Then she turned to her fiction.

As Harriet re-read Chapter One, she could see how laughable that was. You couldn't just string a series of anecdotes together and make it into a title fit for the shelves of Foyles. Besides, she'd dedicated it to Sanjay.

Sod Sanjay. She'd based their two-year relationship on

the fact that Sanjay liked cats. And the shag-fest of their first weekend.

Harriet deleted the dedication.

As she returned to Chapter One, she spotted another problem: getting characters in and out of rooms. She could make them walk, amble, sidle, hobble, swish, or, with the aid of the thesaurus, employ any of a wide range of other means of locomotion. But in how much detail did she have to describe everyone's movements?

They got up from the table. Suzi pulled the dress down over her stretched stomach. They all went into the living room.

Whether they walked or sashayed, they surely didn't all go through the door at the same time. The setting was only a 1930s semi, not a stately home.

And what were they going to do once they got to the living room?

Suzi sat herself by the window where she could enjoy the last rays of the sun and spy on her mysterious neighbour at the same time.

That was all very well, but if Harriet didn't mention Theo, Martha, and Greg, wouldn't the reader wonder whether they were all still standing around like lemons, while Suzi was the only one sitting down?

Theo and Martha shared the sofa, while Greg leant against the wall and puffed on his cigarette as if there was no such thing as a smoking ban.

The guy was a dick to smoke when there was a pregnant woman in the room. Harriet scratched her head. Fiction was ridiculously involved.

It would only get worse in Chapter Two, which brought the dilemma of what to do with their limbs when they were hugging, and, even more complicated, having sex in Chapter Three. If Theo's left arm went under Suzi's ribs, where did her right arm go? Did authors have to mention which arm went where?

Another pang as she remembered that, had she and Sanjay still been together, she could have checked her scenes for feasibility.

Maybe her characters could all be contortionists. Much simpler.

It was half past midnight and she couldn't sleep. Across the street, people were having fun.

Very noisily.

She wrapped the pillow round her head to block out the noise. Lucky old deaf lady downstairs.

It was supposed to be a quiet residential street. How dare they make all that noise? The longer she was awake, the more she thought of Sanjay. A vicious circle.

She dozed off eventually, and woke with a dry mouth in the middle of the night. She automatically stretched out her hand right to the other edge of the bed. He wasn't there.

When changing the sheets that morning, she had found two of his hairs on her pillow. She had twiddled them together, entwining them just as he and she had been when together. That made them stronger. Then she had safely placed the hairs under the bedside lamp.

At about half past four, she got up to use the loo, giving the hairs a feel as she went. As if it would help bring him back.

You never knew.

CHAPTER SIXTEEN

LAURE

Poor Jack. Not even autumn yet, and here he was with a stream of green candle wax from each nostril.

Laure tried to wipe the snot away as he wriggled and kicked. The hard edge of his first proper shoes hurt her shins. "Keep still, little man. I've just got to wipe your poor nose." She was using cotton wool because it was softer, as she'd read in one of her childcare books.

He was still drinking from a cup and eating his meals, but it all took longer. Breastfeeds were especially fraught, and the green stuff got on her skin.

His first winter, Jack had been plagued with a string of colds, along with coughs and snuffles. He'd also gone off his feeds for no reason, and developed ear infections, strange rashes, and unexpected fevers, which made it little short of a miracle that he'd reached his first birthday. Agonizing bouts of teething had preceded each of his four teeth, and no doubt there'd be plenty more of that to come.

Not to mention all the trouble the other end.

Laure had studied and restudied the parenting guides, from

Leach and Stoppard to Cooper and Collins. It still amazed her how often babies had the runs, and consequently how quickly buttocks could become as red as a monkey's. Baby experts said parents needed to be aware of all the signs of dehydration. Nobody could have been more aware than Laure of sunken eyes, dry tongue, lethargy, irritability, and a sunken soft spot. Just as assiduously, she observed the contents of each nappy. She could have drawn her own baby stool colour guide.

Dan would come home to find the bin stuffed with peach-coloured nappy sacks. "Bloody hell!" he'd say. "How much did that little lot cost? Cheaper to wrap his bum in ten pound notes."

Then he'd go and play with Jack, making him crack the loudest laughs ever, until they both got tired and crashed onto the sofa.

Dan had no idea what it was like looking after Jack twenty-four seven. It was the most satisfying thing Laure had ever done, and the most frustrating. Since when had commercial contracts wailed for two hours non-stop? Or up-ended her handbag and pulled the books off the shelves?

Jack was toddling now, with a confidence far in excess of his ability to balance. To stop himself falling, he'd grab at whatever came to hand. It could be a tablecloth or a lamp. Today he got brave and weaved his way unaided across the middle of the living room, screeching with pride once he reached the little table on the other side of the room. He lifted one foot after the other off the floor, then took both hands off the table. He squealed with glee a few more times and promptly fell, mouth open, onto the edge of the table.

Laure rushed to gather him in her arms. The bleeding was torrential. Had he torn an artery in his mouth? Or knocked out one of his new teeth? She struggled to take a look but he screamed and wriggled and kicked and cried. Each scream pumped out scarlet blood mixed with saliva.

"Poor baby, poor baby," she incanted as she got paper towels from the kitchen. Now she could see a jagged wound right through his lip to the inside of his mouth. No wonder he was howling.

She felt her breathing change. Harsher at first, then faster. And her heart was beating all over the place, especially in her chest and her temples. Her hands trembled despite herself.

"There, there," she intoned, barely audible above his screams. He had spat out the paper towel. She could smell his blood, his baby smell, her own helplessness.

Who was there to call? The health visitor was elusive after 10 a.m., and the GP was never available. She'd had to leave a message on countless occasions. He or she would always ring her back later, by which time it would be too late. As she rummaged through the first aid kit, she realized there was nothing suitable for injuries such as this. Briefly she considered Accident and Emergency, but a long wait would be inevitable.

The bleeding was easing off. Calmer now, Jack dribbled a little blood-stained saliva onto his beloved blankie.

In the end she rang the practice nurse who suggested ice and assured her that it would heal in the end. "But you can come in if you're worried, and I will take a look."

Jack didn't like the ice. As he was happily playing with his toys now, Laure left it. She also left the bloodied paper towels on the kitchen counter as exhibits for Dan when he got in.

He breezed in from work, his kiss reeking of garlic.

She gave him a blow by blow account.

"Relax," said Dan. "He's learning to walk."

"He could have really hurt himself."

Jack chose this moment to beam at Dan and say, "Car," as he offered him a wooden vehicle.

"But he didn't. It's only a cut."

"It's a very deep cut. Have you actually seen all this blood?"

"It's stopped now," Dan pointed out.

Sometimes Jack had been feverish and off his feeds all day, and Dan would insist he was the picture of health. Which showed how obtuse Dan was about kids. It was impossible getting the right attention from him.

Laure wished she could have hit Dan over the head with something, got it out of her system by clubbing him with a bottle of extra virgin olive oil. But the bottle was plastic and she wasn't the type. So instead she got upset and the horrible pounding in her chest would begin again. She went to the bathroom cabinet for some of that Bach rescue remedy, while knowing it made no difference.

GEOFF

"What are you going to do about this?" complained Geoff.

"Do about what?' said Daisy, even though it must have blindingly obvious.

He threw the sheet back dramatically, hoping to amuse her. "This."

She laughed as if it was of no consequence, a mere bagatelle. The woman was so inconsiderate.

"Please?" he went.

She covered her head with the pillow and said, "I'm not a morning person," she said.

Sunlight streamed through the window. Geoff checked the clock. "We've got at least ten minutes before we need to get up. You don't have to do anything. Just sit on it for a bit." It was worth a try, just in case she saw the funny side and relented. His situation was ridiculous, given that a year ago he had to take two Viagra for anything to happen at all. Last night he had only taken one tablet. Maybe he didn't need it anymore.

"I'm not sitting on anything," she replied, her voice muffled.

"Please," he tried again.

"Mrff."

"You're an actor. You could at least fake some enthusiasm."

"No."

"Or some sympathy?"

She removed the pillow to say, "Go take a cold shower."

"The amount of effort you're spending putting me off, you may as well put me out of my misery."

"Sounds like you need a vet."

"You were keen enough last night."

"Like I said, I don't do mornings." She covered her head once again.

Geoff had got used to early starts as a hospital doctor. Now he actually liked mornings, especially for sex. He assessed his predicament again. It was showing no sign of going away. "I suppose a blow-job is out of the question?" he asked as a last ditch attempt.

Her response was inaudible from the depths of the pillow.

"You can't even see how much I'm suffering. It's probably against the Geneva Convention."

Sighing, he got up to make tea. In the hall he paused in front of the mirror and told himself he was magnificent. He turned from side to side for a full appraisal. Yes, he was in the peak of condition and rather proud, in every sense of the word. The Viagra headache and red eyes had subsided, and the Greek column that was his knob drew the eye away from an early pot belly, especially if he tensed his abdominal muscles.

It was all he could do not to scald himself making the tea.

"Thanks," Daisy said as she took the mug. "Now tell me, is there anything in your brain except sex?"

"Nothing whatsoever. All the blood's gone somewhere else. Which is hardly surprising. There you are with your heaving bosom and here I am with my throbbing Mr Wibbly Wobbly. What do you expect?" He gave it a little wave to emphasize his point.

"Nothing's heaving except my stomach," she said as she flounced off to the bathroom, taking her green tea with her.

SANJAY

As he tucked into Mum's chicken for the second time this week, Sanjay thought it was no bad thing being single. Although he could have done without the brush-off from Daisy.

She'd been breathing heavily when he called. Probably vaping again. Yes, of course she remembered him from the dinner party. "You're the guy with a plastic testicle."

Sanjay quickly said, "Also tall, dark, and handsome, as I'm sure you recall."

She had laughed throatily at that, but, even so, he'd been unable to tempt her to meet for a glass of something. "I'm very busy right now, both workwise and socially. But do keep in touch if you'd like to."

It was slap in the face, but he'd have to toughen up if he was going to be young, free, and single as well as tall, dark, and handsome.

He wiped the last of his sauce up with a chapatti and suppressed a burp. After they'd eaten more food than anyone needed for a week and heard all about the vagaries of the import-export business, Dad went off to deal with the dishes. Was he moving a bit more slowly than usual, Sanjay wondered. Perhaps it was just his imagination.

"Let's go to the park, yeah?" said Sita.

Sanjay stared at her. Sita hadn't wanted to go to the park with her brother since she was about twelve.

"Yeah. OK." Although he didn't smoke anymore, he automatically patted his pocket for cigarettes and a lighter. That used to be the only reason for going to the park with his sister.

Sita grabbed one of her hoodies on her way out. It came down nearly to the hem of her short red skirt, but at least it covered up the wonky unicorn on her shoulder.

They sat on the swings in the deserted playground. Sita's bum overflowed the seat and the metal chain must have been digging into her thighs but she didn't seem to mind. They gazed into the night as it fell. In the distance, a hopeful ice cream van was still doing the rounds.

Sita went on the swings. "If I swing really high like this, I can see the church," she said.

"If you swing really high, I can see your *punani*."

"That's horrible." She brought the swing to a halt and her face crumpled, ready for tears. Then she hooted with laughter. When she finally stopped, she turned to say, "So what happened with you and Harriet?"

"Fucking hell! Not you as well."

"Aren't you going to tell me?"

He focussed on his feet. "She's got AIDS."

"You're shitting me."

"Yeah, I am."

Sita set her jaw. "Bro, that is so not funny. Plus, even if she did have AIDS, it wouldn't be a reason to dump her."

"Maybe not. But AIDS would be kind of hard to explain to the folks."

"Fuck! Yeah, so it would."

"Don't swear, Sita."

"You swear all the time, innit. And Dad too. And there's me, all I can say is the occasional *damn* or something."

"You say *innit*. That's way more annoying than swearing."

"Anyway, what happened?" Sita persisted.

He looked at his feet, scraping the ground under the swing. They should have had that special safety surface, but maybe it had worn out. Sanjay tried to work out how much to tell Sita. Fuck it! She didn't need to know he missed Harriet. "It ran its course," he said at last.

The moon was up now, and the ice cream van had finally given up. A cool breeze played with his hair, and with a crisp packet caught in the railings.

Sita was studying him. He shrugged, to make it more final. "What about your boyfriend?" he asked her. "What's happening there?" He was pretty sure that, whoever the guy was, he was married.

She sat in the swing, dangling her feet. "Nothing really."

"You've been with him a while now, haven't you?" he ventured.

"I guess."

He wasn't going to get much more out of her. "Well, as long as you're happy."

"He's married, innit." She made a face as if she'd smelled sewage.

"I knew that."

"Suppose I shouldn't be surprised. You always know everything. Bloody smart-arse."

Instead of reminding her that, as a graduate, she was a bit of a smart-arse too, he said, "How could you, Sita?"

"How could I? Don't lecture to me. You started shagging Harriet while she was living with someone else."

Technically that was true, but at the time Simon and Harriet's relationship was clearly terminal. Sanjay said only, "That was different."

"Yeah. Right."

"Has he got kids?" he asked.

He'd forgotten how quickly Sita's face could set when she was in a strop. This was an award-winning sulk, no less eloquent for being silent.

"So that's a Yes then."

She gave a tiny shrug.

"How could you, Sita?" he said again.

"I know it's not ideal. But bro, do you actually know how hard it is to find a guy? One that's actually single and available? And who's not terrified of commitment?" Her voice was rising. "I've had more commitment from him than from anyone else in the last five years."

She paused to wipe her eyes with a corner of her hoodie, and Sanjay saw the rims were red. "Anyway, if you remember, we were talking about you. What do your friends say about Harriet?"

"Don't know."

She responded with a look.

"And before you tell me I don't have enough friends, I have plenty of friends to talk to." That was a slight exaggeration. Ben and Shofiq were his closest friends, but they didn't do a lot of talking about relationships. Hell, Sanjay didn't want to discuss Harriet at all. Had it not been for his family's persistence, he wouldn't even have been thinking of her.

HARRIET

There were lots of good points about the break-up, Harriet told herself. She would make a list of them. Only right now, poised with pen and paper, she couldn't think of a single one, bar the fact that she hadn't been dumped by text.

The pain at night was almost palpable, waking her with a kick in the guts. There'd be a moment before she remembered what it meant, then the sobs would start.

She had to move on, she told herself in the morning. Today was a new day and all that.

Harriet showered and applied foundation with a brush to cover the circles under her eyes. Maybe she'd see Dan, have a coffee or a drink with him at Lolo's. Hadn't he said she could drop by? Plus, from the little she'd seen of him, he made her laugh.

Harriet checked her phone again. The daily photos of Shelley had stopped coming, as had anything else from Sanjay. This constant checking had to stop. She put on the rest of her make-up and decided to go to Lolo's today.

As she applied mascara, she wondered what Dan's word of the day would be. Harriet found herself managing perfectly well with quite a limited vocabulary, especially lately. This included the phrases *fuck him*, *more wine*, and *I hate the bastard*, especially when she was with Virginia. Which she didn't quite mean, because if Sanjay turned up now she'd probably tear off his clothes and drag him to bed.

She hadn't been to Hampstead Village for a while, perhaps only once since Lolo's had opened its doors. It was far too expensive.

It was another fine day, so she put on a hat and walked all the way, taking the road past Keats's house and then up Rosslyn Hill, past the fabulous deli and all the cafés. The shops in Flask Walk were spilling over with flowers and bric-a-brac. By the time she could see the Flask Pub and the front of Lolo's, the back of her neck was melting like one of Oddono's gelati.

Dan looked hassled, his face was shiny and wet, his apron rumpled and stained with something that could have been red cabbage. At least, she hoped it was red cabbage.

"Hi," said Harriet.

He made a face and replied, "Bad time."

"I'm sorry. Looks like you're busy today." She'd been about to sit down in this elegantly cool dining room, with the high windows and ceiling fans, hoping to have a cappuccino and maybe some of those wood-hard aniseed biscuits while they chatted and laughed during his break. Instead she just stood there, holding onto the back of a chair.

He shrugged one shoulder. "It's been pretty much like this all week. Sorry."

She smiled and repositioned her handbag strap on her shoulder. "Is there a better time maybe?"

"I don't know. I mean..."

"That's OK. See you around."

She left before her eyes turned into leaky taps again.

Dan had definitely said *any time*. As bad as *let's do lunch*. Or *the payment's in the system*.

Lying should be made illegal.

Harriet exited as fast as she could to Hampstead High Street, the land of gourmet bites, pricey fashions, exquisite antiques, and the myriad lovely things that other people had in their lives.

CHAPTER SEVENTEEN

KAREN

Crap! She'd forgotten all about Thomas and his suit, and there he was at the door, beaming like an idiot. Impeccable timing, as ever.

"You've just missed Damon and Ashley," Karen informed her ex.

"That's OK," he said, charging in as if the place still belonged to him.

"Well, I know they'd like to see you a bit more often. As would the other two." She, however, did not, though she vaguely recalled he wanted to pick something up as well as his suit. "What do you want?"

"I've come for my suit, if you remember." He grinned. "Though mad passionate love on the futon would be nice too."

"Don't be such a tosser. I found your suit. It's right here," she said, opening the hall cupboard.

"What about my spoon?"

"What spoon?"

"I said in my text," he whined. It was a silver spoon, apparently, which had belonged to his grandmother.

Ah. Not a spooky after all. "I imagine it's still somewhere in the kitchen," she said.

Most annoyingly, he'd already scooted off to the kitchen as if he still lived there. Even worse, he proclaimed, "God, it's filthy in here."

She ignored this. "Let's look in this drawer." Miracle of miracles, an ornate but tarnished teaspoon was lying about among the string, receipts, rubber bands, and money-off coupons. "This it?"

It was, but that didn't satisfy him. He had to pronounce on the state of the drawer too. "That is in a real state. I don't know how you can live—"

The shoe was in her hand before she could think. Had she taken it for re-heeling on her way back from school as intended, it wouldn't have been lying on the kitchen dresser, just waiting for her to pick up and thwack him on the shoulder. He was lucky she couldn't reach his head.

"Ow!"

Karen was equally shocked. She had never hit anyone before, not even when the kids pushed all her buttons or did something really dangerous. She shouldn't have done it today, either, but when someone was that rude, that patronizing, that infuriating, what options were there?

He rubbed his left shoulder. Then came the killer. "You're so beautiful when you're angry."

Men said that a lot. It was condescending and it wasn't even true. How could anyone be attractive when they were spitting teeth? She should have just left the room coolly, patting him on the head as she went. The snag was that she never remembered to do this. Also he was six foot three.

Was it possible he still fancied her? There'd been that episode with the DVDs two years back, but not a whiff of chemistry since, which was exactly as it should be.

Now he was by the kitchen window. Doing nothing apart

from rubbing his shoulder for attention while staring out at her much-abused lawn.

She was going to set him straight. She strode towards him, level with his chest. She was damned if she was going to apologize, at least not until she'd levelled with him about the kids.

"Sit down for just one minute. I've got a bone to pick with you." Had she ever used that expression before? Never mind. This time she was going to tell him what was what.

He made a non-committal sound and installed himself on the seat by the window. In this light the hair above his ears had silvery glints. For one brief moment, she saw what she had missed.

"I've got a bone to pick," she said again, even less sure this was the right phrase. "The kids need a dad from time to time. Especially Edward. How can you ignore your duties as a father and just waft in from time to time when you're concerned about material possessions?"

He glanced down at his lap.

Crap, thought Karen. Now the bone was only too obvious.

He grabbed her hand and tried to plant it on his crotch. Then he had the nerve to grin at her.

"Confession time," he said. "I haven't come round for my suit. I'm here to see you."

She pulled away. "Yeah, well you could have fooled me all the time when you were going after your floozies."

He grabbed her wrists. "Karen, Karen."

"That's my name. Don't wear it out." She said it lightly, but already her heart was pounding far too loud and she feared another hot flush. She wrenched her hands away. The afternoon with the DVDs came back to her as clear as ever. He'd come back to sort through them and take his, and then, for no reason whatsoever, they'd shagged on the carpet in front of the bay window. She'd been furious with him that day as well, and her rage had spilled over into something it shouldn't have.

"Karen, it's you I love. I mean it."

She shook her head. "Not going to happen."

"But you wanted me that day." He obviously remembered it too. "And if you want my opinion—"

"Which I don't. I don't want your opinion. And I don't want your personal problems. What your kids need is some input from you. So just go," she finished, pointing to the door. It gave her huge satisfaction to throw him out, with his suit, his spoon, and his hard-on.

GEOFF

Whoever said people couldn't offend you without your permission had never been a GP. Today one of the regulars was mouthing off about a receptionist.

I know what you mean, Geoff thought. Prize bitch, that receptionist. But even the most even-tempered member of staff would have found Mr Tooth a challenge.

There he sat, an aggressive misshapen fellow with a BMI of thirty-five (according to the computer), and still a smoker despite his lung disease. His most distinguishing feature was the solitary tooth left in his head. It wobbled in the breeze whenever he talked, which he did far too much, accompanied as usual with the squeaking of his accordion lungs. Geoff felt like sticking up for the prize bitch at the front desk.

"Sorry to hear that," said Geoff. "It's been a busy old week out on reception. But don't you worry, I will have a word."

The man's tooth oscillated as he spoke. "You better had, doc. She was well out of order."

One of Geoff's regulars was next, an elderly woman with osteoporosis.

"How's that broken wrist of yours?" he asked.

"It wasn't a break, doctor. It was a *fracture*."

Geoff remembered now. She never just had flu. She always had full-blown influenza.

Glad to get a breather, Geoff nipped to the room next door to borrow a proctoscope. His colleague Helen was slumped at her desk in tears. She waved a letter at Geoff. "It's from a solicitor," she wailed.

The letter alleged she hadn't monitored a certain patient closely enough. Said patient remained in good health, but had suffered massive emotional damage which, according to him, ran into thousands of pounds.

Geoff handed the letter back. "It's never as bad as it seems," he said, which was complete balls.

She wiped her nose. "I've never had a formal complaint before."

He smiled. "Then it was your turn." Helen was one of the smartest and most dedicated doctors he knew, but it made no difference. Every medic got at least one scare like this.

"I don't understand it." She sniffed. "I've done all my appraisals. I've just been revalidated, for God's sake."

Ah, revalidation. It had grown out of the Shipman enquiry and was now the jewel in the crown of the General Medical Council. An expensive and time-consuming process which diligently counted up all the things that did not count, while not counting anything that did. He handed her a tissue.

"Thanks. I want to retire."

"You're thirty-five," he pointed out.

"All right then. I want to be a plumber."

"No, you don't. Trust me, you'll feel a lot better after your ring your defence organization." Then he added rashly, "Call them now."

Which was how he ended up seeing twice as many patients as were originally booked for him. Were Helen's patients grateful? Not exactly.

"I specifically asked for a lady doctor," said the first one.

"Where's the doctor I was booked to see?" barked a woman with a squint and singularly mean lips.

They even had the gall to use her first name. "Where's Helen today?"

The patients were depressed, disgruntled, or had a foul discharge. No wonder Helen talked of hanging up her stethoscope.

When Geoff finally finished, he made himself a cup of tea and rummaged through his old emails. Wasn't there something a while back about regular sessions in A&E?

CHAPTER EIGHTEEN

KAREN

Karen licked the spoon. It was a new chicken recipe. You could never have too much lemon, a TV chef once said, but this tasted as if she'd marinated the chicken thighs in Lemsip.

At least the kids ate it, with the exception of Charlotte who had a Quorn cutlet. Then, while the kids amused themselves, Rose popped round because they hadn't had a proper natter for at least two days.

"Did you shag him when he came over?" asked Rose as soon as she sat down.

"Thomas? Of course not!"

"Well, wouldn't have blamed you. Better than the football coach," continued Rose.

"How do you know? You haven't even met him."

"I know he's using you," Rose said.

If anyone was using anyone, Karen was using him. "I don't think so. Anyway, how are you and Keith?"

"Same old. You know."

Karen knew. Keith hadn't wanted sex since 2006. Rose always said it was because her husband had got lazy, but Karen suspected he'd found someone else.

Rose fiddled with the handle of her mug and tilted her head. "What's it like with the coach?"

"Well," Karen said. "Makes my pulse race and my skin tingle." It also made her legs shake for hours afterwards, though that may have had more to do with the rickety bench than with Footie Dad's prowess.

"So the earth moves, huh?" Rose was practically drooling into her coffee.

Karen lowered her voice. "The whole pavilion moves." One moment she had him clamped between her thighs, and the next she was back in the car, patting down her hair in the rear-view mirror, and acting for all the world as if nothing had happened, save that she was grinning from ear to ear and driving like Lewis Hamilton to collect the kids on time.

"Mummy!" came an anguished cry from the living room. "No yellow ones left!"

"Look under the sofa, Edward," she hollered back. There was bound to be something there, if not the Lego bricks he wanted, then something else that might occupy him. Distraction was a great tactic.

Rose was staring at her. "Why are you smiling like that?"

"Sorry. Miles away. Thinking about football shirts."

"Really?" said Rose.

Karen told her about all the lovely clean kit that the man with the Porsche had brought back. "The mums' shirt-washing rota got me down, so last week I managed to offload a batch of them. And they came back clean." It was entirely possible the Porsche driver's wife had washed them, or the au pair had, but at least Karen hadn't had to.

Rose shook her head. "You're weird."

"I am not! Why should mothers be stuck with all the wash-ing after Sunday football?"

"Because that's how the rota is?"

"Because that's how *society* is. Because despite legislation, and universal suffrage, and all the other pretences at equality, we get lumbered with all the menial stuff. The posset is always on the woman's shoulder, you know. It's deliberate. And it's not fair." Karen paused to mop up the coffee she'd spilled in her fervour. Now she could see how women's lib could easily turn into an armed struggle if people were going to be so obtuse.

"Well, I don't often say this, but I've got to go," Rose said, without actually moving an inch.

"Mummy, look." Edward had just appeared at the kitchen door, holding out five yellow bricks, a Lego pirate hat, and an old sock. "Treasure."

"That's lovely, darling," said Karen as Edward padded out happily.

Rose resumed her favourite topic. "Whatever happened to that doctor guy you met speed-dating? He sounded nice."

"Ah, him." That was two years ago. Geoff was nice. They'd been together only briefly, then he'd upped and gone to be an Army medic just as things were getting interesting. "He's back from Afghanistan. I had an email a while ago."

"You had an email? What are you waiting for, girl?" asked Rose.

Karen surveyed the sink full of dishes. "I don't know. He's very buttoned up." Most likely a chauvinist too.

"You've still got his phone number, haven't you?"

"Rose," she warned. "One can't turn the clock back."

"Did I say anything about clocks? Just give him a call. See how he is. Say you're concerned for him in view of Lyme disease, mumps, or some other outbreak that's keeping him busy. Nobody will be thinking of him. Trust me. Men love being fussed over."

"I don't need that kind of man."

"They're all like that. Get used to it."

Karen gave an exasperated sigh.

"All I'm saying is, give him some attention," Rose continued. "See what happens."

Karen wasn't convinced. Of all the people she'd ever met, Geoff seemed the most self-contained, except when he talked about his son. "OK. I'll text him."

"Make sure you meet up. What are you going to wear?"

"Stop it. I haven't even messaged him yet."

Rose appraised her regardless. "Don't forget your hair. Once in a while maybe you could go to a salon instead of doing it yourself with nail scissors."

Karen crossed her arms. "Right. So, apart from my clothes and my hair, what else have I got to change?"

"You could stop being so animal rights and women's lib."

"Stop it right now!" Karen said as she chucked a tea towel at her. "Listen, you, I've got a riddle for you."

"Shoot," said Rose.

As Karen explained, there was a man out driving one day with his son, and they had an accident. The father was killed outright, but the boy survived. On arrival in Accident and Emergency, the surgeon on duty took one look at the boy on the stretcher and said, 'This is my son.' "So," finished Karen, "how can this be?"

Rose hadn't a clue. "Maybe the boy's stepfather is the doctor?"

"Try again."

"You said the father was killed? Are you sure?"

Karen gave her a stare. "Positive. It's really not that hard."

"A case of mistaken identity?"

Karen had already tried the riddle on Charlotte who'd shrugged. 'Like maybe the surgeon was the boy's mother? Can you take me to Belinda's house in half an hour?' Ashley had a few questions of his own. 'Where were they driving? How did the accident happen? Bet they weren't wearing seat belts. Are you sure the father died? Cos if he did, then who called an ambulance? Cos someone must have. Unless the ambulance was just driving around doing nothing.'

"Rose, you're a hopeless case. The surgeon is his *mother*."

"Right," said Rose, getting up. "Now, what can I make my family tomorrow night with flour and water? Apart from glue."

"I'm the last person you should ask."

LAURE

Daisy took a sip and made a face. "It's too black," she told Laure.

Laure added more milk, reflecting she'd never have made that comment herself in front of someone Afro-Caribbean.

"Thanks." Daisy looked up from stirring her coffee. "So tell me. Why is he called Jack?"

"It's a nice name."

Jack had tipped out all his wooden blocks and was trying to stack one on top of another.

"There are lots of nice names. Why did you pick that one?" Daisy paused, head tilted, eyes fixed on Laure with a look that said there was a reason for everything.

"Well, *Jack* is simple. And it can't be shortened. It's also easy to write and spell," she added, thinking of a child from toddler group who'd been saddled with *Seraphina*. That kid was going to be the last one in her year to master her own name.

"I suppose you can always change it if you don't like it. It's not like he answers to it yet or anything."

As a matter of fact, he did, but that wasn't the point. "We do like the name."

Daisy considered this. "Well then, he can change it himself when he gets to eighteen. Want me to take him for an hour or two? You're looking very tired."

Laure's reaction was an inner howl. She couldn't leave Jack

with anyone. Although Daisy wasn't just anyone. And the books did say to accept offers of help.

"You've never looked after him before," said Laure.

"But I have nephews, and you know I'm good with Jack." Daisy added, "He won't come to any harm, I promise."

It was true that she was good with Jack, and he seemed to love her. "Perhaps just a walk in his buggy then?"

"Sure."

"OK. Just half an hour," said Laure. "Don't go too far."

"I wouldn't."

"Don't take any buses or anything."

"Of course not," said Daisy. "Just a little walk in the buggy. We'll only go up the High Street."

"Don't get him out of his buggy. And if he screams, just come straight back."

"I will. But it's not a problem. He's an easy baby."

"You wouldn't say that if you'd been here in the middle of the night."

After sorting out the sunscreen and the changing bag, just in case, and waving them goodbye, Laure ran a bath. She added cranberry bath oil and got in. Then she wondered if she should get out to phone Daisy and find out how Jack was. She told herself not to be so stupid.

I am calm. I am serene. All is well.

She did some deep breathing, which made her feel light-headed. Perhaps that was the heat of the water. She got out of the bath.

Put your worries in a box, she told herself.

Unable to manage that, she started tidying the toys on the living room floor.

The doorbell went right on time. "It's us!" trilled Daisy. "He's been a little poppet. Haven't you, Jack?"

Laure thought she could detect quotation marks around *Jack*. "Has he been good for his Auntie Daisy?"

"He has indeed."

"Oh, good." Laure refrained from mentioning the wee hours of the morning. "Go anywhere nice?" Jack kicked out his legs and made happy noises as she bent to pick him up.

"We went to the High Street. He did a poo, and I changed his nappy in Caffè Nero. I got him a macaroon, which he liked. Actually I think half of it may still be in the buggy." She retrieved a soggy object from its depths. "Don't suppose he wants it now." She held it up before dropping it into the bin.

Laure put Jack down. He clung to her legs as she got him a beaker of water, then he took it with both hands and chugged noisily. "Did you vape?"

Daisy paused over the open bin. "Only once. You know, Laure, you should lighten up. You're too uptight about your son."

"I'm not uptight. Just sensible."

"So you say. Anyway. Changing the subject, are you and Dan going to get married? Because if you are, there's a fabulous dress in the window of *Mon Mariage*. It would really suit you."

Jack gave back the empty beaker and zoomed off to the living room, where he emptied the contents of the toy box onto the floor.

"Thanks. A dress may not be a reason to get married, though."

Daisy gave a short laugh. "There aren't many other reasons to get married, *chica*. I should know. A great dress eases the pain considerably."

So she was opposed to marriage? The woman was baffling. "I should have thought there were plenty of reasons to get married. Companionship, for one."

"Believe me, it's not companionable when all one of you wants to do is watch the golf on telly or make home-brew in the basement." Daisy arched an eyebrow. "And sex goes out the window."

Laure ignored the comment about sex. "Dan and I don't go out a lot, but we spend a lot of time together." When he was home he was either asleep or playing with Jack, but that was a minor detail.

Daisy arched the other eyebrow. "Only because you don't have a basement."

The more Daisy pointed out the drawbacks, the more obstinately Laure defended marriage. Daisy might not have had a good marriage, and Laure's own parents hadn't done that well either, but plenty of people had wonderful marriages. Well, maybe not wonderful, but—

"They can be long. Or they can be happy," observed Daisy, as if reading Laure's thoughts. "They're rarely both."

Laure began to heat up some chicken stew for Jack. "And you're the expert?"

"Pretty much. And I'm the one who's been married, as you know."

That only made Laure want to rush out and buy the latest issue of *Brides Unlimited*, shop for wedding dresses, and design lacy invitations. Perhaps she could carry a brooch bouquet, as seen in the hands of various celeb brides. There'd be her oldest friends as bridesmaids, she thought as she stirred Jack's stew, plus most people from her office. The first dance. A fantastic cake. Great shoes in which to walk down the aisle.

Jack began to grizzle. Laure made soothing noises and put him in his highchair, complete with his car.

"Something to think about, anyway," said Daisy. "Don't forget to pop round for a Kir Royale some time. Oh, I forgot. You're still breastfeeding. Maybe just a tiny—"

Whatever else Daisy had to say was drowned out by Jack's delight at finally getting his meal.

CHAPTER NINETEEN

HARRIET

Harriet had something else up her sleeve for the editor of *RightHere!* She was considering something like *Smouldering sex with a fireman—why the blaze never goes out*, but she only had to say one word. "Firemen."

"Ooh," the editor said, practically salivating down the phone. "I like a fireman."

Harriet sat down to make a plan. She'd check all the info online about London Fire Brigade, including Facebook, then visit a station. There was no particular deadline, the editor had said. The downside with pieces that weren't topical was that they often got elbowed out of the way by those that were. That wouldn't exactly help with October's rent demand. She fired off another batch of speculative emails to other publications, without much hope.

At first, Harriet thought she'd imagined the knock on the door. When she checked, it was the old lady from downstairs, wearing a pleated skirt, bright pink ankle socks, and a lavish application of red lipstick.

"Hello, dear. I'm just wondering if you can help me."

"I'll certainly try," said Harriet. She hoped to God it was an easy task like opening a jar, rather than helping her shower or something.

"Well, you see." She paused to adjust her bra. "I need to go to Morrisons."

"I don't have a car," said Harriet.

"It's not like that." The woman batted the air with her hand. "I can get there on the bus, but my balance isn't so good these days. It's better if I have someone nice to help me, you see."

Harriet saw. "When do you need to go?"

"Any time now. If that's all right, dear."

They exchanged names on the way to the bus stop. "Call me Nora," said the old lady. She had dressed for the shopping trip in a well-used gabardine coat and a transparent rain hood, and her pockets were stuffed with plastic bags.

"I'm Harriet. Do you have much to buy?"

She waved the air again. "No. Only a few bits and pieces."

They waited ten minutes for the 24 bus, during which time Nora did a wobbly little jig, one hand on the bus post.

Harriet had to help her onto the bus. Nora weaved her way to a seat meant for elderly or pregnant passengers, grabbing every single rail and pole as she went.

"There!" she said triumphantly as she sat down.

Harriet took a seat next to her.

Despite the huge number of bus lanes in North London, they were stuck in traffic.

"Do you have any family, Nora?"

"Yes. But it's not like that." She paused to rearrange her bra again. "I've lived in Savernake Road since I retired, you see."

"Retired from what?"

Nora lifted her chin, looking as regal as anyone could while wearing a plastic rain hat. "I was a translator." She grabbed the rail as the bus lurched forward.

"So you speak lots of languages then?"

"Only six now. I speak Russian, Polish, German, French, Serbo-Croat, and of course English. I didn't keep up my Hebrew." She leaned forward confidentially. "Don't tell the rabbi."

A woman manoeuvred her buggy into the space in the middle of the bus. Nora said something else about translating, but Harriet was busy helping the mother with the buggy.

"And what do you do, Harriet?"

The bus was moving again now.

"I'm a journalist."

Nora studied her. "What sort of journalist?"

What sort, indeed? "I write articles on all kinds of things. Basically, whatever people will pay me to write."

"That's nice." Nora managed to convey the exact opposite. "Who do you write for?"

"I'm freelance, but I write a lot for *RightHere!* magazine."

"I need the toilet," said Nora.

"There must be one in Morrisons." At least, Harriet hoped there was.

At Chalk Farm, Harriet guided Nora off the bus, which proved to be more complicated than getting on. First Nora put one foot towards the pavement, then changed her mind and tried the other one. This went on forever, it seemed to Harriet, with Nora holding onto the yellow support pole all the while.

As soon as they were in the supermarket, Nora tottered all the way to the customer toilets. Harriet went into the cubicle next to her, even though she didn't need to wee.

There was silence from Nora's side.

"Are you OK, Nora?"

There came a long wee followed by shuffling noises.

"I'm fine," said Nora as she lurched out, clinging onto a basin. "Let's shop."

Harriet pushed the trolley while Nora used it for support. They accumulated at least five boxes of breakfast cereal, a tiny packet of sliced luncheon meat, crackers, chocolates, fruit, and lots of panty liners.

"Do you ever use a walking stick?" asked Harriet when Nora threatened to topple over yet again.

Nora replied, "I can't reach the pickled onions."

"Here you go."

Finally they were done. Harriet packed all the shopping into six of Nora's bags and wondered how they would get them all back.

"I can take three bags," said Nora.

She clearly couldn't. Even carrying her own purse threw her balance out of kilter. She was stooped and short, and a shopping bag just trailed on the ground.

"Let's see if they sell shopping carts," said Harriet. It was either that or a taxi.

They did sell them. Nora fretted about the cost.

"I'll pay," said Harriet. "It's a present."

"Thank you, dear."

On the bus home, Nora sighed and stretched both legs out straight, displaying her ankle socks and her brown Mary Janes.

"Did you enjoy translating, Nora?"

"Oh, yes! Well, I was very good at it. People from everywhere asked for me. But I had to work at it, you see." She gave Harriet a meaningful look.

At the door of her flat, Nora gave Harriet a bag of Fox's Glacier Mints and said, "Thank you very much, dear."

"Thank you, Nora."

Harriet realized as she opened her own door that she hadn't given Sanjay a thought for hours, and she'd only checked her messages once. There was really no point, if there were to be no more one-liners from Sanjay or photos of Shelley.

She met her friend Virginia in Café Rouge that evening, when sadness had descended again.

Virginia drained her Pinot Grigio. "You have to remember, Harriet, happiness is like a cat's tail."

Harriet had heard it before, but Virginia was unstoppable. "If you run after it, you'll never catch it. But if you forget about it and go merrily on your way, it'll follow you everywhere."

Harriet made a sceptical face as she speared an olive.

"I know you don't believe me, Harriet, but trust me. Good things happen when you least expect it. You'll see."

Harriet still wasn't convinced, so she was totally unprepared for the buzz on her intercom that night.

LAURE

Laure tried to prise open Jack's fingers. He resisted, holding onto the flex of the lamp for all he was worth.

"Come on, Jack," she wheedled.

He responded by grinning and wobbling from side to side, still gripping the flex tight.

"Cheeky monkey. You know you're not supposed to play with that."

"Ga ga ga ga ga GA!" He thumped the table with his free hand for added emphasis.

Although his legs were planted wide apart, his stance was precarious. The wound on his mouth had healed, but then the other day he'd fallen spectacularly while furniture cruising. In the park yesterday, people had stared accusingly at the massive bruise on his left temple.

Jack tugged the flex experimentally. The lamp inched towards him.

"Oh, Jack. Do I have to remove literally everything from this room until you grow up?" It used to be easy to distract him with a nipple. She was still breastfeeding, but he was less into it these days.

"Gag. Gag. Gag."

"At least you're happy today."

"Ag!"

He could understand every word, she was certain. But surely he should be speaking more by now, especially with all the encouragement she gave him? "Let's read a story, shall we?"

Repetition, said the experts, was good for a child. Before Jack, Laure wouldn't have believed she'd be reading *Each Peach Pear Plum*, let alone know it by heart. It was amazing how completely she'd slipped into the mummy role. If she'd gone back to work, she'd have missed his first few steps.

The downside was that motherhood wasn't great for the nerves. She feared each of Jack's mishaps might be his last. How was it that footballers could fling themselves onto the hard ground from a height of six feet and get up with barely a scratch, while a chubby one-year old picked up injuries at the slightest tumble on the carpet?

She'd panicked, of course, on seeing all that blood in his mouth when he'd cut his lower lip, just as she'd reacted when he'd fallen on his toy box and the side of his head grew a lump the size of an egg.

"I'm going to move that lamp," she told Jack.

He found this hilarious.

Laure pulled the sofa out to unplug the lamp. Then she put the lamp on a high shelf, coiling its flex out of reach. Jack chewed thoughtfully on his blankie as he watched her push the sofa back again.

Nothing bad had happened to Jack today, but even so her hands shook. This was new, her body misbehaving even when Jack hadn't stumbled.

She had to control her breathing. There was a paper bag on the shelf near the lamp. She grabbed the paper bag before her vision grew dim, and her fingers began to tingle and became stiff and straight, because, once they did that, there would be no hope of holding paper bag, Jack, or anything else.

Jack sat on the play mat, a toy car in each hand. He stared at her with wide brown eyes. "Ga?"

"Mummy's fine, sweetheart." The paper bag distorted her voice.

Only last week, her doctor had told her again that it would pass. That it was normal to worry about your baby, especially if you didn't have family around to support you. All mothers worried, said the doctor, her eyes barely flicking in Laure's direction. As usual, the GP was mesmerized by her computer screen.

It was the same with every doctor in the practice. Laure knew because she had seen them all. There must have been something deeply thrilling about the display on the monitor. Then, after a bit, they would glance at her and ask something off-topic, like smoking or contraception.

Laure couldn't see how a coil or a contraceptive implant might help. "Is an implant good for panic attacks?" she'd asked last time.

"Of course not," Dr Bell had tutted. "I just thought you might find it more convenient. A lot of ladies have trouble remembering their Pill after they've had a baby. But you can change to the combined Pill if you want."

"Then no. I mean, no thank you." Laure added, "I'm still breastfeeding, actually."

"I see." It could have meant anything.

"I'd like to go on as long as possible," Laure said.

Dr Bell wasn't listening anymore. She was tapping keys furiously, then swearing at the screen.

Laure's breathing finally settled and she put the paper bag aside. Fresh air might help.

"Shall we go to toddlers?"

Jack made approving noises.

Motherhood was a funny thing, reflected Laure as she crossed the road with the buggy. She was no longer an international lawyer, a description which people usually prefaced with *high-powered*. She was, far more often than she wanted, a supplicant begging for medical attention for her child or for herself.

Dan had turned into the bread-winner. He hadn't had a bean when they'd met at speed-dating. Now, as he'd said himself that morning, he was the paterfamilias.

Laure parked the buggy and heaved Jack out. Was there such as thing as a materfamilias, she wondered.

The church hall was already buzzing. About thirty toddlers were popping in and out of the play house, hitting the hammer pegs with the wrong implement, and shoving each other in their haste to get down the little slide. At the easel, one mother was teaching her child to write her name. "Isn't Tara clever? She's only two and a half, you know."

Laure noticed that Tara wasn't holding the felt tip herself.

The place was obviously teeming with viruses. But Laure now realized that they were necessary to build up an infant's immune system, at least according to the hygiene hypothesis.

Another mother gave Tara's mum a superior look and said that her own daughter was destined for Cambridge at an early age. At that moment, however, the child prodigy was attacking someone with a wooden hammer.

Jack clambered all over the soft play area then spent time on the play mat with its network of roads. It was exactly like the mat they had at home, only stained. But the surroundings were different, Laure reasoned, and interaction was as important as immunity, especially for an only child. Her mind boggled at the amount of worry involved in raising two or more children.

Although Jack should have been tired after all that activity, he sprung out of the buggy when they got home and wanted to play.

"Brm, brm," he went, running a plastic car along the wall in the living room.

The place was overrun with cars. She'd once tried to give Jack a doll. He'd shown no interest.

From a parenting book, she'd picked up the idea of giving Jack a duster to amuse himself while she cleaned. That would help deal with dust and stereotypes simultaneously. Jack had found nothing remotely interesting about a square foot of yellow cloth.

Neither did she, truth be told.

She glanced at the clock. Dan was later than expected.

"Look, Teddy's tired," she said, picking up a discarded bear from the floor. "Shall we put Teddy to bed?" she asked hopefully. It was too early for Jack's bedtime, but a quiet soothing routine was a good thing, said the experts.

"Brm, brm," replied Jack as he crawled out of the room and down the hallway, scraping the wall with his little car as he went.

Laure padded after him. "Teddy needs you to help him sleep, big boy," she pleaded. What would her colleagues at the law firm have thought of her?

Jack had disappeared down the corridor.

She sighed. Jack needed constant watching. The minute she took her eyes off him, he'd find some mischief to get into. Then her panic would set in.

No wonder the flat was cluttered. Once an oasis of feng shui, it was now home to things like discarded beakers and even a little box of raisins he'd clutched in his warm mitt. The mess only made Laure more stressed.

Finally Jack settled on the kitchen floor and got saucepans out of a cupboard. It was not quite the peaceful run-up to bedtime recommended in *Baby & Child*, but as long as Jack was making a racket with pots and pans, he wasn't doing anything dangerous. Now Laure could enjoy a mint tea and concentrate on her breathing. Laure handed him a wooden spoon.

"Good boy," she said. "Just like your daddy."

CHAPTER TWENTY

HARRIET

She peered at the grainy profile on the entryphone. How did Dan even know where she lived? Ah. She'd given him her card during dinner that night, hadn't she? And because only a dodgy dealer would leave off their address, she'd included hers, along with the words *Freelance: features and comments,* her Twitter handle, Instagram, and Pinterest.

"Come on up," she said. What else could she have said?

"Didn't you get my text?" he said when he appeared at her door.

"No." She'd resisted checking for messages, and had mostly succeeded. Looking at her phone now, she read *Sorry about the other day. OK if I pop round?*

"Is it OK then?" He looked great in a white shirt, smart leather belt, and blue chinos.

"Um, yes, of course. Come in. Would you like a coffee?"

"Thanks." There was a not-unpleasant whiff of onions. So he had come straight from work.

She made it black, no sugar, just as he'd asked. He smiled, took the mug, put it down on a shelf, totally ignoring the coaster with a tabby cat on it even though it was right there.

Dan was close now. Very close. Enough for her to feel high voltage electricity. It had been a year since that had happened with Sanjay. She held her breath and waited for a moment to be sure what she'd felt.

"What about Laure?"

"I know." He mumbled something she didn't catch.

Before she knew it, his tongue was inside her waiting mouth. She thought she might die.

His hands found the small of her back beneath her jeans. He rubbed the crease of her buttocks, then eased up her T-shirt as far as he could with their lips still locked. She pulled away to let him remove it altogether.

An image of Laure and Dan together flashed before her. A handsome couple. With a baby. She dismissed it.

His chinos were on the floor beside her clothes.

"Come here, you little pulchritude." He paused. "Doesn't sound quite right, does it?"

"Not quite." But that didn't matter because right now she tingled all over. She moved the laptop and the desk was there, ready to take her weight. It was an old reclaimed school desk she'd rubbed down and varnished, without ever quite losing the smell of old pencils. It was where she did her most productive work, as well as the other kind.

She perched on the edge. A moment later they were fused.

All too soon it was over. He kissed her and was gone. She sat on the sofa in the semi-darkness, not knowing what she felt, apart from glowing.

LAURE

Dan wasn't cooking that night. He'd finished in the kitchen after lunch, but there were loads of things to sort out, he'd said, so he wasn't home till after six. He was in time to get the full evening's performance of whiny Jack.

"Aren't babies supposed to become happy and smiling at some point?" he asked. "He's a year old now."

Laure, bouncing Jack on her hip to keep him quiet, had no idea. He wasn't due another feed yet. He wasn't due anything. He'd even refused the last breastfeed but she resolved not to take it personally. As sad as it was, Jack was just growing up. "That's what he's like."

"Well. I'm wiped out." Dan threw himself into the sofa instead of horsing around with Jack as he usually did. "The guvnor only turns on the charm for customers. He's a bloody tyrant in the kitchen."

Laure shrugged and put Jack down on the floor. "Goes with the territory, doesn't it?"

"I suppose. Was Jack any better earlier today?"

"No. A complete terror again, apart from a brief respite." Daisy had looked after him for an hour, but couples didn't have to tell each other everything. "He's actually better now that you're home."

"Yeah. Well. He's not that chuffed to see me, is he?"

Jack was on the floor, flinging one plastic car after another in Dan's direction. Most of the time he missed, though one missile got Dan on the shin.

"It's normal," Laure explained. "He's developed eye-hand coordination just enough to be able to throw things, but his skills don't extend to being careful."

Dan heaved himself up. "I need a drink."

"I could use an elderflower, if you're offering."

There was much clinking of glasses and slooshing of liquids

from the kitchen before he asked, "Have you thought any more about stopping breastfeeding?"

"Not yet."

"Shall I make dinner?"

"That would be lovely," she said. "Seeing as one of us has to look after Jack."

"You don't mind? You've had him all day."

"It's fine."

Since that morning, Laure had made progress with the new box technique. You took all your emotions about the thing that worried you, put those in a box inside your brain, then shoved the box into a corner.

Through the hatch, Laure could see Dan opening cupboards, chopping things, and boiling up stock. The little parsley pot was shorn. He cut a lemon, pressed a couple of garlic cloves, and found a tin of *ras el hanout* which he sprinkled onto chicken pieces. Before long, a spicy North African aroma filled the flat.

Laure shepherded Jack into the bathroom.

"Barf barf barf," hollered Jack. As he watched the water rise, he continued with a running commentary, some of which actually made sense.

Once in the bath, he splashed, poured water from one beaker to another, and fiddled with the hot tap while Laure tried to distract him with wind-up toys. Basically Jack loved everything about bathtime, except getting out. He made a boot-face as Laure heaved him out of the water.

"Drying time!" Laure announced, holding out a big towel. Jack cheered up and made a beeline for her, covering her in moist hugs and kisses. He then wriggled and giggled as was a she dried his hair. He smelled delicious.

She took him to the kitchen to say 'nite nite' to Daddy, then put him in his cot, read him *The Big Hungry Caterpillar* again, gave him one last breastfeed, kissed him goodnight, and crept out backwards while praying fervently they'd be able to have dinner in peace.

Back in the kitchen, Dan was shuffling dishes. He shut the oven door and flung a tea towel over his shoulder. "Got a question for you. Is there anything odd about calling something a *little pulchritude*?"

"Sounds bizarre. Where'd you hear that?"

Dan concentrated on the wooden spoon in his hand. "I think it was at work. One of the customers."

"Really?" It was exactly like a word Dan might have picked out from the dictionary.

"Well, I overheard it. Somewhere. Thought it sounded offbeat. That's why I'm asking."

"It comes from Latin and isn't much used."

She went to lay the table and to listen out for Jack, then returned to the kitchen. "What sort of thing would you associate with pulchritude?" she asked.

"A large lobster on a platter." He grinned. "And you, of course."

He'd hesitated a fraction too long, but it still made her smile.

"Dinner in about five minutes." Dan stood against the wall with a glass of wine, watching things simmer. On the counter his mobile vibrated twice. He ignored it.

She folded a tea towel and placed it on the oven door. "Dan. How do you see our future?"

He put down his glass. "Well. If I look too far into the future, I see things like ISIL beheading half the world, or meteors crashing down. If the polar ice caps don't melt and drown us all first."

"I wasn't thinking about the world. I meant this family. Us."

"You'll stop breastfeeding one day," he said. "And maybe we'll have another baby. Or you'll go back to work. Or maybe even both."

"I don't want to go back to work. You know that."

He drained his glass. "You will one day."

One day. When Jack became smelly and spotty, his bedroom

was a bomb site, and he was falling over his own feet, grunting in a new voice several octaves lower. Maybe then. Not now.

"It's not as if you have a wonderful time at home with him," continued Dan.

"But I do." She began to list all the ways that Jack was adorable, and all the reasons why she couldn't be parted from him. Then, aware they were getting off the point, she said, "But we'll always be together, all of us, no matter what. Right?"

He smiled. "Of course. Just about to serve up now."

She put her elderflower drink down and went to give him a full-on kiss.

"Whoa. Mind my denture. Needs a bit more glue." Even so, he was beaming.

Now was a good time to test him out. "How would you like to do that in front of a happy crowd?"

"Like on the balcony at Buckingham Palace? Or in a film? I'd need to bring a tube of Fixodent, just in case."

"No," she said carefully. "In front of a large congregation. Doesn't have to be a church, of course. It could be a registry office." She looked up to assess his reaction.

He ran his tongue from side to side over his palate. "You mean a wedding?"

She nodded.

He said no more, but at least he hadn't run out of the room screaming.

She considered it all later, in great detail. When you had a baby, nights were best spent sleeping, but that night Laure pondered instead. What did Dan really think of getting married?

And why hadn't he answered his mobile as he usually did?

CHAPTER TWENTY-ONE

GEOFF

Too much going on, thought Geoff as he put a ready-made lasagne into the oven. Patients to see, students to teach. And there was Daisy. Which reminded him: he needed a fresh supply of sildenafil. He poured himself another glass of red. It might not be the best thing for erectile problems, but it de-stressed him. Was he crazy to take on extra work like the new TV programme he had signed up to?

Well, it kept him busy. Davey—correction, Dave—was still away. It was two years now. His time away would be up soon, by Geoff's calculations, but it had been a long famine, sustained only by short Skype calls.

'Went to the beach,' Dave would say. Or sometimes, 'Had a barbie.'

Geoff set the oven timer and downed his wine. Then he installed himself in front of the screen and fired up Skype. His pulse missed a beat when his son appeared.

Today Dave wore a T-shirt with a blue fish on it.

Geoff beamed. "Hi, Dave. Doing anything nice today?"

"Going to a birthday party at the whacker." Dave pronounced it *pairty*.

"Right," Geoff said. "What's the whacker?"

An impatient look prefaced his reply. "The WACA. It's the cricket ground in Perth." Once again he'd said *crickid.*

"That sounds nice," Geoff said. If the WACA was like everything else in Perth, it was miserable and soulless. "Keeping up your footie?"

"Nah."

Sonya was hovering to the left of the screen as Geoff asked, "What else are you doing this weekend?"

Dave shrugged. "Iron-no. Sump'n." He shrugged again. There was a sound Geoff couldn't make out in the background, then Dave said, "Bye, Dad."

The screen had gone blank and the lasagne still had fifteen minutes left. Such a short call, thought Geoff as he refilled his glass. He tried to Skype again the following week, but Sonya was offline. That was no way to be a father.

On Monday afternoon, Geoff was ready to perform. The production company had required the most basic of screen tests, nodding and giving the thumbs-up after just a couple of minutes. And now here the team were, crowding out his little consulting room.

A couple of his long-time patients had got wind of the filming, so they were hanging around in reception, hoping to catch some of the action. No matter how well qualified you were, patients thought TV was the highest achievement ever. The downside was reliving experiences from Helmand, but then that was the whole point of an interview on military medicine.

A Kiwi woman with a clipboard pumped his hand. "Hiya, Geoff."

"Good to see you again," said a guy who looked like a male model.

Geoff was sure he'd never seen him before. He remembered patients' bodies better than faces.

"We'll just set up here, all right?"

They began to move his desk here, and trail wires there, and then move the desk halfway back again, putting the chair just so, chattering amiably all the time.

Filming was a break from the usual routine. No doubt about it: even though he was a GP, Geoff still hankered after acute care. But his first casualty in Afghan had been nothing like Accident and Emergency patients back home. In Camp Bastion there were no pulseless junkies, no old people with strokes, no tendon injuries from opening food packaging.

The first squaddie he'd treated reminded him more of a hedgehog he'd tried to save when he was fifteen. Hole in his side. A crater with blood, leaves, maggots and spines. The hedgehog had died.

The squaddie was unresponsive but breathing, just. One leg was shot to pieces and his guts were all over the show, along with tattered uniform and other debris.

Was that really his liver? Dear God. A right-turn resuscitation, they called it. The whole team worked together in theatre, resuscitating and operating simultaneously.

Someone had the job of removing all the lines when the team finally had to call it a day.

"Right. Nearly ready now, Geoff," said one of crew as he fiddled with the mic.

Geoff had scripted most of what he wanted to say. The heat. The sweat. The pride. The panic. All of it came tumbling back. He had a fine line to tread. Even when talking about the tragic toll of war, there was a danger of glorifying it, and Geoff never wanted to do that, no matter how much respect he had for those on the front line. The programme would have several other segments too, taking in the Gilles archive and the work of Dr Andrew Bamji at Sidcup. It was important to give a sense of history, and to show how far some specialities like critical care and reconstructive surgery had progressed in a short space of time, even though human nature, especially in the form of politicians, still lagged behind as ever.

"Aw right?" said a short man with a mop of grey hair. Geoff had no idea who he was either, though he was pretty sure he'd seen dogs with the same hairdo. The kind you never rubbed under the chin because front and rear looked identical.

"Right then," said Male Model, gesturing towards the chair. "I'll ask the questions. Look at me, not the camera. And remember my questions won't be included, so please make your answers stand alone as complete sentences."

"Complete sentences. Right."

The first few questions were easy. "What were the greatest challenges in your time as an Army doctor?"

"Having so many critically injured and ill patients in one go."

"Stand-alone answers, please."

"Sorry." Geoff paused. "For me, the greatest challenge was having so many critically ill and injured patients in one go. That doesn't happen in civilian practice."

The sound man wasn't happy. "Can we have that again? There was a lorry."

"For me, the greatest challenge was having so many critically ill and injured patients in one go. That doesn't happen in everyday civilian practice."

"Sorry. Airplane."

"So what were the greatest challenges?" Male Model prompted.

"For me, the greatest challenge was having so many critically ill and injured patients in one go. That doesn't happen in everyday civilian practice." By now he had said it so often he was beginning to doubt it. Wasn't the greatest challenge of his life being away from Davey?

"And what were the most common injuries?" asked Male Model.

153

"Blast injuries and—"

"Stand-alone sentences, please."

"Sorry." Geoff paused. "The most common injuries during my time there were blast injuries and –"

The sound man was shaking his head. "Leaf blower."

"What?" Geoff was mystified.

"Leaf blower outside."

The leaf blower showed no signs of stopping, so they shut the window. The room quickly became baking hot. Geoff thought he could still detect the staleness from the last few patients, like old Mr Thing whose bladder hadn't been quite the same since his prostatectomy.

There were more questions, about friendships forged, and colleagues lost. Geoff banished the lump in his throat.

Outside, a woman exhorted her child to hold hands and stop dawdling, promising him an ice cream if they got up the road before it rained. All the everyday sounds nobody noticed until a film crew turned up.

The mother and child moved on, but the rain began, lightly at first, then hammering down onto the aluminium windowsills.

Male Model checked his watch. "Shall we take a little break?"

Geoff opened the fanlight temporarily to get some air, and mopped a few beads of sweat.

As soon as the downpour eased off, the questions resumed. "How much of the skills you gained in Afghanistan can you use here in the NHS?"

He'd never need that emergency know-how again. "The skills you hone in the theatre of war can be of immense use once back in the NHS. For a GP like myself, it's not so much the clinical aspects as the leadership skills you– Oh, fuck."

The sodding phone. All the mobiles had been powered off but this was the extension on the desk.

Geoff picked up. "Yes?" he said irritably.

"Them new tablets what you give me, like, they don't half make me break wind."

Fuck. It was Mr Bowel with his microscopic colitis. "Well, just make an appointment to see me, or even better the nurse. She'll sort it all out for you."

Deep breath. Working in Afghanistan hadn't helped one bit in dealing with difficult patients. If anything, it made it harder. How had Mr Bowel got his direct number? And how could anyone moan about farting and belching when there were lads in their teens with limb stumps and mutilated genitals?

"So," resumed Male Model. "How much of the skills gained in Afghanistan can you use here in the NHS?"

"The skills you acquire in the theatre of war can be immensely useful back in the NHS. For a GP like myself—"

The sound man rubbed his ear and shook his head. "I can hear something."

They looked out of the window to find a lorry. Two work-men jumped down and began unloading scaffolding. Geoff wondered when a chapter of Hell's Angels would turn up and raise hell, or whatever else they did when they got together.

"Can we call it a day soon?" asked Geoff. "I have an after-noon clinic to do."

The mop-haired guy peered out of the window. "They'll soon be done, I think. Shall we break for a cuppa?"

The Kiwi woman offered to get tea.

Geoff switched his mobile back on as he simultaneously checked the appointments screen on his desk. Sixteen patients to see this afternoon, the first of them in fifteen minutes from now. He looked across the screen at his colleagues' appoint-ments. There were still a few gaps.

His mobile peeped with a missed call. Sonya never called, not from Australia. Was something wrong? She hadn't left a voicemail, though, so probably not. He'd ring back later.

Right. Back to the appointments screen. Could he ask to shift some of his patients across, perhaps to Helen? Quid pro quo, and all that. Then one name on Helen's appointments jumped out at him from the monitor: Daisy Isabella Long.

It had to be her. Dear God! She was a patient of the practice?

He'd only just got over his last difficulty with the General Medical Council. Swearing at a patient's relative, as indefensible as it was, was one thing. Sex with a patient was in a different league. He'd be struck off.

His head was spinning. He looked away, took a couple of deep breaths, blinked hard, and returned to the monitor. Of course, her name was still there.

Daisy Isabella Long. And what was that just after her name? It said *Mrs*. Oh, fuck! The bloody woman was married as well.

His hands hadn't shaken like this since his first casualty in Bastion. Just as on that occasion, Geoff had no idea what to do.

The hairy guy's face came round the door. "Mel got you some tea. Hey, doc, you awright? You look like you've seen a ghost."

CHAPTER TWENTY-TWO

LAURE

Hunched over his tray puzzle, Jack was hell bent on making the horse fit into the slot for the sheep, and didn't want any help from Laure, however gently she guided him.

Daisy had another afternoon off. She was currently spending her Daisy time on Laure's sofa, looking sassy in a pink fedora.

"Is that Tinder?" asked Laure.

Daisy looked up from her mobile to give her a pitying look. "Tinder is so dead. I'm using DingDing."

"Never heard of it."

"Yeah, you don't get out much." Daisy got out her e-cig, fiddled with the end of it, and took a long drag.

"What are those things like?" All Laure could detect was a vague smell of strawberries.

"They serve a purpose," said Daisy. "Though I'm still waiting for someone to come up with a product that gives a hit like the real thing."

Frustrated, Jack gave a little scream and shoved the wooden horse into his mouth. He was teething again. According to the books, his upper lateral incisors could be through any day now.

"Why don't you just give up smoking altogether?" Laure asked. "Dan quit ages ago."

"Why would I want to give up when it looks so cool?" Daisy tipped her pink fedora a little lower on her head and gave a wicked smile.

"I'm not sure if vaping's cool, or makes you look like an addict." Had she offended Daisy? Well, served her right.

Daisy took it as a compliment and winked.

Laure continued, "I'm not convinced vaping is safe either. Especially around young children."

"There's no tar."

"But there's nicotine."

Daisy tutted. "That *is* rather the point."

"And trace elements, like heavy metals and God knows what." Laure couldn't remember all the additives she'd read about but, according to newspaper articles, those could all harm brain development. A new fear gripped Laure. What if the damage had already been done? She glanced at Jack, still unable to master a simple tray puzzle, and wondered.

"I'm the one vaping. Not Jack."

"But it could still affect someone else. The long-term effects aren't known."

Daisy returned to her phone. "If one of us gets ill, I'll sue. Simple."

"Oh, Daisy. It doesn't work like that. I know this. I'm a lawyer."

Daisy's eyes threatened to pop out of her head. "You're a lawyer?"

Laure nodded as she stroked Jack's head. He'd just dropped the barn into its rightful place. "Good boy!" she said.

"A lawyer?" Daisy was unblinking. "I'd never have guessed."

"What did you think I was?"

Daisy shrugged. "A mummy. Never really thought you'd be anything else."

"I've only been a mummy for a year. Besides, I don't think you can tell what someone does just by looking at them. Some of my clients have turned out to be quite surprising."

Daisy considered this as she inhaled deeply.

"As an actor," continued Laure, "you play many different roles. Surely it crossed your mind that in real life we don't just play one part?"

"I suppose," said Daisy. That was as much of an agreement as Laure had ever got out of Daisy.

Laure reflected that she knew relatively little about Daisy, considering they saw each other so often. Only that she was an actor, liked kids, and had been married. Possibly still was, for all she knew. Daisy was hazy on details.

When Dan came in from work, Jack squealed with delight.

Daisy said, "Hello Dan. I've just found out that your Laure is a lawyer."

"A-ha," he said, hugging Jack. "We all play many parts." He began reciting Shakespeare, declaring him the greatest geezer of all time. "Pure class."

"Indeed. And most probably a homosexual," added Daisy, enunciating every syllable. She made it sound irresistible.

"Shakespeare a poof?" said Dan. "Get away!"

"Not that there's anything wrong with that," Daisy added.

"Maybe he played many parts too," suggested Laure as she went to the kitchen to prepare Jack's organic dinner.

"What are you cooking tonight?" Daisy asked Dan.

"I'm making my lovely lady roast poussin with tarragon."

"Lucky Laure!" said Daisy.

The reality was that Dan hadn't cooked at home for ages.

"We'd ask you to stay for dinner," said Dan, "but..."

"No, no, I wouldn't dream of imposing," said Daisy.

"Maybe another time," said Dan.

Laure wished he hadn't said that because Daisy was round at theirs several times a week as it was, whether she was invited or not. She often brought them something, though rarely anything they wanted. Last time, Jack had scattered her pot pourri all over the carpet. And they now had three unopened bottles of *crème de cassis*.

Daisy pulled her hat down on one side and made a funny face at Jack. He frowned back, then a smile cracked his face wide open. Daisy picked a few bricks from the carpet and put them in his shape sorter. Jack just as promptly tipped them out again.

Daisy was still smiling but under her fedora a vertical ridge had formed between her eyebrows. "Naughty Jack," she said.

Jack launched into a long scream and started banging the table with one hand.

"He's feisty today, isn't he?"

"He's always feisty," Laure said.

The fact was that Jack had been remarkably good today. He hadn't thrown a full-on wobbly, and now Dan was cooking poussin. Laure's breathing was nice and even. It was beginning to work, this box technique.

After Laure had given Jack his last breastfeed that night, Dan did his usual retreat to the bathroom, locking the door to do his dental manoeuvres. He emerged to ask, "When are you going to wean Jack?"

"He's already weaned. He has solids three times a day."

"I mean off the breast."

She applied cream to her face in the bedroom mirror. "I haven't decided."

"He'll be off to uni before you know it."

She shot him a look. "Cheeky sod."

"Well, he will be. And he'll still be attached to your tits."

Laure said nothing.

"Why don't we do an experiment?" said Dan. "Let him sleep in his own room tonight. We might all sleep better for it. You never know."

So far Jack hadn't spent a single night in his own room, even though it had been decorated for him long before he was born. Laure agreed, but insisted on leaving the monitor on, just in case.

Dan shuffled the cot out. "Let's put his toys in there as well."

Jack didn't seem at all perturbed by having his cot relocated to another room. He immediately said, "Night night," and lay down on his front.

He was old enough to sleep on his front without risking instant cot death, but so many other things could happen. What if he was sick?

The box, Laure reminded herself. Put it all in the box. Then put it away. For good measure, she held her temples and told herself *I am calm. I am serene. All is well.*

Back in their own bedroom, she watched Dan take off his shirt. He tossed it on the chair. Undid his belt buckle.

"Take your T-shirt off now," said Laure. "Do it slowly."

"If Madam says so." He languidly removed the white T-shirt.

He was in good shape. She'd forgotten just how good.

Dan threw the T-shirt at her.

She crumpled it in her hands and inhaled a subtle blend of man and—what was it? Rosemary? "What have you been cooking up?" she asked.

He took her hand and placed it on his crotch. "Trouble."

She undid his flies.

He stepped out of his jeans.

She'd also forgotten how much she could want him. "Perhaps you should take your socks off too."

"Have we got any oil?" he asked.

At first she thought he meant cooking oil. It had been that long.

He found the massage oil and carefully trickled some onto her back.

161

"Mmm," she went into the pillow. "But I want to see you." She turned onto her back and spread her legs.

This felt alien after so long. They began with exquisite slowness, and quietly, so as not to disturb Jack. On the bedside table, the monitor crackled.

"Don't stop," she said.

I am calm. I am serene. All is well.

Her tiredness had vanished. Now every bit of her felt alive, energized. It was all going to be fine. She pumped in time with him until at last her pelvis tightened into a red-hot knot before letting go.

Dan rolled off.

Laure lifted her head. "Where are you going?"

"Check on Jack."

Laure shoved the last few negative emotions into the box and snapped the lid shut. "I'm sure he's fine."

"Never heard you say that before."

GEOFF

Geoff stared at the screen the next day. Bloody Daisy. How could she be a patient of the practice? She lived miles away. Although, Geoff mused, hadn't she said the Hampstead address was purely temporary? He'd have to tackle her later. With the utmost delicacy, obviously.

First he had to try Sonya again. It went through to voicemail. A pretentious voicemail over a background of Vivaldi. He left a short message just to say he'd called back. She wasn't on Skype at the moment, so there wasn't much else he could do.

Right. Back to his audit of over-seventies with atrial fibrillation. The whole point of treating AF patients was to prevent strokes and other catastrophes. Around twenty per cent of stroke patients died of their stroke. As Geoff knew, the other eighty per cent wished they had. That made the condition well worth preventing.

Geoff opened the list of elderly patients on the database.

Now his mobile was going. Sonya. He picked up immediately.

"Hey, Geoff," she said conversationally, as if weeks hadn't passed since they'd last spoken.

"Hey," he replied, although he hated the word.

"Drew and I are back in the UK," she continued. "And of course Dave."

Geoff's heart trampolined in his chest. Maybe he had atrial fibrillation too. "How is Davey? I mean Dave. Everything all right?"

"Dave is absolutely fine?" She sounded like an Aussie too now.

"Not ill?"

"Not at all."

"Great. Can I speak to him?"

"Well, he's rather jet-lagged. As we all are. I suggest we leave it for a few days. Just wanted to let you know we are home a few weeks earlier than planned."

"That's fine," said Geoff. "I'll call tomorrow."

"Make it the day after?" said Sonya.

Geoff put his phone away and looked in the mirror above the sign reminding him to wash his hands properly between patients. He really was grinning like an idiot. Now that Davey (make that Dave) was back, Geoff would be able to spend Saturdays in the park with him again. They'd do things like go to Burger King, or make breakfasts of pancakes and syrup in Geoff's kitchen where the quest for the perfect pancake could, and often did, take all day.

Geoff had lived through weekdays just for those weekends.

He'd lived through two tours in Afghanistan for Dave's

return, sustained by the belief that, unlike the parents of the fallen, he would see and hug his child again.

Now that time was nearly here. He was glad the practice manager couldn't see the little victory dance he did round his consulting room.

Dave was home. They'd have fun together at weekends. Be like a normal father and son.

Geoff checked the mirror again. Yep, idiot grin still in place.

CHAPTER TWENTY-THREE

SANJAY

"Mate," said Ben. "That was amazing."

"Yeah, wasn't it?" Sanjay agreed.

The credits had rolled, and they were wading through popcorn and empty paper cups up to the door of Screen Two, slowly because Ben's leg still wasn't right, plus there was a fucking enormous crowd of people. Shofiq used to join them at the cinema, but these days he had gone off nudity in films. Ben, however, was as much in favour of it as ever.

"That Gemma Arterton's fit," Ben said.

"Oh, yeah. And Ben Affleck's a great actor."

Ben nodded. "He's always value. Though not in *Good Will Hunting.*"

"Fair enough," said Sanjay, though he couldn't remember that film. Why was he always agreeing with Ben? Probably because he still had two arms, and Ben had lost one of his while on patrol in Lashkar Gah. "Actually," he added, "Justin Timberlake was OK."

"Yeah, bro. He was. Saw him in *The Social Network* too."

They'd now made it to the entrance. "Where shall we go for that drink?"

The nearest pub was across the street.

They settled in front of their pints. Sanjay ran his fingers up and down his beer glass, wiping moisture off, thinking that Ben was pretty good with his left hand.

Sanjay was in no hurry. What else would he be doing anyway, except lying on the sofa at home reliving Brit Pop and making Shelley purr? When you were pushing forty, you actually had to plan your fun, even if you felt like a kid inside. Social life no longer just happened. Funny that nobody warned you.

"This guy at work," Ben was saying. "He's got a really bad cold..."

Sanjay nodded. Actually nothing really equipped you for life. He'd survived. Now what? Bollocks! He should be out having fun, as should Ben. If you didn't make the most of your time, you were letting yourself down. And letting down all the poor saps who hadn't been as lucky. The ones who actually had cancer. Or who'd died from other things. Had the remaining Red Hot Chili Peppers lived their lives differently after losing Hillel Slovak? Now there was a question.

"I was thinking of doing a degree," Ben said.

"Yeah, mate. Why not?" Sanjay had no idea how they had got from the colleague sneezing all over everyone's desk to choosing an Open University course.

"Meteorology maybe," mused Ben.

"Yeah?" said Sanjay again. All these things he was doing, and Ben was doing, were basically marking time. May as well be in a giant waiting room while the Grim Reaper decided which number to call out.

"Or else Sanskrit?"

"That's an idea. Sanskrit's a great language," said Sanjay, although he wouldn't have recognized Sanskrit if it had walked into the pub and punched him on the nose. "Mate, how did you cope when other soldiers died?"

A glint of anger appeared in Ben's eyes. "How do you think? You just have to."

"I mean, did you want to live life differently because you'd survived?"

Ben got it. "Like I owed it to them?"

"That's it!" Sanjay banged the table.

"Yeah. Thing is, we all owe them anyway. So, I haven't figured that one out yet. You're better off not over-thinking."

Sanjay almost asked Ben if he'd had therapy but went to get refills instead.

"Thanks, mate," said Ben when Sanjay returned with the drinks. "You know what? That was actually a shit movie. But I could give Gemma Arterton one."

"Aren't you a bit old for Gemma Arterton?"

HARRIET

As Harriet struggled through the front door with her shopping, she greeted Nora from downstairs. Today the old lady was fussing about on her doormat.

"Hello, Harriet," she replied, showing teeth with red lipstick stains. She had another bundle of newspapers under her arm.

At least someone was still reading print papers, thought Harriet. "Are you OK for groceries, Nora?"

"I'm fine for now. Thank you, dear."

Harriet opened her own door and sat for a while on the sofa.

With Dan, it was lusty, guilty, and quick. Furtive sex. That was to be expected. However, with a bit of visualization Harriet could make each moment last much longer.

She could put herself in a trance in which she lay cocooned in his arms, bathed in a sustaining glow. Which she needed to do, she reflected as she got her laptop, because sex on the sly couldn't go on forever. Nor should it.

Exercising her imagination had the benefit of blocking

out the blare of the TV from downstairs, and everything else. Unfortunately that made it harder to churn out the trivial lifestyle pieces that kept the roof over her head. She checked her online statement. A payment had just come in. That would help cover the rent, though nothing else.

Eight o'clock. Harriet went into the cupboard that pretended to be a kitchen and wondered if Dan would be home now, enjoying a family meal instead of the diminutive omelette she was about to make herself.

She added cheese, cherry tomatoes, and a pinch of basil. There was a solitary slice of ham left in the fridge. She chopped it up and sprinkled it on top. Was that how they served omelette at Lolo's?

Dinner was tasty, but just now she had an odd pain in her gut again, made worse when her thoughts turned to Laure. She barely knew the woman, but still felt bad.

Harriet resolved not to dwell on that. Dan had obviously wanted to be with her. She should make the best of it.

Virginia's advice came back to her now. She'd said it late one night in Café Rouge, and it owed more than a little to the special offer they had on red wine.

"Harriet," Virginia had said, clutching the empty bottle for strength. "The best way to get over a man is to get under a new one."

It was a load of drivel, but still.

As Harriet cleared up after her omelette, she thought of taking Dan to Primrose Hill. It was such a romantic place, especially with that new inscription at the top of the hill. A quote from William Blake, which Harriet couldn't quite remember, but it was Blake's usual mysticism. Dan would absolutely love it.

DAN

Christ! She kept trying to hold his hand.

He wasn't even concupiscent anymore. Though obviously he had been, that first time. It was like when he'd been let out of jail, concupiscent twenty-four seven. After being inside, he'd have shagged anything, including an ironing board. If he'd had one, that is.

Now Harriet was smiling at him as they waited for the lights by the church. One of the nicest and priciest parts of London, but as they stood on the corner the place began to give him the creeps. He guessed the church was Gothic. Windows were long and eerie, anyway. Also had the most pointed spire he'd ever seen, sharpened to a spike that could do you serious grief if it ever came down to pavement level.

Primrose Hill was her suggestion. It was a bit close to home, especially in broad daylight. But he'd been stupid enough to agree. So here they were. On their way to one of the most popular spaces in the whole of London. With a woman who wasn't Laure. Why the fuck had he agreed?

As they walked up Prince Albert Road, two Porsche Carreras went by in quick succession. Then a Maserati, no less.

"I've longed to see you," said Harriet. There was concupiscence in her eyes. Bad sign.

"Really?" They'd done it twice more since that time on her desk. And they'd got away with it because they'd kept it secret, but it would be harder if Harriet was going to be demanding. Still, he'd started it. His bad.

"It's good to be out together," she said.

When he didn't answer, she said, "Isn't it?"

He fired a glance her way. "You know we shouldn't."

"I know, but."

Dan said nothing. Didn't she realize he was as good as married? Actually he had no idea what the woman was like. Christ!

He barely knew her. Shafting someone on the sly didn't mean you understood the person. She'd pestered him for outdoor sex too. He thought of rows of vegetables. Chamomile lawns. A screen of runner beans. A train to Watford rattling past. But it would have been impossible.

Even walking along together was risky. What if there was a crash? Which was on the cards the way people drove around here. He and Harriet might have to make statements. Appear as witnesses. All that hassle.

"Hold my hand," she said as he wriggled away.

"Can't." It was the hand with the scar, he explained. The burn another lag had inflicted on him.

So she tried to hold the other one. "You get the best blow-job ever and you won't even hold my hand for five minutes."

"That's not the point." Though she was almost right. It had been the only blow-job in a long while.

They walked past a row of houses. In a bay window, a rocking horse tore at Dan's heart. Harriet tried once again to clutch his hand.

"You're a big girl, Harriet," he said. "Why are you suddenly unable to cross the street without hanging onto my mitt?"

Harriet looked like she was about to cry.

On Primrose Hill, there were rich people with dogs. Poor people with picnics. And all kinds of people with prams. Every bench, every tree could be hiding someone who might recognize him.

"Shall we walk up to the top?" asked Harriet.

He didn't want to, but it was a foregone conclusion. So he kept his head down and concentrated on his feet.

The hill was steeper than Dan remembered. A woman brushed past them, struggling to keep up with two Dalmatians. One with a pink collar. The other with a blue. Bounding ahead as if they ate springs for breakfast.

Dan and Harriet sat down at the top of the hill. You could

see the BT Tower. The dome of St Paul's. The London Eye. The pointy glass of the Shard. The Gherkin. All those things. Tourists pored over the engraved plaque and tried to figure out what the hell those buildings were. Loads more landmarks in the making, too, judging by the cranes on the horizon.

Dan turned away from the view. "You still love Sanjay, don't you?"

She didn't say anything. Kept staring at Canary Wharf in the distance.

He continued anyway. "I've always loved Laure. I can't imagine that ever changing." He wanted to give his view of what had happened. That his dick had got some ideas into its pointed little head. That he knew it shouldn't have happened. But he didn't have the balls to say it.

"Have you seen this?" she said, pointing at the ground. "It's by William Blake."

Dan glanced at it. Two sentences carved into the stone. Something about seeing the spiritual sun on Primrose Hill.

"It's lovely, isn't it?" she said.

"I suppose." He didn't know about the spiritual sun, but the last thing Dan wanted was to be seen on Primrose Hill.

"I'd like to buy you something," she said after a bit.

He felt like smacking himself on the forehead. Exchanging presents and having sex out of doors were things people did when they were in a relationship. "No," he said. "We are not going to exchange presents." They'd shagged three times. That was all.

Harriet obviously thought that was a big deal. In a way it was. But a woman and a child at home, those were much bigger deals. Laure had believed in him, had his baby, and was the most exquisite woman he'd ever met. Then he'd gone and been concupiscent with someone else. It was great sex but it felt shit. It hurt his chest even to think about it, and none of the words he'd so carefully studied and practised were in any way up to the job of explaining.

We just needed to break out, he wanted to tell Harriet. To see our own lives away from our partners. Maybe Sanjay needed a break too.

He'd rehearsed it all, but it was impossible now that Harriet looked so teary. Maybe someone else, a proper wordsmith like Julian Barnes or Martin Amis, could have told her, but Dan just couldn't.

At least he convinced her not to get each other presents. She bought him a cannoli in the end, from one of the shops in Regent's Park Road. It smelled fantastic. Dusted with sugar. Crammed with cream. Hint of chocolate and mocha.

They sat on a bench and shared the cannoli. It tasted too sweet and too rich. Made a mess of her T-shirt, and his.

CHAPTER TWENTY-FOUR

SANJAY

Fucking result! Sanjay nearly jabbed his finger right through the screen.

She was still called Shelley Ritchie, same as in Year Twelve when he'd last seen her. Not that it meant anything. She could have got married ten times since leaving school and not changed her name even once.

"Thank you, Facebook. You're a fucking genius," he told his iPad. How did people track down anyone without it?

Under the table, his cat snaked around his legs before jumping onto the table with a "Prrt." That had to be the loveliest noise ever, but he didn't need her on his Mac now.

"You'll have to wait, Shell-Shell. This is important," he said, returning to his research.

Shelley Ritchie, London, had gone to Durham, her profile said. Which he knew. He wondered where she worked. She was probably in advertising or something equally dubious. A lot of people were. He studied her profile picture again. Her face was thinner than he remembered, but the hair was still fair and her front teeth slightly lopsided. Definitely her.

He couldn't see all her *About* info, but it didn't say she was in a relationship, and from the small selection of photos that were on show there were no subtle clues like wedding dresses or a naked guy in her bed.

She hadn't posted much in the last little while. Sanjay hoped she was OK. It was bat-shit crazy to worry about someone he hadn't seen for about twenty years, but he'd thought about her a lot. Eighteen months ago he'd wanted to get back in touch. No surprise really. Wouldn't anyone hammered by the Big C want to see their first love again?

But he hadn't actually got back in touch. He hadn't died of cancer either. Then there'd been Harriet. Lovely, slightly dippy Harriet with her microscopic self-esteem. He sighed.

He hadn't forgotten Shelley, and he would always, but always, remember the night he spent beside her. The whole entire night. He'd told his mum he was at Shofiq's house. They didn't sleep a wink. They lay like spoons the whole fucking night, minus the fucking because nothing had happened. How stupid was that?

Sanjay had scarpered about five the next morning, out of her window, down onto the roof of her parents' extension and then into their neighbour's garden, toppling over the bins. He could still remember the gash he'd got on his arm on touchdown.

He brought his mind back to the screen in front of him. Now to send Shelley Ritchie a message. He tickled his cat under the chin for inspiration.

LAURE

Laure stood by the window and practised her abdominal breathing, counting to three with every breath in, and up to six with every breath out, all the while making sure her belly filled with air as much as her lungs. How long were you supposed to do this before the calming effect kicked in?

She focussed on daily signs of normality outside. Cars went by, as did the occasional delivery van. Dogs trotted alongside their owners. Children dragged their feet. The postman strode past with his red trolley, wearing shorts as usual, no matter what the weather.

I am calm. I am serene. All is well.

Didn't work.

She had already tried the mental box. Nothing she did altered the fact that Jack was snuffly again. He was sitting on his play mat chewing one of his plastic cars and lacing it with snot. Earlier this morning, his airways were so blocked that he'd struggled for breath. Now that she observed him closely again, she thought she could hear some soft wheezing.

Hadn't she better check his resps again?

"Come on, Jack." She lifted him off the mat. He was a big boy, his weight over the seventy-fifth percentile at the last clinic visit.

Still clutching his slimy car, he went, "Mam mam mam bob," as she undid the poppers and lifted up the vest that kept his nappy tidy. She waited for him to stop babbling, then watched his chest movements for fifteen seconds.

His respiratory rate was normal. The new app said so. She did it again, just to be sure.

Even so, there was something wrong. A mother just knew, didn't she? Not her own mother, obviously. Things had been very wrong, all those years ago, and her mother, so interested in everyone else's business, had understood nothing of what went on under her own roof.

Laure ordered herself to take a few more controlled breaths. All that belonged in the past. Now Jack was her concern. He sat on her lap, a touch more docile than usual. That wasn't right.

"Do you want a drink?" she asked.

He made a face. "Nome."

Wasn't his hand more curled up than normal? Although he'd let go of his precious car, his fingers weren't completely straight. She quickly checked her phone. The app didn't even mention finger position. Well then, that surely meant curled fingers didn't signify anything.

Laure tried to persuade herself that all was well, but Jack really was too quiet.

Maybe he was allergic to something. So many children had allergies. Jack didn't cry all the time as he used to, but he often had the sniffles or a delicate tummy. The night he'd spent in his own bedroom, he'd vomited copiously without her even realizing. Laure had gone to check on him later in the night, and found the side of his face covered in the stuff, his golden locks matted with sick and sweat. It just showed parents had to keep their wits about them all the time.

What the hell could he be allergic to? She glanced around the flat.

There were scented candles, gathering dust since Jack's birth. She'd got rid of the pot pourri, but Daisy had brought flowers a few days ago.

"Dory, dory," clamoured Jack.

"Shall I read you a story?" she asked.

"Ess."

She read him a Spot the Dog story. He went, "Dog! Dog dog!"

That was normal enough, but, as she put her arm around him, she noticed a fine rattling sound from his chest. She felt the small of his back and the nape of his neck. Neither hot nor sweaty, but still. Perhaps she had better call the doctor to be on the safe side.

Two days ago she'd been mortified on taking him to the doctor's. She thought it was smart to have taken a photo of his vomit, but the duty doctor was rushed and uninterested in the offerings on Laure's iPhone. As soon as Laure confessed Jack had only vomited the once, the doctor's minimal interest levels plunged further. There were, the GP had informed her, no signs whatsoever of dehydration, or any focus of infection, as she'd called it.

Laure went away that day realizing she'd worried over nothing. Well, this time she was going to be sensible and not give the medical profession any cause to think she was neurotic.

But that wasn't a reason not to call the surgery if something really was wrong, was it? She wasn't neurotic. She was an intelligent caring mother.

The Spot story was over. Now Jack's eyes were shut, his long fair lashes resting on his cheeks.

Laure took a couple more deep breaths and told herself nothing was wrong. But her body wouldn't listen. Now her vision was blurring and contracting into a tunnel.

GEOFF

Damage limitation, thought Geoff as he parked outside the medical school. Probably nobody had made the link between Daisy and himself. Best keep it that way.

But Daisy herself must have realized he worked at the practice when she'd registered as a patient. And why had she chosen that health centre anyway? It was miles from where she lived.

He got out and slammed the car door. He would ask her today, after the teaching session.

Now one of the actors was playing the role of a man with painless rectal bleeding, while a student made a complete hash of it. Geoff checked the clock. Already nine of the allotted ten minutes had gone and the talentless rugger bugger was firing irrelevant questions on alcohol consumption. At this rate, the original symptom, a red flag for bowel cancer, would be over-looked entirely.

Sure enough, by the end of the consultation the student had failed to ask for any examination findings. It was bloody terrifying when the lad was going to be a doctor within fourteen months.

Geoff leaned back in the chair and listened to the other students comment on the consultation.

"I thought your body language was good," said the young woman in the hijab.

"I liked the way you stood up and shook hands when he came in."

"You built really good rapport with him."

The actor's feedback was more restrained. "I thought you were very positive. That's always good in a doctor."

The student lapped up this load of flannel.

As per the rules for role play feedback, the tutor went last. Geoff fixed on the student for a moment before saying, "If you don't put your finger in it, you put your foot in it. Anyone heard that before?" He glanced around the room.

A glimmer of recognition appeared in Rugger Bugger's physiognomy before a red wave crept up his neck.

"If anyone consults you with rectal bleeding, what should go through your head?" continued Geoff.

"Cancer," said the hijab student.

"That's right. Now remember, it's all very well building a rapport. But you're supposed to keep people alive, not kill them while charming their socks off."

They all nodded.

Daisy played the next patient, a flighty young woman called Vanda who harboured several sexually acquired infections. The students missed a lot of clues.

As Daisy said during the feedback, "Why did you assume the patient was straight?"

The student gulped audibly. "Well. Vanda looks, you know, er..."

"Sexy?" suggested Daisy, crossing her legs and making her stockings rub together.

"Erm. Yes, I suppose."

Daisy persisted. "Surely lesbians can look sexy too?"

Geoff watched with amusement as the student squirmed. "Well, I don't know many lesbians."

Daisy scoffed. "Then I suggest you go out and meet some. As well as gays and transsexuals. You should all go and mix with as wide a range of the population as possible. Because very soon, most of you, though probably not all," and here she paused to survey the room meaningfully, "will be doctors. And you will have to care for the biggest cross-section of human beings imaginable."

As well as their dogs, thought Geoff, recalling an elderly patient who couldn't afford the vet.

One brave student ventured, "Can't it wait till we meet them as patients?"

Daisy turned her gimlets on him. "Research shows that doctors spend more time with patients who are similar to themselves in social class and interests. You need to understand those who are different to yourself. And to relate to them. Not just without prejudice or preconceived ideas, but as fellow members of the human race."

She rolled the R deliciously on *race*, sending a tingle right down Geoff's spine and into his dick. Of course, she was right about the students getting to know the world that they would meet as patients. No time like the present for them to get the message.

As usual, Daisy wanted a lift after the session, ideally anywhere nearer the centre of town.

"No problem." Geoff smiled as he opened the car door for her.

He started the ignition. Enough of the kid gloves.

"Daisy, is there any reason at all why you're still registered as a patient with my practice? Seeing as you're living practically in the middle of Hampstead."

She got out her vaping kit for a fix. "You know Belsize Lane is just a temporary address," she said. "I'm staying with a friend until I find somewhere."

"In that case, you could temporarily register with another doctor in that area. And then register with someone else when you decide where to settle."

She looked out of her window and inhaled deeply. "I suppose it's inconvenient for you, is it? For me to be on your practice books?"

"Oh, so you did know you had registered at the practice where I'm a partner?" He craned his neck, hoping he wasn't about to get stuck in a box junction.

"I suppose I did."

"Daisy. This has nothing to do with inconvenience and everything to do with regulations and professional standards. Surely you know that the GMC takes an extremely dim view of relationships between doctors and their patients?"

"I'm not actually your patient though. And we started fucking before you even realized I was at your practice."

This was getting him nowhere, except into a long queue leading up to a roundabout and, as he could now see, a lane closure ahead. He stole a look at Daisy. Her face was giving Mount Rushmore a run for its money.

"Change of plan," he said. "I'm going to make a detour via the practice. OK if I drop you off near here?"

"Fine," she replied. "There's a tube station just up ahead."

KAREN

Every time Karen considered contacting him, she felt fifteen again. Suppose he brushed her off for some reason?

In the end Rose made her promise to contact 'that doctor guy.' "If you chicken out, I'll never babysit for you again," she warned.

Karen wasn't at all sure about Geoff. He was someone from her past, from an evening at the Jacaranda. They'd parted nearly two years ago, just at the peak of their passion. "Rose, when you get back in touch after a long while, you can't tell which way it'll go."

"So find out," said Rose. "He's emailed you. Means he's interested."

His email now lay at the bottom of her inbox because she'd delayed responding to the simple short message saying that Afghanistan had been memorable, and here he was back in the GP saddle, for his sins.

Who used expressions like that these days?

Besides, if he'd been interested, he'd have phoned, rather than vaguely suggesting it might be nice to meet at some point for a glass of something.

When Rose left, Karen opened his email again. He had definitely said 'nice'. What the hell did that even mean? People said, 'Nice weather for the time of year,' or, 'Have a nice day.' Years ago, her mother had extolled the usefulness of nice navy blue skirts, which were horrid ugly things no teenage would have been seen dead in.

When Karen did get in touch, Geoff sounded pleasantly surprised, so here she was, her children fed and watered, inspecting herself in the hall mirror. She had chosen, under Rose's instruction, a cobalt blue dress that apparently brought out her eyes.

"It's not a bloody prom," she told Rose.

From the living room came the sounds of Damon educating his brothers at full volume.

Karen adjusted one shoulder. The Oxfam shop had labelled it a size twelve but it was more like a fourteen. Karen had meant to take the dress in, shorten the sleeves, and add bands of contrasting ribbon near the hemline, but never found the time.

"Stand up straight," instructed Rose. "Makes your boobs more obvious."

"I don't need to thrust my boobs out." After four children, Karen thought her breasts were best supported by scaffolding and covered in heavy duty tarpaulin.

"You won't get anywhere being a man-hater," said Rose.

Karen scowled. According to Rose, anyone who believed in equal pay was a hairy-legged man-hater.

"And don't frown," Rose added. "At our age, we've already got all the wrinkles we need."

Karen poked her head into the living room to check on the kids. With Charlotte at Belinda's for a sleepover, just the three boys were left.

Damon was holding court. "Who here knows how many bricks it took to build Battersea Power Station?" He glanced expectantly at his mother.

"No idea," said Karen.

He gave up on her. "Come on, boys. How many bricks do you think?"

"About thirty-eight gazillion," shouted Edward.

"How big are the bricks?" asked Ashley. "Because that makes a difference."

Damon scoffed. "They're standard bricks. And a gazillion doesn't exist. Go on, guess."

"Are the walls double thickness?" asked Ashley.

"They're single thickness," said Damon. "So come on, how many bricks?"

"A bazillion," shouted Edward, flapping his arms.

Damon gave him a withering look because a bazillion wasn't a real number either. "As you don't know, I'll tell you. Sixty-one million."

"Now, boys, I'm going out. Be good for Rose," said Karen.

"Bet it wasn't exactly sixty-one million," said Ashley. "It could have been sixty million nine hundred and ninety-nine thousand and ninety-six bricks. Or sixty million nine hundred and ninety-nine thousand and ninety-seven—"

"Bye, boys," she said, just as Edward emptied out a crate of Lego onto the floor.

CHAPTER TWENTY-FIVE

KAREN

The place had subdued lighting. Rose would have approved.

Geoff was running late, as his text had said he'd be. He arrived, wreathed in apologies, and kissed her on the cheek, all the while explaining that he should have known his clinic would overrun. The frustrations of general practice, he said.

It wasn't her imagination or the tea lights on the table. He was as good-looking as she remembered.

"I bet it's strange coming back from Afghanistan," Karen said.

"Very. I actually went twice." Before Karen knew it, he was telling her all about Bastion, the biggest trauma unit in the world. "A lot of the time nothing much happened, then it was action stations. I was lucky. I wasn't out in the field."

She fiddled with the corner of the drinks menu. "Why did you go?"

"I realize the timing wasn't ideal. But it kept me busy and challenged while Davey was in Australia with his mother."

"Davey's your son, right?"

He nodded. "He's seven now."

"Same age as Ashley, my middle son. I expect he's a bit of a smart-arse sometimes." Her lot were all smart-arses, though Damon was the one who had it down to the fine art.

They ordered a bottle of wine.

Geoff fiddled with the stem of his glass. "Actually, I don't know what Davey's like any more. Or rather Dave. That's what he wants to be called now that he's been to Oz."

"You're lucky it isn't Dave-o," said Karen.

He nodded. "I've only seen him once since he got back from Australia. It was a little strained."

She observed him as she sipped. It was a rather nice Vouvray. "I imagine it was."

Instead of giving her details, he sat with a helpless air and rubbed his thumb. "You know a lot about children."

"As I'm sure you do."

"Ah, I know a lot about children's diseases. Not quite the same thing." He gave a thin smile. "It's hard to reconnect with someone after nearly two years."

She nodded. That was also almost exactly the length of time since she'd last seen Geoff. "You have to give it time. Do things together. Try not to be pressurized," she said. "Or to pressure."

"Yes. Absolutely."

"Rediscover common ground between you," she continued. "And of course accept what has changed."

He appeared to be thinking. "A lot can happen in two years. New experiences and all that."

She took another sip. He was right about new experiences. She'd done two years as a teacher, and had become a lot less malleable, or, as Rose would have put it, turned into a raving femi-Nazi. What was Geoff talking about exactly?

He gave her a distracted smile. "Would you like a bite to eat? I've hardly had a thing all day."

She glanced at her watch. "Why not?"

"I think they do quite good steak and chips." He cast around for a menu.

"Erm, do they have vegetarian dishes too?"

A raised eyebrow. "I didn't know you were veggie."

Funny how people often said that with exactly the same tone. "Heading in that direction. I still cook some meat for the kids, except for my daughter." She explained it had been her daughter Charlotte who had first wanted to give up meat. There was so much cruelty in food production.

Geoff's face turned to genuine surprise. "I thought the UK was better at animal welfare than most other countries."

"Well, we're possibly the best of a pretty bad bunch. According to Compassion in World Farming, there's a hell of a way to go."

She ordered a veggie burger from the limited selection, hoping it wouldn't give her, as Edward put it, lots and lots of bottom burps.

Geoff had a porterhouse steak which, even in this light, looked very rare. He cut into it with gusto, explaining that it wasn't a proper porterhouse unless it had some nerve or other running on its underside. "Sorry. Too much information?"

"Yes. Nerves are off-putting. I was at the school gates one day, and this really irritating woman with a voice like a scratchy violin was explaining how she prepared foie gras. I think she was just trying to impress, but what got to me was how she described removing all the nerves out of goose liver."

"Ah," said Geoff. "It's not just the nerves. There are veins too, and I imagine quite a lot of connective tissue."

She made a face. "Thanks for that."

That blip aside, the conversation was easy. They talked a lot about children, and how quickly they changed before your eyes. A rudderless conversation, thought Karen. The kind of thing parents discussed just about anywhere.

She dabbed at her mouth and ventured, "So what else has happened to you since we last met?"

He leaned back in the chair. "Well, I am seeing someone."

Karen failed to detect much enthusiasm, but maybe he was trying to let her down gently. "What about you?"

"I've trained as a teacher and work part-time. Feels like full-time, though. And I'm seeing someone too, but—" She shrugged. Just mentioning Footie Dad would put their encounters on a more important footing.

He nodded. "That's the way it is, sometimes."

She broke the awkwardness with a challenge. "Right. Let's see if you can answer this riddle. A man and his son are out driving one day."

He topped up her glass and sat unblinking as she told the familiar little story. Good. She had him hooked.

But then his eyes twinkled in the candlelight. "The surgeon is his mother. Sorry. I've heard it before."

She tilted her head. "Did you get it the first time?"

"Nope." He shook his head slowly. "It was a long while ago. I'd like to think I'd get it now, if I heard it afresh, but..." His voice trailed off. "I know what the reality is. I've seen kids of just three or four run after one of my female colleagues calling her 'Nurse, nurse.'"

"Not that there's anything wrong with being a nurse," Karen pointed out. Or was there? Shit! It was complicated once you scratched beneath the surface.

By the time they had coffee, it was getting late. "It's been fun," said Karen, "but I need to hurry along home now."

"We should do this again," Geoff said. "Only please let me pay next time instead of splitting the bill."

She found it hard to read him, but she agreed anyway. "And try not to worry too much about Dave. We all worry far too much about our kids."

"Very true," said Geoff. "At least ninety-five per cent of the time it's completely unnecessary."

"You're absolutely right," she replied as he kissed her on the cheek.

GEOFF

The room was stuffy and redolent of new carpet, which, Geoff saw, was still shedding bits of green fluff. Someone opened a window and the meeting began, presided over by the practice manager. Around the table were also three GP partners, including Geoff, two sessional doctors, a new IT geek, and three nurses, along with a selection of coffee mugs, home-made sandwiches, and tubs of salad, all being consumed noisily.

Geoff unwrapped his cheese and cucumber roll. It had lost its shape after a morning in his medical bag.

The practice manager spouted forth. There was a new duty doctor system, which he was describing at a laborious pace, covering every single development since the system had first been mooted eighteen months ago. One of the nurses sneaked a look at her fob watch.

Geoff suppressed a yawn. Meetings never were conducive to concentration.

Karen was a nice woman. She would have been a far safer choice, Geoff knew. She was sensible, stable, and actually quite attractive, whereas Daisy, apart from being sex on legs, was almost everything Geoff didn't need. Damn!

"Are you with us, Geoffrey?" asked the practice manager.

"Absolutely," said Geoff.

They were discussing the part-time doctors now, meaning the two women who each shouldered far more than the half-time hours they were paid for. The senior partner made a perfect sphere of his cling film and flicked a few crumbs off the table. "I think I speak for us all when I say how much we appreciate the dedication shown by our part-time sessional colleagues," he said in a poisonously quiet voice usually deployed when stabbing someone in the back.

Daisy was part-time at the teaching hospital. She probably had several other jobs. Geoff just hadn't figured what she was up to, or why her mobile was often off for hours on end.

He recalled angiograms from his hospital days. The registrar in the angio room always turned off his bleep. Geoff had totted up six long angio sessions a week, an improbable number given the modest size of the cardiology unit. Clearly the registrar was poking something other than a wire up the groin of angina patients.

Now Geoff sensed people looking at him. He glanced around the table and said, "Despite current pressures, I do think our part-time doctors should be properly remunerated."

"We're on item four now," the senior partner pointed out.

"The new vaccine schedule," added the manager helpfully. "If you'd care to refer to your agenda."

After that, the meeting discussed a patient who'd died. What a shame, they all seemed to think. The old boy had been with the practice for forty years, such a nice old chap, agreed the nurses, nodding. Geoff recalled most of the staff couldn't stand the man while he was alive.

The complaint against Geoff's colleague Helen was on the agenda too. It was obvious that the complaint had little substance, but still had to be answered.

"A vexatious complaint," declared the senior partner.

"He's just a chancer," said the practice nurse in between mouthfuls of flapjack.

All agreed that patients had become too litigious for their own good.

Geoff struggled to stay awake for the rest of the practice meeting and rang Daisy as soon as it had ended.

"Where shall we go this evening?" she asked in a rare show of consideration.

Geoff hoped to sit somewhere quiet, ideally where they might not be noticed. "A movie?" He didn't even mind which one.

The reality was less relaxing than he'd anticipated. According to Daisy, the male lead was too old and the one playing the young anti-hero was trying too hard to be a Benedict Cumberbatch. The female lead couldn't have acted her way out of a paper bag. Anyone could see that her tears were totally unconvincing. Besides, the make-up was all wrong for the period.

Geoff gave a furtive glance to see if anyone recognized him.

When Daisy wasn't making her observations on every scene, she intermittently pawed his crotch. He thought again of her abundant lips and pert buttocks, as a result of which he missed a crucial twist in the plot.

"Oh no!" hissed Daisy. "Now the blackmailer will be after them."

"What blackmailer?" asked Geoff.

"Shh," went a voice behind them.

After the film, Geoff feared she'd decide to go back to her own place. It would have been typical of her to be contrary and return to her flat alone.

"My place?" he asked.

"Why not?"

Maybe she wasn't so contrary after all. To his delight, she held his hand all the way back to the car while she vaped with the other hand like a woman possessed. Woman possessed was good. It presaged a great shag.

He was about to unlock his front door when she kissed him on the lips. "I hope you're inviting me in."

He beamed and pushed open the door.

She took a hesitant step into the hall and surveyed the hideous striped wallpaper, mass-produced prints, and low-energy lighting typical of all the rental houses he'd seen in the area.

"Nice place you've got."

"For fuck's sake, Daisy. You've been here before."

"I'm seeing it through new eyes. Have you got any Kir Royale?"

Surely she remembered he didn't keep any. "I don't have any cassis, but if you'd like a glass of wine or Prosecco..."

"Never mind." She arranged herself and her skirt primly on the sofa. "Coffee is fine."

They sat nursing their instant coffees.

"Shall we take our drinks upstairs?" Geoff said after a while. It had been three hours since he'd taken a tablet.

Her eyes grew wide. "Is that where your bedroom is?"

Perhaps she didn't even know she was being weird. There was a condition called multiple personality disorder, which Geoff only dimly understood.

She did at least allow herself to be led upstairs by the hand.

"Whoops," she said as she negotiated the turn on the stair-case.

In the bedroom she took her clothes off carefully, folding each garment, including stockings and underpants, on the chair by the window. It was pale pink lingerie today. When Geoff put his arms around her, she responded with all the ardour of a rag doll.

Once in bed, she lay flat on her back and observed the ceiling rose. He kissed her. She didn't kiss back.

He prodded her hip bone with Mr Wibbly Wobbly, who was by now throbbing and far from wobbly. She didn't push him away, but she didn't encourage him either.

He stroked her breast. "What's the matter, Daisy?" He asked knowing this to be the worst question a man could ever ask. The answer was only ever 'Nothing' or 'How can you possibly not know?'

She went for option A. "Nothing's the matter," she said, and shut her eyes in the manner of someone enduring coil insertion.

"You're normally a bit more, well..." He searched for the right word. *Responsive, interested, passionate*, or *active* would all have done, but, given Daisy's tendency to flare up over semantics, he finally plumped for, "You're just a bit different tonight." Maybe she wasn't an evening person anymore either.

"People aren't the same all the time, you know. They'd be

stereotypes if they were." She said all this with eyes closed.

Best avoid the subject of stereotypes. "May I kiss you?"

"If you like."

"Daisy, listen. It's about doing things we both like."

"I'm perfectly happy."

So he kissed her. She obediently opened her mouth and let him in. Next he sucked on a nipple. She didn't move at all.

"Is this OK?" he asked before working his way down with his lips. Other than obligingly parting her thighs, which he took to be informed consent, she lay perfectly still. He kissed what was left of her pubic hair, then had a go with his tongue. Nothing. It was about as passionate as putting together flatpack furniture.

He got on top. What was wrong with her? She was as dry as a bone. Applying a little of his saliva first, he entered, only for Mr Wibbly Wobbly to play the dying swan.

She opened her eyes. "Is everything all right?"

"Fine. Having the time of my life." *Come on, Wibbly.* He added an energetic rub. Nothing doing.

She smiled. "Shall we just go to sleep?"

Sometimes those were the six best words in the English language. Even if they did remind him of being married.

CHAPTER TWENTY-SIX

GEOFF

Monday morning. Today it was good to be up to his neck in other people's problems. It took his mind off his own.

After the frustrating evening with Daisy, the weekend hadn't been a complete disaster, but it was close. Dave had been meant to stay overnight.

"I've got your room ready," Geoff said brightly on the phone.

There was silence on the line before Dave said, "My room's here."

"I meant the room you've got in my house."

"Yeah?" said Dave without a hint of enthusiasm.

"Let's just make it a day visit," said Sonya when she got hold of the phone. "Easier all round. It's been a while, after all."

She was probably right, conceded Geoff. Dave had been away nearly two years with his mother and a man who wasn't his father.

So Dave was deposited at Geoff's late Saturday morning. Geoff had made no plans for that evening just in case. If it went well, Davey could still stay overnight instead of being collected at six.

Holding him close was the same as ever. The best thing in the world, bar none. Of course, Dave had grown. He was wearing a Cricket Australia T-shirt and he needed a damn good haircut. But he was surely the same boy inside.

If Geoff remembered correctly, Bowlby had said in one of his books on attachment theory that the hunger of a child for love was as great as his hunger for food. Geoff would provide both.

"What would you like to do today?" Geoff asked Dave. He'd already asked the very same question on the phone a few days previously, and got nothing useful.

By way of response, Dave pulled something flat out of his bag. That was when Geoff realized he'd be playing second fiddle to an iPad mini.

Bloody hell! That was a new development. Geoff was about to lay down the law, but the kid had only just got here. Cut him some slack, he told himself.

Sure enough, Dave put it away for lunch.

The boy was quieter than he used to be, with a wariness about him. To be expected, of course. He was older now, and hadn't seen his father for months. But Geoff hadn't expected him to have gone off pancakes. He preferred pizza now, apparently.

After a twelve-inch loaded with everything, Dave returned to his iPad.

"What are you doing there?" Geoff hoped he wasn't being groomed or downloading porn.

"Killer Diller?" replied Dave.

"What's that?" said Geoff.

"It's a game?"

Geoff was none the wiser. "What sort of game?"

"You have to zap these guys over there. They come out of the shadows if you're not careful. But if you get extra points, they have to use extra shot to kill you. And you can kill them if you find the dwarves first."

Geoff glanced at the screen. It could have been worse. "Right. Well, don't play Killer Diller all day." He cursed Sonya for allowing Dave to bring the damn thing. "We could go to the park. I've got a new football."

"I've got my iPad," Dave reminded him.

"OK," said Geoff. "So maybe a bit later we can have a kick-about."

"Cool?" said Dave without looking up.

Geoff busied himself for half an hour, during which Dave sat hunched over his little screen, laughing helplessly at something.

"Something funny?" asked Geoff.

"Kinda," replied Dave, but the laughter had gone.

"Want some juice?" Geoff had got in a large supply of Dave's favourite tropical juice drink, the kind that stripped tooth enamel faster than battery acid.

"Got any Seven-Up?"

"I don't think so." That was another dental disaster, but the occasional can wouldn't hurt. "Do you have Seven-Up every day?"

"Nah."

Eventually Geoff prised Dave off his game with the promise that they'd stop for some Seven-Up on the way back from the park.

In the park, Dave become almost animated, but that, Geoff reasoned, was probably because he was letting him get all the goals. Dave was barely even trying.

"Did you play much football in Oz?"

"Nah." Dave was back to his sullen self.

The afternoon dragged by. How was that possible, when previously time with Dave had always galloped? Geoff had plenty of time to think of Bowlby.

Dave chugged his Seven-Up while Geoff tried to find out a bit about his friends in Oz, what he'd enjoyed most about Perth, and what kind of animals he'd seen. He asked a lot of open questions. According to received wisdom on consultations, that was the type of question most likely to get people talking. But those who endorsed this style of questioning had obviously not dealt with stubborn seven-year old boys.

Geoff also tried, "Do you remember when...?", but got only non-committal replies.

Finally Geoff brought out some Lego. It was the best toy in the world and he'd kept it all, every single brick. The fire engine that Dave had made years ago had been on display since long before the boy had gone to Perth. Just last week, Geoff had bought a small, more advanced set.

Geoff pulled the box out from under the table and beamed at his son.

Dave stared. "Lego's retarded."

To prove that it wasn't, Geoff sat on the floor and made a locomotive. Dave didn't even watch him. He went back to Killer Diller.

It was six fifteen. Sonya was late and Dave was staring at the living room carpet. Geoff could hardly bear it. He wanted so badly to hug his son.

When Sonya arrived, twenty-three minutes late, he did put his arm around Dave as they said goodbye.

Dave looked back as he got into the car.

He was so hard to read, Geoff mused later over a large glass of wine. Even so, I should have managed that a lot better, he thought, going for a refill.

The guilt ebbed slowly away over the course of the evening as he worked his way down the bottle.

HARRIET

Love triangle, ménage à trois, or grubby little secret? Call it what you will, the chances are that many women will one day fall into the role of the Other Woman. It's a difficult part to play, but you can minimize the hurt to yourself and others if you keep your eyes open and follow the rules.

Harriet paused. There were no rules. This would be yet another breezy piece that would catch the editor's eye. *Write what you know* was the mantra. She felt more than a pang of guilt, but Laure need never know, ever.

Harriet cobbled together a few more paragraphs before making her pitch.

To her amazement, the editor of *RightHere!* didn't bang the phone down after five seconds. "Right, Harry. I want 900 words by close of play Monday. And I want all the dos and don'ts."

Piece of cake, thought Harriet.

"And I want case studies."

That was harder. "I'm not sure I can get all of them to agree to photos or using their real names."

"Just get lots of quotes then."

"OK." Harriet could interview herself all weekend if need be.

"I take it you're writing from personal experience?"

Harriet swallowed. Spilling out her secrets to the nastiest commissioning editor in London could only lead to trouble. "My lips are sealed. That's rule one, by the way."

"Remember to cover the guilt, Harry."

As if she could forget.

DAN

Atavistic. Dan rehearsed the word silently. He was in the grip of an atavistic fear.

The fear of being found out. That went way back. Back to the first time he'd banged Harriet. He'd been so careful. Avoiding being seen. Spending as little time with her as possible. Not calling from his mobile if he could avoid it. Using a condom, obviously, apart from the first time at her desk. All those things.

He shut the side door behind him and made his way down Flask Walk.

He tried to keep everything in separate compartments. Just like the spices at Lolo's. But he couldn't avoid feeling fucking awful. Now he felt guilty about Harriet too. As if he owed her. Jesus!

Dan walked uphill to Hampstead tube station. The other fear was, as usual, money. His big idea for being a media chef had stalled. Nobody had asked him on radio again after that BBC interview.

Funny, that.

It was good working at Lolo's. But he, Laure, and Jack were going to need more dosh.

Dan caught the southbound tube to King's Cross, then a westbound Met line train. This time he knew precisely where to go.

In Harrow, a fine drizzle was falling. He pulled his baseball cap down over his forehead.

The runner beans had lost most of their leaves and nobody was shagging on the allotments. A damp smell of mould hung over the place. Still smelled a fuck of lot healthier than in town.

Dan made his way to the tip of the triangle where the old biddy hung out. There she was. In the door of her shed. A pile of greenery in front of her.

"I've got your broccoli raab," she said. "This is the best time for it."

She was wearing funny pointed shoes and had raindrops in her hair. Looked like an old pixie.

"Thanks." He picked up a couple of stems and brought them to his nose. "Wow." Almost no scent at all apart from fresh air. Unlike regular broccoli. Though that would likely change when they were in the pan.

She looked pleased, as if you'd said her baby was cute. "And I've got all the carrots you wanted."

"Great," said Dan, fishing the money out of his jeans. "Don't suppose you do receipts?"

She took the cash and shook her head.

That was OK. There were always bits and pieces at work that were bought cash. He'd get paid back.

At the station he got some flowers for Laure. Not much choice to be had, just a few boring daisies. Better than nothing.

On the tube back, Dan sat with the flowers in his lap and two enormous carrier bags of carrots at his feet, topped with the new broccoli. Lying on the seat beside him was a discarded copy of the *Metro*. Looked well-read.

There was a free sheet just launched in Hampstead. The guvnor had been going on about getting some publicity in there.

It hit Dan just as the train rattled past Northwick Park. An article on trends in veg. New veg for old. And Dan could write it.

The idea buoyed him up until the next stop. He couldn't fucking string two sentences together, could he? Another atavistic dread seized him. Fear of failure. The most atavistic one of all. Went back to his time in jail. To his schooldays. Maybe even before that.

"Fuck it!" he said aloud.

He startled a man with a beard and a long white tunic.

"Sorry, mate," said Dan.

The geezer in white said nothing and went back to mumbling over his book.

But writing only took practice. Even that guy in the tunic had had to learn his holy book. Dan could put all the ideas down for an article and get someone to check all the words. Maybe Harriet, seeing as she was a writer and all.

Fuck, no. Not Harriet.

Laure could do it, right? He'd give it his best shot, and then she could take a look.

The train was approaching Baker Street station now. Dan gathered his carrier bags and the flowers. For a moment he considered whacking up his claim for the veg to cover the flowers, but decided against.

He wasn't a cheat. Was he?

CHAPTER TWENTY-SEVEN

SANJAY

Bloody Shelley Ritchie.

Sanjay checked Facebook every day, to make sure he hadn't overlooked any messages or notifications. He checked the messages under *Other*, just in case she'd got in touch to tell him that no, she wouldn't be his friend if he were the last person on Facebook. But she wasn't even doing that. She was fucking ignoring him, just as she used to at school when he slipped her notes during General Studies.

Now, a full six days after getting in touch with her, he was lying on the sofa listening to Tinie Tempah's *Not Letting Go* wash over him, while feline Shelley stood kneading right where Sanjay's piri piri chicken and chips were currently situated.

Shelley circled a few times, sweeping his face with her tail as she tried to work her way into a comfortable spot. In the early days of his TB treatment, he needed afternoon naps. If he lay down for twenty minutes on the sofa, you could guarantee that Shelley would spend eighteen minutes making herself snug. He bloody loved that cat, even if her tail always ended up somewhere under his nose where it tickled most.

Ping went Messenger. He extracted his arm from under the warm fur and reached for his iPhone. Who could resist looking at a message as soon as it came in?

OMG! Of course I didn't forget you.

He sat bolt upright to give it his full attention, and furry Shelley went flying.

Which bits did she remember most, he wondered. He still had very clear memories of that night.

Other fragments of the past came back. Her hair, almost white in summer. The cowlick she always tried to defeat. The way she wrinkled her nose when she laughed. The curve of her hip bone when she lay on her side. A glimpse of pubic hair, hardly visible she was so fair. And her breasts, of course. The first real-life ones he'd ever seen. He spent a few moments reminiscing.

Now he tried to imagine her in this flat. For some reason, he couldn't clear his mind of his old single bed at his parents', under the ridiculous Kajagoogoo poster and the paper lantern with a huge rip in its side from Sita's trainer because she'd wanted to show that she'd totally nailed juggling.

If Shelley was here now, he wouldn't just lie next to her trying to decide what to do. He'd bloody know what to do and he wouldn't hang about.

Her email was mollycoddles@nowmail.net. Seriously, *mollycoddles*? Who was she mollycoddling? He composed his reply.

Hi Shelley Ritchie. I'm pleased to see you're as gorgeous as ever and have the memory of an elephant. It would be great to hear more from you, if you can drag yourself away from your high-flying job, your ten kids, and your billionaire husband.

He pressed *Send* then realized how lame his message was. How could a message possibly not be lame after all this time? He gazed at the cat scratching the side of the armchair as he counted the years.

GEOFF

People normally spilled the beans and told Geoff everything, whether or not he wanted to hear the lies they told their employers, or how it turned them on to shove biros up their urethras.

Daisy was not a run-of-the-mill patient.

She refused to tell him why she was registered as a patient at his practice. Nor would she say where she went to on the days she didn't work at clinical scenarios.

First he had a go at subtlety. "Have a good day. Whatever you're doing."

To which she replied, "Thanks."

The next time he went for, "Are you free this afternoon?"

She wasn't, as it happened. It was a 'Daisy day', whatever that meant. His expectant expression did nothing to elicit any details.

"I could do with some Geoff days," he said.

She bestowed a lustrous smile and said she hoped that one day he would get his wish.

"How was your day?" he asked her later.

It had been average.

"Wouldn't you like to do acting work every day?"

"I do act every day, believe me."

"Oh, right. What are you doing today then?"

"Going to work." She said it with such finality that there was no chance of a supplementary question.

He might have to follow her one morning. It shouldn't be hard. He could schedule a day off from the masses of annual leave owed to him. Surely it wasn't stalking? It was natural curiosity.

He took his Geoff day on a Tuesday. She didn't do role play on Tuesdays. Geoff made sure they spent Monday night together, just her, him, and the little blue pills. And an irresistible dinner.

He already had a mammoth headache and a stuffy nose by the time she knocked on his door.

"Ooh, carbonnade of beef," she said as soon as she came in. The overnight bag in her hand was a good prognostic sign.

"I hope you like carbonnade."

"Love it." She kissed him for ages, as if she hadn't seen him the previous evening.

It was going to be a great night. Followed by a revealing morning.

The night fulfilled its promise. She rewarded him for serving her third favourite dish by riding him on the dining room carpet.

In bed the next morning he woke with a hard-on and a head that felt like a bass drum. She was unimpressed with his condition and said she had to get a move on.

"Where are you off to?" he asked while rummaging in a drawer for aspirin.

Her answer was to have an inordinately long shower, then spend ages applying make-up. Normally all she wore was a dab of something on her cheeks and a bit of lipstick. Today she gave her face the Sistine Chapel treatment.

She rejected the first piece of toast he offered her on the grounds that it was too dark. Geoff made her another slice.

She must have forgotten about getting a move on, because she ate her toast with elaborate slowness, pausing frequently to tell him a convoluted story about a woman who had fainted on a District line train at Earls Court. "The woman next to me wanted to pull the emergency stop," said Daisy. "But a man persuaded her not to, or the journey would be even slower."

"The District line is the slowest anyway."

She took another tiny bite of toast. "It is. I try to avoid it as much as possible. So many strange people on the tube, anyway."

Finally, after a second piece of toast and two cups of hot water and lemon juice, she was on her way. He figured it would look odd if he just trailed her from his house, so he said he'd walk as far as the corner with her. "I'm going to the newsagent's," he explained.

"Don't you read *The Times* online?"

He did. "I'm not getting a paper. I'm putting an advert in the shop window."

She arched an eyebrow. "Looking for flute lessons?"

"Of course not. Just hoping to offload some junk from the loft. You know," he added, although he didn't at all know.

This seemed to satisfy her.

"Right-o. Well, I'm ready if you are." He scooped up his keys from the hall table.

"You haven't brought a card," she observed as they shut the door behind them.

"What?"

"A card. Or a piece of paper. For the newsagent's window."

He nodded sagely and patted his pocket. She wasn't to know it was empty.

As predicted, she carried on walking past the newsagent's. Geoff poked his head into the shop and waved at the woman behind the counter before he shot out again.

With a long flowing skirt and a halo of curls, Daisy was easy to spot as she sauntered down the street. She turned right at the corner without noticing Geoff. This was simple, he thought.

Now would she go to the tube station, take a bus, or be picked up by a punter? If so, trailing her would become much harder. He cursed himself for not having a proper plan or tech backup. Why hadn't he gone to Spymaster or whatever that shop near Oxford Street was called?

He did have an Oyster card on him, though, so in theory he could get the same bus or tube. But what excuse would he have if she saw him? He'd be caught on the hop, which was typical of his whole relationship with Daisy.

Those thoughts occupied him as he kept her in his sights,

so he failed to notice the short woman with a limp until she shrieked, "Hello, doctor!"

Unsurprisingly, Daisy turned around and recognized Geoff. He gave an uncertain wave.

Following her was now impossible, so he had to settle for talking to Mrs Short. "Ah," he said, wondering what the hell her real name was.

She peered up at him with flat brown eyes. "Are my X-rays back yet, doctor?"

He couldn't recall her name, but he did know it was the third time she'd asked this week. As he struggled to find a suitable reply, Daisy disappeared into the distance on the way to her secret life.

CHAPTER TWENTY-EIGHT

KAREN

"Are you going to see him again?" Rose asked over the rim of her coffee mug.

Karen fiddled with her mug instead of replying.

"You really shouldn't keep cracked mugs. The cracks harbour bacteria. So are you going to see him again?" Rose was such a bully.

The mugs were a lost cause. Karen's entire house was a germ warfare repository. "I might."

On the hob, a pot of three-bean casserole bubbled away. Karen considered getting up to stir it, but it was too much effort on top of a day's teaching. "We mostly talked about his son," she said. "Not exactly flirting."

"Well, acorns, oaks, and all that." Rose took her mug to the sink. "Got any wine?"

"Help yourself. It's open." Karen got a bottle of Valpolicella off the shelf behind her and pushed it towards Rose. "He told me he was seeing someone."

Rose stared at the bottle with a distracted air. "Do you fancy him?"

For just a moment, Karen revisited the last session in the pavilion. In place of the customary football kit, she imagined chinos and a button-down shirt on the floor, and the hard bench had transmuted into a king-size bed in a boutique hotel. While straddling him, she gazed not at a cracked windowpane but a tasteful antique print, and, instead of exiting furtively to her car, she planned to lie in his arms for a while, because every woman knew she didn't have to be strong and independent every single minute.

This reverie came to an abrupt end with a crash and a scream from the living room.

"Argh." It sounded like Edward.

Karen heaved herself up and went to the living room in time to hear Damon go, "You fucking dipstick. Look what you've done."

Edward began to cry.

"Don't swear," said Karen.

She now saw what Edward had done. The computer monitor was on the floor, in pieces. It would have been a lot easier if someone else would help her clear up fragments of glass and deal with the kids at the same time, but Rose chose that precise moment to remember she had to get home.

"I want Mr Cow," howled Edward.

"See you later," said Rose from the doorway.

"You don't need Mr Cow," Ashley informed Edward. "There's lead in the glass. It's poison and you're going to die."

GEOFF

Sonya opened the car door to let their son out and announced, "He's all yours."

Geoff smiled at Dave then noticed his hold-all. "Aren't you collecting him at five, Sonya?"

"I thought you'd sound a bit more pleased than that. Anyway, I can't pick him up, no."

"No worries." Geoff was learning. "I can drop him round."

"Well, no. Drew and I are going to the theatre."

"That's all right then." Geoff beamed at Dave. He could make Sonya pay for this later. Meanwhile there was no need for him to know his father had theatre tickets for tonight too.

"Nice case, Dave," he said when Sonya had gone off down the road.

"Yeah. It's cool, isn't it, Dad?"

"It's very cool. In fact, it's ice." That was one of Geoff's oldest quips.

Dave duly rolled his eyes. "Not *that* kind of cool."

"Oh," said Geoff, feigning confusion. "Now. Why don't you put your things into this little old bedroom of yours? I'm just going to make a quick phone call."

He pointed out the duvet cover, the same one as before. Dave threw his bag into the corner and sat on the edge of the bed, bouncing up and down on it.

"Be right back," said Geoff and went to his own bathroom.

Daisy picked up right away.

"Look. I'm really sorry, but I can't do tonight. Apparently Dave—"

She went ballistic.

"I know. I wanted to see *War Horse* too," he replied.

"You need to sort out your priorities," she proclaimed, enunciating every syllable.

In his view, he had done exactly that. "Can't do much about the tickets, though. Perhaps you'd like to go with someone else?"

She yattered on about the difficulty of it all until he said, "Look, don't worry about the bloody tickets. If I have to write them off, I'll write them off. Call you tomorrow."

He turned to see Dave in the doorway to the bedroom. How long had he been standing there?

"Hey, Dave."

"I forgot my toothbrush," he said with infinite sadness.

"That's OK. We'll buy you a new one."

"To keep here?"

Was that a question? "Sure. Why not?" said Geoff, trying to keep it light.

Dave didn't reply. He was so unknowable since he'd become a laconic Aussie.

In his room, he'd tipped out the contents of his hold-all. A book on cricket, his beloved iPad, two of his usual inhalers, and a soft toy that was just about recognizable as Lil' Bun. Since Geoff had last seen it, it had lost its tail, one eye, and a substantial amount of fur. Reconstructive surgery was much needed.

"He lost his eye, see?" said Dave.

Geoff examined the toy rabbit closely. "I know what we can do today."

Dave brightened. "Ah, yeah?"

They had pizza for lunch. It was another ridiculous flavour like sweet and sour, but Dave wolfed it down and agreed to go to the park afterwards.

"Does Lil' Bun do parks?"

Dave was indignant. "Course not!"

Geoff realized on arriving at the park that he'd forgotten to bring the football. Dave had to content himself with watching others play.

"I don't supposed you go on the swings anymore?" Geoff said after a while.

"Nah. They're for liddle guys?"

That didn't stop Dave making a dash for the playground area. He leapt onto the roundabout and made it accelerate with just one foot.

"Wow. I'm getting dizzy just watching," said Geoff.

Then Dave ran towards one of the swings. "This is my one."

It was indeed. It was the swing Dave had favoured long ago,

when his parents lived together and all was well with the world, except of course on days when another child got to 'his' swing first. Then Dave would throw a monumental tantrum that was totally inexplicable to anyone who was under the illusion that all five swings were exactly the same.

Geoff refrained from pushing the swing, although Dave always demanded it, pre-Oz. A five-year old was a very different animal to a sophisticated seven-year old. So Geoff stood by one of the other swings, fingering the chain. Little fingers could so easily get trapped or pinched between the links. Dangerous place, the world.

As if to prove it, a child of about three dashed behind the row of swings. Through no fault of the girl next to Dave, her swing was heading straight for the toddler as it swung back.

Geoff bounded towards the swing and stopped it. The injury had been averted, but, shocked by the suddenness of it all, both children started howling. Geoff didn't dare hug either of them. Strangers couldn't do consoling in the twenty-first century, even if a child was injured.

The cries brought their distraught parents onto the scene. Geoff explained briefly what had nearly happened.

It wasn't until the mothers had gone their separate ways with their children that Geoff noticed Dave had abandoned 'his' swing and was standing right there.

"That was cool, Dad." Was that pride in Dave's voice? "But you could have fixed the little kid's head if he'd been hit, right?"

"Well, Dave, I'm not so sure about that. Heads are delicate things. They can't always be fixed."

"But the bone's really hard, yeah? It hurt when Aaron Gapes hit me with his head at school once."

"Yes, the bone is hard. It has to be. The brain inside is really soft and squishy, like a marshmallow, only more important. It needs a strong box made of bone to protect it. But, you see, Dave, boxes can break sometimes."

Dave was giving the matter his whole attention. "Like in a car crash?"

"Yes. Or even a fall in the playground." Thinking of the cases he'd seen, Geoff nearly added, 'or when someone beats the daylights out of you.'

"Then you get a little hole and the brain comes out, right?"

"More or less," agreed Geoff. "Are we finished in the park now?"

"Yeah. I'm done."

"Right. Let's go up Argyle Road then."

"Why, Dad?"

"You'll see."

Dave eyed him suspiciously, but was happy enough to go along with the plan. When they reached the parade of shops, they went into the pharmacy first. Dave stood in some indecision before the array of toothbrushes. Hard, soft, medium. Angled, straight, small. Precision, compact, interdental, zigzag, indicator. Children's brushes with cartoon characters.

Geoff nearly broke the silence, but that often led only to pointless prattling.

Finally Dave chose a plain blue toothbrush.

Next they went to the charity shop. At the till, an old boy haggled over the price of a jacket. Geoff hung back with Dave and waited. When it was their turn, Geoff asked if they had any buttons.

"Why yes, we do, my lovely," said the elderly woman behind the counter, all smiles. She extracted a metal biscuit box from somewhere. "There you are."

There was a mix of buttons in all sizes, colours, and shapes.

"I need one with a thing underneath like a mushroom stalk. Ah, this'll do." Geoff picked one out of the box.

Dave's face lit up. "A new eye for Lil' Bun!"

Geoff also bought a ball of pale blue wool. He'd be able to create some kind of bobble, he was sure.

They went home past the fish shop. Geoff checked to see whether Dave still held his nose as he once used to. He did, but he no longer made retching sounds to accompany it.

Ophthalmic surgery on a stuffed rabbit turned out to be surprisingly challenging, as Geoff needed to embed the eye as deeply as possible.

Dave studied the entire process. "Why do you do knots like that?"

"They're surgeon's knots," said Geoff. "Won't loosen even if you cut the ends short." That was the theory. In practice, they still came undone if you didn't do the job right.

Geoff was quite pleased with his handiwork even if the procedure had left Lil' Bun with one eye a bit proud. He pushed it in as far as he could. "There."

"Can you teach me to do knots with one hand too?"

"Of course. But don't give up if you don't get it right first time. It took me ages when I was a student, although I practised every spare moment. Right. Now for the bobble."

Geoff found a piece of card, wound the wool around it, and created a passable pom-pom. "There. What do you think of that for Lil' Bun's tail?"

Dave's face crumpled. "Don't wannit."

Geoff reflected. "OK."

"It won't be Lil' Bun if he has a brand new tail," Dave explained, his lower lip wobbling like a pre-schooler.

"OK. No worries."

Things changed in two years. Geoff got that. You couldn't graft something on and pretend it was still the same.

"I didn't really want to go anyway," said Daisy when he saw her after the weekend. She was wearing knickers today, as Geoff could tell when she crossed her legs on his sofa. The turquoise ones. "I mean, what is the point of a play where the principal character is a wooden horse?"

"There are people in it too," Geoff pointed out.

"I did know." Daisy unfolded herself and rose to get a Kir Royale. "I suspect they're a bit wooden as well."

"Very funny."

"You can take me to the cinema again though," she said. "Or to Paris one day. Didn't you promise me a long weekend away?"

He honestly couldn't remember. "You must be thinking of one of your other boyfriends," he said.

"Oh well. Worth a try." She dipped one finger into the glass and licked it.

"It's not a bad idea. Though I probably can't get a Friday off for another couple of months. By the way, there's more champagne in the fridge."

"That's what I like to hear." She gave him a wicked look before planting a lingering kiss on his lips and a hand on his flies.

He had taken his last two tablets, which was just as well because Daisy rarely took No for an answer. The turquoise thong was soon on the coffee table, and the two of them were on the sofa in a precarious diagonal position that would have seemed ludicrous, Geoff thought, were it not so exquisite. He had a steel girder of a hard-on, a thumping head, aching calves, and a demon of a partner who spurred him on until they lay spent in each other's arms.

His coma lasted until the oven timer went on off. Geoff gathered himself up and shambled into the kitchen to prod the baked potatoes. Nearly done. He put the hob on for the veg.

"How do you want your steak?" he called out. Daisy was stepping into her thong, a sight which could take anyone's mind off supper.

"Medium rare."

"Medium rare it is, then." Geoff opened the blue plastic bag from the butcher's and took out both slabs of meat. While he seasoned the sirloin with black pepper, he wondered, as he often did, why uncooked meat was so floppy. Surely all muscle developed rigor mortis.

The steaks turned out just right, more by luck than good judgement. Daisy ate as if it were her first meal in a week. She even tucked away a gigantic baked potato and half a head of broccoli, then asked what there was for dessert.

"Apple crumble. So," he said after he'd given her a bowl. "If we have to defer Paris for a month or so, I'm wondering about a little weekend in the Cotswolds."

"I'm not sure," she said. "I do have to go away for a few days very soon."

When she said nothing more, Geoff replied, "OK." To pose a direct question, like where she was going, was asking to be told to mind his own business. "Custard?"

"Please." She held out her bowl.

"They're my neighbour's apples. You really can't beat fresh apples." Geoff had no idea if this was true, but it sounded the sort of patter that should accompany apple crumble.

She made appreciative noises over a few mouthfuls before putting down her spoon. "You haven't asked when I'm going."

"No." He managed to suppress a smile. "Perhaps you'll decide to tell me."

"It's in precisely one week." Daisy rolled the R suggestively. "I'll be away for no more than ten days, I expect."

"OK." Didn't people normally know how long they would be gone for? They usually needed mundane things such as tickets and time off work. "I hope your trip is enjoyable and successful, or whatever you'd like it to be."

She flashed that dazzling smile that did as much for him as the tablets. "It's family business, so I'm hoping for peaceful. I'll let you know as soon as I'm back."

"I hope everything is OK?" he asked.

"Perfectly fine. It's just routine."

'Routine' was what doctors said when they wanted to reassure. "Ah, families," said Geoff.

"Indeed."

"Anything I can offer to do for you?"

"Nothing at all." She licked the spoon. "Thank you."

He wondered if he'd ever figure her out. But that, he reasoned, was part of the attraction. That and her magnificent body.

CHAPTER TWENTY-NINE

DAN

Dan finally gave in. "OK. We'll meet in town."

"Then we could go back to mine."

"We'll see," he said into the phone.

"OK," she said. "It'll be nice just to be out together."

"Just one thing. No kissing. No holding hands either."

That was actually two things. Didn't matter. She said OK anyway.

"We just can't take the risk," he explained. Which meant he couldn't take the risk.

It was madness. It had been madness all along, and now it had to stop. Yet somehow he couldn't help himself. Pathetic, that was. Who was the geezer who'd said a man only had between his ears what he had between his legs? Whoever it was, he was right on the money. Yeah, he needed something Laure had only given him twice in about a year. But he didn't need it badly enough to mess everyone up.

"So where shall we meet?" Harriet asked brightly.

He paused and hid his phone while one of the waiters squeezed past with dirty dessert plates. Everyone at Lolo's knew he had a partner and a baby. Something inside him felt rotten and squelchy. Like the remains of the baked apple that just went by on a plate. He couldn't go on like this. Nefarious, it was. It had to stop.

LAURE

Dan was at work and had said not to expect him till later. 'Possibly much later' were his exact words.

In the meantime, she and Jack were having a lovely day. That morning they were meeting Tante Lina and Tante Victorine for coffee.

Laure tweezed a few errant brow hairs and plucked four tenacious hairs from her chin. That was what you got for the twin sins of having Lebanese genes and neglecting your appearance. How had they grown so long, she wondered as she examined her reflection in the times seven magnifying mirror. She was having her hair done today too. It was high time to get the caramel highlights back into her now mousy hair. Had she really left it since before Jack's birth? Well, now she had an appointment.

The aunts were already at the tea-room, a traditional place full of wood-panelling and old ladies with chamberpots for hats.

"*Chérie, chérie,*" they cried as they fell over themselves to embrace her and Jack.

"*Le petit amour,*" exclaimed Tante Lina, ruffling Jack's blonde curls.

"*Amour, amour,*" echoed Tante Victorine. "*Je veux le croquer.*" Luckily she had never carried out her threat to crunch him.

"Ah-moo, ah-moo," went Jack.

Tante Lina giggled helplessly. "*Mais qu'est-ce qu'il dit?*"

"He's saying '*amour*'. Such an intelligent child!"

Lina tutted. "Of course he's intelligent, Victorine. You're the only dim one in the family."

Jack enchanted them with his appreciative noises and the way he held his croissants, one in each podgy hand.

Anyone could see from the way Jack attacked the pastries that he didn't need breast milk anymore. Laure was finally going to give up breastfeeding. And she was going to stop thinking that he was ill every five minutes.

"*Sm'Allah*," said Victorine as Jack licked his fingers.

Lina added, "*Sahtayn.*" It meant 'two healths' and was a Leb-anese way of praising someone's boundless appetite. They didn't mind that Jack dropped crumbs all over the floor or smacked the table with his sticky little hands.

Despite the promising start, Jack quickly tired of the outing. He was crotchety well before they set off home, but fell asleep in his buggy before they got to their front door.

Daisy looked after him while Laure went to the hairdresser's. "I'll be as quick as I can," said Laure.

"Take your time. We'll be fine," replied Daisy. "Have a manicure as well. God knows you need one."

Despite it being a little impractical, Laure had her nails done. Her hands looked transformed with a neat French manicure, and her hair was amazing. She tossed her head and admired herself in the salon mirror.

"Wow, check you out!" said Daisy when Laure got in. "He's been very good, by the way. But he hasn't had much to drink."

Jack's cheeks looked red. Had the aunts really pinched them that hard? Laure gave him water, which he refused. She tried a beaker with very diluted juice.

He cried. That wasn't exactly unusual for Jack, but he rarely refused juice.

"Well, I'll be going. Drop round if you fancy a Kir Royale."

"Thanks so much, Daisy. You've been a great help."

Laure tried to coax Jack into drinking but he pushed the beaker away every time, as if it hurt to swallow. Did he want to be held close? No, he didn't, she discovered after several attempts. He just wanted to sit up, leaning slightly forward. His forehead felt hot, and he was dribbling as if another tooth was coming through.

Surely there was nothing wrong. He was teething again, that was all. She had an app on her phone that might help. Now where the hell was it?

I am calm. I am serene. All is well.

Trying not to hyperventilate, Laure studied her iPhone as if her life depended on it.

HARRIET

Harriet had a leisurely bubble bath, even though it was bad for your skin. The words from *Are Your Christmas Presents Giving You Cystitis?* came back to her, unbidden. Well, once wouldn't hurt.

Then she selected her best underwear and a pair of super skinny Gap jeans and sat down to make herself up. She nearly didn't bother with perfume, but when else was she going to wear Coco Mademoiselle? She spritzed it on her neck, arms, and chest, making believe with each spray that she was turning into Keira Knightley, only with boobs.

It would have been wonderful to meet in Hampstead, but that was impossible. They could never be seen there together.

He'd asked if she knew One New Change. Did she know it? She'd written about it when it opened in 2010.

Sleek and sophisticated, One New Change is the only large shopping centre in the City of London. With over 50,000 square metres of floor space, its eateries and high-end shops will astound you, but wait till you zoom to the top and take in the breathtaking views.

Harriet stood by the escalators and saw him approach. He was carrying something. It was a slim carrier bag from Daunt Books.

"Hey," he said without touching her, which made her longing worse.

"Hey. What have you got there?"

He handed it over. "Open it later."

She just about resisted the urge to go *Squeee!* and settled for, "Thank you very much."

"Don't thank me yet. You might not like it."

"Silly." She punched his arm playfully. "I'm sure I'll love it." Even if it turned out to be a book about bin lorries, it was the first present he had ever given her, and she would treasure it forever. "It's a book, isn't it?" This wasn't hard to work out. One day, her books might be at Daunt's. Obviously, she'd have to write them first and get them published, but there was no need to worry about such matters now.

It was a clear autumn day, ideal for One New Change. The shops weren't the draw for Harriet, nor the umpteen cafés and restaurants dotted around the place. It was the exhilarating ride to the top floor in a glass-sided lift that sped right past the in-your-face dome of St Paul's Cathedral and up to that magnificent view of practically all of London.

Four tourists got out of the lift as they got in.

"Fancy a drink at the top?" asked Dan.

"Maybe water. You'd need a mortgage for anything else." For a moment, Harriet allowed herself to imagine a margarita.

In the lift, she hugged him and asked if he'd ever thought of shagging in a lift.

Dan pulled away. "The lift would stop and ten Japanese tourists would get in with their cameras. And capture every angle."

The view from the top didn't disappoint. She tried to get him enthused. A selfie, that was what she wanted. Just one of them together. She got out her phone.

He covered the phone with his hand. "No."

He seemed about to say something more, but she led him to the far end on the right, where you could see most of London, and also have a bit of privacy for a hug.

He pulled away. Well, it was still a bit public, she reasoned.

"I don't think we should be here after all," he said. "We shouldn't..."

"Come on then," she said. "Let's go back to mine."

Now he was hesitating. "Well. OK," he finally said.

It was going to be the perfect shag. She knew it. The best ever. He would be rock hard. Lucky Laure. No, she shouldn't have thought that. She refused to give Laure another thought. Or their son. Especially not their son. She'd concentrate on herself. Her pleasure, and Dan's. Wasn't it clear he wanted to be with her?

As they waited for the lift down, a voice inside her head read out a paragraph she'd composed.

Men play around. It's a fact. So do women. In a recent survey, at least 45% of women in a committed relationship cheat, as do a whopping 65% of men. A man often shrugs it off, saying it was nothing. And that's exactly what it is.

All those features were garbage. She refused to listen anymore.

As they left One New Change, she squeezed Dan's hand tight while nobody was watching.

He dragged his feet on the way to the Tube station, yet his pace changed when they got to Kentish Town.

"Wait for me," she said.

The communal entrance was musty as usual, and carpeted with gym adverts and takeaway menus. A police chase blared out from Nora's flat on the ground floor. Harriet wished she'd turn the TV off just occasionally, especially today, when it was important for everything to be just so.

As soon as they got in, Harriet went to the bathroom and sprayed on more Coco Mademoiselle.

Of course it couldn't be just so, because Dan could never be hers to have. But she could pretend. Over the years, creative visualization had helped her turn an acned boyfriend into Brad Pitt, and a timid lover into Daniel Craig, leaping from building to building to reach her. It wasn't hard to suspend reality for a few moments.

She began to unbutton Dan's shirt. He didn't seem as responsive today, but she could change that in an instant.

"Harriet," he began. His tone was all wrong.

She'd got down to his belt now. She could feel his breath as she undid the buckle. He always wore a nice leather belt. When (or if) their fling came to an end, she would remember every detail of his leather belt, along with all that happened when it came off.

Now Nora downstairs was watching a game show at full volume. Harriet's fingers trembled as she popped the top button then unzipped Dan's jeans.

He was wearing horrible off-white briefs. Unbidden, an idea for a feature popped into her mind. No, she told herself. This was not the time for articles on making over your man's underwear drawer. It was the moment to revel in his closeness.

He was trying to say something, but endearments could wait.

She kissed him, plunging her tongue deep. Though less impressive than usual, his hard-on was growing. She thrust her hand into his briefs and pulled them down.

He groaned and muttered as she moved to lick him fully into life.

On the coffee table, his mobile rang out the first bars of Plan B's *She Said*.

"Fuck," he said.

"Leave it," she said as she kneaded his scrotum.

He wriggled away. "Can't."

It was Laure. Harriet knew that even before he said, "Hey, darling."

There was a pause. "OK. Don't panic. I'll be right there."

CHAPTER THIRTY

SANJAY

Mum rearranged her dupatta. "I am going to phone her."

"Bollocks! No!" He tried not to shout.

She waved a hand up and down at him. "There you are, Mister, all grown up now, and what do you know, ha? In my day, all marriage arranged. So now I am thinking, you should have arranged kiss-and-make-up time with Harriet." She went to rattle some pans before adding, "It's not rocket salad."

Sanjay stormed out of the kitchen and came face to face with Sita. A terrifying encounter, as she was in hot pants and a sleeveless thing. Sanjay tried to avoid staring at her cleavage or clapping eyes on that unicorn tattoo.

"Let's go to the park, yeah?" Sita tugged her hot pants in vain to make them cover her arse.

"You might need something first," Sanjay pointed out. "I'm thinking clothes."

She rolled her eyes and grabbed a coat from the hall.

On the way, Sanjay stopped to buy ciggies and a lighter. He hadn't smoked since he was at uni but he just felt like it. Bloody hell, they cost a fortune now!

They sat on a bench by the playground. He opened the ciggies. "Want one?"

She shook her head. "Maybe later."

He lit up, coughing manfully through the first few puffs. His head went spinning off somewhere and he needed a shit or else a barf. He wasn't sure which.

"So are you seeing anyone?" Sita was asking.

"No." He paused to stare at the cigarette packet in his hand and read all the health warnings. "Although I did find the girl from Year Twelve."

"And?"

He forced himself to inhale again. The sick feeling came back in waves, a kind of chemo tribute number. "I kissed her."

Sita nodded, flaunting the extra chin she had grown.

"Don't get too excited. It was the kind of kiss you'd get in Year Two."

"Oh." She decided to help herself to a cigarette now. "Have you heard from Harriet?"

"Nope."

She took a drag and produced a couple of passable smoke rings. "You should contact her."

"No. It's over. Really over."

A kid on a scooter whizzed by, nearly slicing off their kneecaps. In the distance the ice cream van made itself heard. Sanjay's legs were too wobbly from the nicotine to even think of getting an ice cream.

"You and Harriet were really good together, bro."

"Past tense, Sita."

"Mum really might ring her, you know," Sita pointed out.

"Luckily Mum doesn't have her number." From now on, he'd make damn sure to keep his mobile out of Mum's hands. And Sita's.

"Anyway, beside the point," said Sita. "If you want the truth, I'm not that worried about you."

"You're worried about your bloke, right?"

She took a long drag and exhaled. "I'm worried about Dad."

"Dad? Why? The business has its ups and downs, but—"

"It's not the business I'm worried about." She wandered over to the swings.

He followed. "Then what?"

She fixed on him with eyes that were ringed in black and bright pink. "You noticed he's slowed down a lot, right?"

"I guess." She was right. Dad wasn't as quick these days. Doing the washing up was a case in point.

Sita nodded and put her cigarette out on the ground. "I think he's got an appointment with the doctor."

"Really?" Dad never went to the doctor.

"Mum made the appointment."

That was more like it. "When is it?"

"Dunno. Haven't seen his diary." She sat on the swing. "Give me a push."

"What do you think's wrong with him?"

"Give me a push," she said again.

Sanjay gave her swing a giant shove and watched as Sita made it go higher and higher.

When she got bored, she stopped with a scrape of her shoes and looked Sanjay in the eye. "Mum thinks it could be his heart."

An icy shaft went through him, colder than a Calippo lolly on a hot day. He was aware of how ridiculous it was, but he said it anyway: "Give us another ciggie."

Sita didn't scream at him, or even use the word *innit*. She just put the cigarettes in her pocket and said quietly, "You think I want to lose you as well?"

It hadn't been a Year Two kiss at all. First they'd met at the Gourmet Burger restaurant. For a moment he thought the bag on her shoulder was her school bag, which of course it wasn't.

They'd begun by telling each other they hadn't changed a bit. You had to say that, didn't you? Obviously they'd changed. Shelley had lost a few kilos and gained a few wrinkles. Looked harder, maybe, with lips that were a bit less full. Perhaps that was the effect of the lipstick, though. Her hair was a tad shorter and still very fair, with lots of bright blue streaks.

He looked down at her hands. No wedding ring. Not that it always signified.

There was a raincoat on the bench next to them, along with a full shopping bag, both courtesy of the adjacent table. It meant he and Shelley Ritchie had to sit pretty close. Fine by him.

They held their menus without really looking at them. It was funny how things had worked out, they agreed, as they asked about each other's work. Shelley had studied French and Russian, and was in property management now.

"Your Russian must be useful then," said Sanjay. "Seeing as oligarchs have bought up half of London."

"Not so much down my end of the market. What about you?"

"My work's down the same end of the market." He told her about the charity he fundraised for, and he made her laugh with his account of the lad who'd kicked in a door out of frustration and anger, then brought in a chocolate cake and a scrawled apology written on the side of the cake box.

"So what shall we have?" Shelley smiled again, showing those irregular front teeth.

As they waited for her wine and his lager, she said she had a daughter. "My first and last baby. I haemorrhaged from the birth," she explained. "Had an emergency hysterectomy."

"That's sad." There wasn't anything else to say.

She showed those teeth again. "Erin is a lovely girl."

"I'll bet. How old is she?"

"Nearly twenty."

A waiter brought their drinks. Sanjay took a gulp of ice cold lager as he double-checked the arithmetic. "You got pregnant right after you left school?"

"Yep."

Sanjay racked his brains. "Who was it?"

"My husband, Pete. He wasn't at our school. He was at Greenhill." She smiled and her nose wrinkled up just as it always had. "Pete was the bad boy of his year. Then he decided to settle down with me."

"What happened to this Pete?" He leaned across encouragingly.

She hesitated. "Let's look at the menu."

Bollocks! That left masses of room for speculation. Had Pete copped off with his secretary? Died in a crash? Had an op and changed his name to Petra? "Tell me later, yeah?"

She made a non-committal noise.

They got burgers with everything on them, and in them, and around them, including fries, onion rings, coleslaw, and stuff that looked too much like salad for Sanjay's liking. They also ordered more drinks and got into major reminiscing about school. So-and-so was in banking now, someone else had five kids, and the boy nobody liked had somehow made a fortune and moved to Jersey.

"He's probably even smellier now," said Sanjay, "as well as an odious shit."

"Do I detect a smidgeon of envy?" asked Shelley.

"Not at all." He couldn't understand himself how he was still an intolerant sod after his brush with death. Surely it made you concentrate on more important things. "Remember that trick we played on the art teacher?"

Her nose wrinkled again. "When I put laxative into a cake?"

"Classic, wasn't it?" said Sanjay. "I can't believe you actually did that. It was so..."

"Mallory Towers?" suggested Shelley.

"Something like that." Sanjay picked up the last onion ring.

"Another thing I remember is I wasn't any good at art." On the bench, the coat and the bag had gone, but there was no law saying you had to use space just because it was there.

"Yes, you were. You were good at everything." She bit into a French fry and gave him a look that could so easily have been mistaken for lust. "Well, maybe not cross-country."

"You were pretty good too."

"I loved school," she said. "God, whatever happened to that awful Tara? Such a bitch."

He nodded in agreement, said he had no idea. Their fingers were too greasy to use their phones and Google her, so they debated which was worse, a bitch or a cow, without coming to any firm conclusion. His belly was stretched beyond belief, but he wasn't giving up on his burger.

Fit to burst, Sanjay got up to use the loo. When he washed his hands, he noticed in the mirror that he was about ten years younger than he remembered.

Shelley smiled when he got back to the table. She too had a twinkly look, as well as a cute smudge of bright yellow mustard on her chin.

He sat down and recited:
But who hath seen her wave her hand?
Or at the casement seen her stand?
She grinned. "The Lady of Shalott."

"Yep." Sanjay couldn't remember why he'd learned this bollocking poem for her, or rather a random selection of lines from it, but the words came back to him none the less from all those years ago. Pausing to wipe the mustard off her chin, he continued:
Or is she known in all the land,
The Lady of Shalott?
They yelled out, "Onions!" together, just as they always had.

She wiped her eyes and had a sip of water. Then, when she'd stopped convulsing with laughter, she went all serious. He knew

230

it was serious because she was toying with the ketchup. "You didn't say if you had any kids."

He shook his head. Was he really going to tell her an ex had got an abortion without discussing it with him? The good thing was that he still had one real goolie left, which, the specialist had said, was enough to get into mischief. "I don't have any," he said finally.

She tilted her head and observed him.

"Coffee at mine?" he asked.

She didn't need much persuading.

Once in his flat, Sanjay put on The Jam.

"Wow! Brings back memories," said Shelley.

He left her to examine his books and CDs while he went to the kitchen to load his Nespresso machine. Although he'd had it for over a year, it had yet to turn him into George Clooney. As he waited for the brewing to stop, he fed the cat. She had scurried out of sight as soon as they'd come in, but now she was in the kitchen doorway, rubbing herself on the woodwork and giving him silent meows.

"Good girl, Shelley," he said as he stroked the soft orange and black swirls on her back.

He looked up to find Shelley Ritchie standing right there.

"Who you calling a good girl?" She looked anything but.

"My cat, Shelley."

Her eyes grew wide. "You named your cat after me?"

"Yes. She's tortoiseshell," he added unnecessarily. "See? Her back end is tabby, but the rest of her is this patchwork of orange and black."

She showed those front teeth again. "That's lovely. Nobody's ever named a cat after me before."

"That you know of," he pointed out.

She put her hands out to grab the lapels of his shirt, and probably would have planted a huge smacker, but the colossal burger he'd had, to say nothing of all the trimmings, began to make itself felt. "Excuse me a moment. Milk and sugar's just there."

As soon as Sanjay got to the toilet, his guts decided to flush out what must have been the entire meal. Even after reams of paper, he still didn't feel clean.

As he had no bidet, he used the bath. He peeled off his clothes while spraying the room with air freshener. It was the only loo in the flat. Suppose Shelley needed it next? Panicking, he let loose a second barrage of Glade. How much of the stuff did one need to obtain the promised clean scent described on the can? He launched another salvo and got into the tub.

His backside was clean now, but damn, his eyes were stinging like mad. He washed his face and blinked repeatedly.

He'd been in the bathroom ages, he realized. As he walked back to the living room, he said, "Sorry, Shelley, I—"

There she was, lying stark naked on his IKEA sofa, legs akimbo, neck extended, her blonde and blue hair spread out on a cushion. For the first time, her boobs were properly on display. He saw too the deep scar from her emergency surgery, and just below it some faint pale fuzz that passed for pubic hair.

The cat was on the bookcase, staring wide-eyed at her.

They did it right there and then, without a thought for the condoms that Sanjay carried around everywhere (a habit going back to his hopeful teens), and without caring whether the cat would jump down from her perch and onto their writhing bodies.

All this time gone by since they'd last been together. Sanjay could sense it, along with all the events it had brought with it. Sometimes he felt he'd lived through too much. It all came back to him, surgery and chemo, pain and sickness, along with university, relationships, worrying about Dad, and Mum with her leg, and hassles at work, but as he came inside her the warm balm washed it all away, the pain, the loss, and all the regrets he'd ever had.

He was home.

CHAPTER THIRTY-ONE

LAURE

Laure somehow got Jack to Accident and Emergency, her knees banging together in the ambulance despite the paramedic trying to calm her down while she put an oxygen mask on Jack.

"He'll be all right," said the woman, smiling as if she was right.

That was hard to believe. Laure had never seen Jack so unwell, dribbling and practically fighting for breath. She gripped Jack tighter and tried to subdue her own breathing.

He was a touch calmer once they'd got to the hospital and a nurse said he didn't really need the mask. They still rushed Laure straight in with him.

The first doctor looked thoughtfully at Jack.

Laure gave the most coherent account she could. "He was fine this morning and his appetite was great. But then he seemed a bit flushed, oh, I don't know, two hours ago? I didn't think much of it, but then he didn't want anything to drink. No water. Not even juice. That was odd."

As Laure spoke, the doctor took Jack's temperature, examined his chest, and checked his ears. Throughout this, Jack drooled and his breathing was noisy. And Laure's heart threatened to pound its way out of her chest.

"He always loves his juice. I mean, I usually give him water, because of his teeth, but he loves juice. It's not normal for him to refuse." She'd already made that point, but it was vital for the doctor to know how ill Jack was. Laure wasn't wrong, and she wasn't neurotic. He was really ill this time. She couldn't read the doctor's face at all, so she added, "He sat up dribbling a bit, even though he hadn't had any water or juice. He threw the beaker in the corner. He never does that. Ever."

The doctor said he would check Jack's throat now. "We often leave the throat exam as a parting shot," he explained, with a tired smile that told her nothing. "Young children aren't very keen on that bit. Where are the tongue depressors?" asked the doctor, getting up.

A nurse pointed to a box on the wall. Laure held Jack again, putting her hand on his forehead just as she always did when she took Jack to the GP.

"Christ!" shouted some crazy man who had bounced into the room from nowhere. He grabbed the tongue depressor out of the doctor's hand. "Don't do that! You'll fucking kill the child."

"What the hell?" said the doctor.

The new man turned out to be a doctor too. His badge said he was Geoffrey Taylor. "It's epiglottitis," said this Dr Taylor. Laure caught the 'half-wit' he added almost under his breath.

Laure recognized him from somewhere. Was he someone from speed-dating a while back, from the Jacaranda? Never mind that now.

"It's epiglottitis," announced Geoff Taylor again. "Get him into resus."

Jack didn't seem to care about being moved into this huge new room, with loads of different bits of apparatus. Geoff began hurling seemingly random terms like *laryngoscopy*, *cannula*, *airway*, *lateral neck*, *blood cultures*, and *ENT stat*.

Laure had to leave the room while this was happening. Now

Dan was there in the corridor. She tried to tell him what was happening, even though she actually had no idea.

"Let's just relax," said Dan. "Let them do their stuff."

He was holding her hand, and shaking too.

When they saw Jack next, he was in intensive care. He was lying still, on oxygen, surrounded by machines and tubes. Laure had a TV. She knew exactly what intensive care looked like, but until that moment she'd never realized what it felt like.

"It could go either way," one of the doctors had said.

Life in suspension, thought Laure as tears tumbled down her face.

DAN

He put his arm around Laure, hoping she couldn't smell anything. It was hard to find the right words. What words were right when your son was practically dying? And when you'd been banging someone just because you were tempted?

They were in the corridor now. "Just for a few minutes," the doctor had said. "Won't be long."

Maybe it was just minutes, but eternity stretched out forever when your baby was ill and you couldn't be with him. That Einstein bloke was spot on about time and stuff.

Dan squeezed Laure's hand. She'd been right all along. Because finally there was something wrong with their son. Except it wasn't right to be obsessed with things going wrong for weeks and months before they actually did.

Cowards died a thousand times before their death. The valiant tasted of death but once. The mutt's nuts, that Shakespeare.

But Laure wasn't the coward here, Dan reminded himself. He was.

Laure turned to him, pushed a strand of amazing honey-like

hair out of her eyes, and said, "Will you do me a favour?"

"Sure. Anything." He meant it.

"They've got a chapel here. Light a candle for Jack."

"Of course I will." And for us, he thought.

LAURE

Before Dan went to the chapel, the staff let them back in again to see Jack.

Was he really going to make it, as the doctors said he would? One of them said just now that he was finally turning the corner, and Laure had nodded, willing it to be true. By the time she'd finished nodding, the doctor had disappeared. She had no idea people could move that fast.

Now there was just one nurse on the periphery in the unit, doing something to another little patient. Laure sat by the cot for a bit as Jack slept. She heard a rasping catch in Jack's breathing despite the oxygen. There was a drip, pulsed through by some machine into tubing that trailed all over the place and finally went into his little arm. His eyes were closed, his lashes pale against his skin, all of him motionless.

It could go either way.

She looked up at Dan.

Someone came and spoke to them. Epiglottitis was an inflammation of the epiglottis, a little lump of tissue at the base of the tongue. "Normally it acts like a flap," said the doctor, waving her hand to show how the epiglottis stopped food going down into the airways. "When it gets infected, it swells up and can block off the airway. Very serious, of course."

Laure wasn't sure she'd ever heard of epiglottitis. "What causes it?"

It was usually bacteria called *haemophilus*, and it was very uncommon these days, especially as Jack had had all his jabs, but there it was. "The airway can obstruct as a result," the doctor said again. Just a precaution now. Not taking any chances. Things seemed to be going in the right direction, but he wasn't out of the woods yet.

There was a lot to take in, but one bit stuck, that bit about not being out of the woods.

Could be the best part of the next twelve to twenty-four hours, apparently, but no guarantees. Empathic eyes, a wry smile, and another rapid departure down the corridor.

Laure didn't want to leave Jack, at least not until he was out of the woods, but now she and Dan had to wait outside while Jack had another scan thing.

They sat in the corridor by an empty water cooler. Next to it, the recycling bin was overflowing with paper cups. Someone had carved their initials into the arm rest on Laure's chair. Others must have sat here a long time too, thought Laure, feeling like this, terrified and numb at the same time. She leaned her head back against the green wall and let out a sigh that caught and turned into another sob.

Dan squeezed her hand and said he'd be right back.

DAN

He had to wash. He'd already tried in the tiny Gents opposite the chapel where he'd lit the candle. But it wasn't the kind of thing you could do in full view, was it?

Course, it wasn't just his dick he needed to cleanse. It was his conscience.

He had to get back to Laure and Jack, but he also needed a wash. So he went downstairs to the pharmacy where he'd seen a large toilet. Maybe there'd be paper towels there. Then he could soak the towels in water. Take himself off into a cubicle to wipe down Percy.

No paper towels there either. Too bad he didn't have any of Jack's bum wipes. He couldn't exactly go back to Mother Goose ward and get them, though.

He managed to douse his todger under the tap instead. But then someone came in. Which left him holding a dripping wet dick in his hand. He inched sideways in the direction of the hand-dryer.

Fuck. It would be one of those Dyson Air Blades, wouldn't it? Great for dipping your hands up and down. Not so fine and dandy for dangling your tackle into. His jeans were soaked, the crotch dark like an adolescent accident.

He made it into a cubicle and used toilet paper, which did what it always did when it got wet. Left bits of paper wherever it had been. Took him fucking ages to remove. How could he be spending all his time doing this while their son was bloody nearly dying?

Laure was in exactly the same place in the corridor. "Are you OK with beef and horseradish?" he asked.

"I wondered where you'd got to." Laure looked up, eyes red.

"I lit a candle, like you said. And then I got us these sandwiches. The only ones left in the shop. I think the red bits might be redcurrant," he added as he peeled open one of the packets.

"I'm not really hungry."

He wasn't either.

"They're still busy with Jack." There was anguish in her face. "I peeked through the door a minute ago."

He nodded.

Laure twisted her fingers together. "I found out why Jack was sitting like that. The doctor said it was to take the pressure off the swollen epiglottis. He was sitting like a human tripod, drooling because he couldn't swallow his own saliva."

He nodded again. Maybe Laure felt better if she kept talking.

"I can't understand how he got ill so fast. Within hours, he had every symptom in the book. High fever, trouble swallowing, hoarse voice. And something else, I can't remember what the doctor said." Laure paused to study him. "What happened to your crotch?"

He shrugged as casually as he knew how. "Went to wash my hands. The tap had other ideas."

"Poor you." She dabbed at his flies with a paper napkin. Which didn't make it any drier. Just served to remind him of what Harriet had been doing a few hours earlier.

He squirmed. He finally smiled when she stopped patting his crotch.

"Best I can do." She smiled back at him.

"That's the first time I've seen you smile today," he said.

She was knitting her fingers together again. "Guess I'm just trying to convince myself everything will be OK."

"Me too." He meant Jack, of course. And other things too.

She put her arm around him and buried her face in his neck. Then she moved away and sniffed. "Have you bought yourself some new scent or something?"

"Erm." Now what could he say?

She sniffed again. "It's a bit..."

"Poncey? Yeah, I thought that too."

"What's it called?"

Keep calm, he told himself. She probably couldn't actually feel his heart beating at double speed, trying to bash its way out of his chest. "No idea. Tried it in a shop. Had a squirt or two at lunchtime. Won't be doing that again." He meant it. "Let's try to see Jack now."

CHAPTER THIRTY-TWO

SANJAY

Ben had a new flat and a new arm. He showed Sanjay both of them as soon as he opened the door.

"See? I can move the fingers and everything."

"Cool," said Sanjay.

"I've got a big lounge area," continued Ben.

The flat could have done with a coat of paint, and probably a dehumidifier, but Ben said he'd been lucky to get it. "Look at the kitchen," he said, waving his new arm in the direction of a hob, microwave, and tiny fridge.

"It's good, mate." Sanjay paused to appraise Ben. "What's the deal with the uniform?"

"Mate. What do you want me to wear? In civvies I look like a sad fucker with one arm. In uniform I'm a fucking hero, even if I've only got a desk job now."

"True." Ben still looked like a sad fucker though.

Ben wanted to go the pub. It was one of those places where you could have a pint and a burger for just six ninety-nine, provided it was a Wednesday between four and five in the afternoon. There was something called a beer garden which was basically a load of waste-bins with drunken wasps circling round in desperation.

So they went back inside and installed themselves beneath a TV screen that took up an entire wall. The place was dingy, the walls stained with years of nicotine and neglect. Half a moose hung crookedly above a fireplace, and a fruit machine flashed away to itself, all alone in the corner except for the multiple notices that warned you to leave quietly or else the neighbours would put you on a hit list.

Sanjay brought their pints back to a table that was marginally less sticky than the rest.

"So what's up?" asked Ben, testing out his new fingers on the edge of the table.

Sanjay took a gulp and told him about Shelley Ritchie. Just the bare bones. He'd seen her again and they'd done the same thing on his sofa, to his cat's disgust, but mates didn't need to know everything.

"Mate," said Ben. "That was a long time coming. Now what?"

"Truthfully? I don't know."

"She sounds a gift," Ben observed.

Sanjay looked into the depths of his pint. "Maybe."

"Back after a slash." Ben limped off to the back of the pub.

This left Sanjay time to think. Back at school she was always Shelley Ritchie, never just Shelley on its own, and she wore a shed-load of make-up even though it was banned at school. Her maroon skirt was hitched up as far as she could have got it without getting ticked off and being sent to change, and her tie was always knotted really short, like a policewoman's cravat. He imagined the long thin end of the tie nestling under her shirt, probably tucked into her bra to keep it out of the way. He sighed at the memory. She'd lean against the wall outside the school, and if she'd run out of ciggies, or there were teachers about, she'd just pretend. You couldn't get a detention for smoking a pencil. Her school bag would have been chucked onto the pavement because she was way too cool to be seen carrying it, and anyway someone would soon carry it for her.

In Sanjay's ears was the relentless sound of Donna Summer. *This Time I Know It's for Real*, the song was. Getting on for twenty-five years ago now, and he wondered if Donna Summer was right.

Ben got back from the Gents and sat down. "You needn't feel sorry for me, you know. I'm fine. I've got my new place. I've got a job. Obviously it's not like being in Afghan, but all that's coming to an end soon anyway." He took another slurp and wiped his mouth. "I'm on my way back in there." He raised his new arm in defiance.

Sanjay didn't need to ask what Ben meant by 'in there'.

It was Ben's idea to think up different types of shag. "There's the posh totty shag," he began.

"The slag shag," added Sanjay.

"Yeah. And the jail-bait shag. Not that I've been there, you understand," Ben added quickly.

"The old times' sake shag," offered Sanjay.

"Well, mate. You'd know about that."

"What about the old-timer's shag?"

Ben made a retching sound. "Don't forget the knee-trembler."

"Yeah, mate. But that could be any one of the others." Sanjay paused. "Especially for the granny."

"Don't. How about the nympho shag? I'd like that. Or the banter shag, the one you can't help bragging about." Ben was warming to his theme. "Hey! Office party shag!"

"More likely I'd end up with the pity shag," said Sanjay. "With the sad bird nobody fancies even though it's 3 a.m."

Ben laughed and added that he'd have settled for that, as it had been a while.

Sanjay put down his glass. "You know what else has been a while? You haven't been for a meal lately."

Ben asked, "Is your pakora as good as your mum's?"

"Working on it, mate. Another one?"

"Sure." Ben drained his glass. "Tell you what. Forget dinner at yours. Wangle me an invite to your folks' instead."

"Deal. As long as you don't shag my sister. Or my mum."

Ben duly laughed.

Bollocks! Who'd trust him with that look in his eyes?

In the event, there were no signs of Ben wanting to hump any of the residents of thirty-two Cornwall Gardens. Sita lumbered to the door to greet him, wearing skin-tight jeans with integral ventilation holes in both knees.

Mum's dupatta kept slipping off her shoulder in her excitement. She wanted to know how Ben was, and how his new flat was, and his new job, and oh my God all the new things that had happened since they had last seen him, now when was it, maybe six months or even longer, but as everybody knew when you were old person like herself and Mr Shah, time went flapping by whether you liked it or not.

"Flying by," Sanjay muttered.

"Flapping, flying. What is difference, ha?"

She got Ben to follow her into the kitchen, where Sanjay heard her say, "Now to find nice girl for you, *beta*, har?" as she started clattering about with pots and pans. It was a subject to steer well clear of, as it was just a matter of time before she turned her focus onto Sanjay.

Sanjay installed himself on the sofa opposite Sita and nodded in the direction of the knee poking through denim. "I'm sure Mum can lend you a needle and thread."

Sita adopted a superior expression. "I'll have you know that this is what all the trendy young people are wearing."

"I know. That's why you'd better have a needle and thread."

She pretended to throw the remote control at him. This made her sleeve ride up, exposing the unicorn tattoo. Sanjay couldn't bear to look, but was powerless to resist.

Dad came in, poked his head into the kitchen, and seemed pretty pleased to see Ben too. "Drink?"

Dad wouldn't take No for an answer, insisting Ben should have whatever he liked from the cabinet in the corner of the dining room. Some of the collection was seriously ancient, like the peach schnapps. Ben was eventually browbeaten into a Dubonnet, which Dad poured right to the top of a large tumbler.

Ben manfully worked his way down the glass while Dad talked. After admiring the new arm, Dad gave him the latest on the import-export business. Ben listened politely to the litany of woes, from shoddy products that were not as described to inefficient no bloody use book-keepers and receptionists. "And they feather own nests!" he added, waving his arms around.

Ben shrugged. "Way of the world, Mr Shah."

Dad put a CD on, because that was what British people did. Mercifully he'd moved on from Celine Dion to Robbie Williams who was, he proclaimed, "As British as the shoes I am standing up in."

He was sitting down at the time, Sanjay noticed, and the shoes were most probably Brazilian.

A spicy whiff came from the kitchen. Mum shooed Sanjay away as Sita was already helping, so he had nothing to do but sink into the leather sofa and think about Shelley Ritchie. He didn't want to meet her daughter, or go away for a weekend. He wanted Shelley Ritchie to stay just as she'd been back then.

It was the same with going back to uni. The first time Sanjay had gone back for a visit, he'd felt the cobbles underfoot, smelled the polish in the hall, imagined the prickly wool of his college scarf, and relived the bad case of impostor syndrome that had lasted his entire first term. The next time, none of that was nearly as potent. Exactly the same would happen with Shelley Ritchie. He knew it.

He'd hinted at this on the phone to Shofiq the other day. Newly engaged, Shofiq didn't have a lot to contribute, except for pointing out, "When you know, you know." Over the years, Shofiq had said pretty much the same thing about at least twenty other women that Sanjay knew of.

Mum called them to the table. She had cooked on the assumption that Ben hadn't had a meal since he was last there. To give him credit, Ben ate like she was right.

"You like?" She preened.

Ben nodded vigorously. "You don't get these in restaurants," he said through a mouthful of pakora.

Mum beamed.

"My wife is wonderful cook," declared Dad, but nobody was listening. Mum and Sita were too busy treating Ben like a maharajah.

"Wish I could cook like this," said Ben.

"But is so easy to make pakora," she said. "Is not rocket salad."

Sanjay rolled his eyes.

Mum launched into an account of exactly how simple it was to make the most delicious pakora in no time whatsoever. Accompanied by appropriate hand movements, she explained that you had to cut the onions very thinly lengthwise just like so, and chop the potatoes, aubergine, courgette, or cauliflower, though Sanjay never did like cauliflower, as everyone knew. You needed turmeric, jeera, a little bit of red chilli powder, some garam masala. Oh, and ginger, and of course coriander leaves and dried methi, as much as you liked really. You shouldn't use methi seeds though. "After you mix this together, you add the gram flour. But you must sieve it first, *beta*, and then—"

"*Beti*," said Dad. "If Ben wants to know, maybe you can write recipe down for him?"

In Sanjay's view, pakora had a lot in common with relationships. Everyone led you to believe it was a cinch, but then, before you knew it, it got hideously complicated and called for ingredients you had no idea you'd need.

Dad went to have a lie down after dinner, saying he'd had a bloody rough day. Sita made a start on the dishes and declined help from Sanjay.

"I'll give you a lift back, mate," Sanjay told Ben.

"Your family's great," Ben said in the car.

"Yeah." Sanjay gripped the steering wheel a little tighter. "I'm worried about Dad."

GEOFF

Evil infection, epiglottitis, thought Geoff as he left Mother Goose ward.

He tried to recall exactly where he'd left his Prius. Piss poor at names, ditto for faces, and not much better when it came to remembering where his car was parked. Still, he hadn't forgotten epiglottitis.

The little tyke was doing OK now. On the ward just now, they were talking about him going home soon, but it had been literally touch and go earlier. One contact with a tongue depressor and the throat could have closed up completely.

Curtains.

Epiglottitis was rare these days, mused Geoff as he reached the bend in the corridor. Hib vaccine had seen to that, but it could still happen at any age and take everyone unawares. Diseases did that.

He was halfway out of the door when a bald guy stopped him and tried to pump his arm.

Ah. Epiglottitis father.

"Thank you so much, doctor. We really owe you, his mum and I." The man clearly meant it.

"No problem," said Geoff. After all, it had been a barn-door diagnosis. "I hear he's doing all right."

"Yeah. They're saying we can take him home tomorrow. Funny how quick things change, eh?"

"Ah, yes. Especially with kids. And you don't always know which way it's going to go."

The man nodded. "Have you got kids, doctor?"

"A son, aged seven. Dave lives with his mother." Geoff made a face.

A nervous laugh. "Dave, eh? Like the prime minister."

Geoff wasn't keen on recent changes in the health service, and even less enthusiastic about those to come. "Not really like the prime minister."

Embarrassed, the slap-head contorted his body awkwardly. "Well, as I say, it's down to you. My partner and I are so grateful—"

"I'm just a GP who happened to be doing a stint in A&E," Geoff said.

At that point the father, whose name was Dan something, squeezed Geoff's upper arm and said he should be bloody proud of himself, mate.

Maybe the bald fellow was right, thought Geoff as he surveyed the serried ranks of cars. Ah, was that his Prius? He should stop saying he was 'just a GP', as if he was only qualified to treat colds and athlete's foot.

When he started seeing patients that afternoon, it was business as usual, reminding him very clearly that he was just a GP after all. Lady Lactose saw to that.

Although she had no royal title, she behaved as if she did. She was convinced she had several food intolerances which caused her simply dreadful symptoms requiring increasingly frequent consultations. Now she wanted a private referral for a new skin affliction which she considered nothing short of disfiguring.

Geoff peered at the offending rash. It covered an area

roughly one square centimetre on the back of her hand. He put on his most intelligent face but still had no idea what it was. However, he was sure it would improve in no time with a little hydrocortisone ointment.

She wasn't impressed. "I want to see a specialist. And as I have private cover, it's no drain on the health service, if that's what you're worried about."

He was meant to be grateful she wasn't clogging up the already vastly overstretched dermatology clinic. On the other hand, his last private referral had resulted in a high-handed request for a barrage of costly blood tests. They bore the most tenuous relation to the original diagnosis, and the NHS had had to pick up the tab.

Geoff took a deep breath and dived in with his take on it.

After a long and mutually unsatisfactory discussion, he ended up signing the referral for Lady Lactose. And running late.

There followed a smoker with a cough, wondering why he coughed so much. Was it the ciggies, like?

No shit, Sherlock.

Geoff was just explaining exactly how cigarette smoke poisoned the lining of the lungs when the receptionist rang through to say some hapless patient had lost one of the prescriptions he'd got last week, and she couldn't figure out what he needed since she didn't speak Sylheti.

After sorting out a replacement prescription for Mr Pills, Geoff saw a baby with nappy rash. Geoff prescribed clotrimazole cream and told the mother to leave the nappy off as much as possible, ideally three times a day.

He was good, he reflected later over a large glass of wine in his living room, at giving advice to other people. Not so good at sorting out his own stuff.

Last weekend with Dave had been promising. He'd even

shown Dave how to take penalties. But when Geoff phoned the next day, Dave didn't even want to speak to him.

'It will happen, but it will take time,' Bowlby had said of the parent-child bond.

Geoff wasn't sure that was all it needed.

CHAPTER THIRTY-THREE

LAURE

"Ma ma ma?"

Laure beamed. "Hello, sweetheart."

Long sleeps seemed the norm since Jack had come home. This nap had lasted an hour. His blond hair had gone curly and the back of his neck was damp. Perhaps his cheeks were pinker than usual. Laure checked his forehead and concluded that it wasn't hot.

She hoisted Jack out of the cot and changed his soaking nappy. "There! That's better."

"Betta?"

Nobody needed a doorbell to tell her Lina and Victorine were here. They were on the landing, as animated as usual.

Jack padded to the door with Laure and squealed with joy when he saw the aunts who'd brought him a toy tractor.

"*Chérie, chérie,*" Tante Lina squealed back as she covered Jack's head with kisses. "*Le pauvre petit.*"

"He suffered so much," said Victorine. "*Haram.*"

"*Le pauvre, le pauvre,*" said Lina as she searched for another part of Jack's head to kiss.

Victorine was more restrained. She installed herself on a chair, her hands clasped together in her lap, the image of a saint. She had lit a candle, just as her sister had. But there had been other candles lit, other prayers unanswered. "*La vie est triste.*"

Life was indeed sad, thought Laure, but Jack was home now.

Laure put on the kettle. The lull, she knew, was temporary. Soon she'd be oscillating once again between elation and anxiety. During her pregnancy she'd asked her GP if she could stop worrying after thirteen weeks, when the risk of miscarriage dropped. The doctor had actually torn herself away from the computer and locked eyes with Laure before agreeing that this was so. Then she'd added, "Of course, you won't really stop worrying until your baby is safely in your arms." She'd returned to the keyboard for a moment before remarking, "Actually, that's not true. A mother worries for the rest of her life."

Worrying was the universal curse of parenting. Thank God she'd been vigilant.

Laure had barely brought cups of Earl Grey into the living room when the aunts fired questions about everything that had happened to Jack.

He had to have a drip? "*Quelle horreur!*"

"But *chérie*, how did you get him to hospital?"

Laure explained she'd called an ambulance, and Dan had followed later.

"And where was Dan?" asked Victorine.

"At work," said Laure, though she couldn't recall his rota for that week.

"*La prochaine fois…*" Lina wagged her finger. Next time Jack got ill, Laure was to call them immediately for help.

Laure recounted what had happened in A&E. It shocked her to think how close Jack had come to have a tongue depressor down his throat, with fatal results. And now here he was, back to his old tricks, pushing the new tractor up the wall while going, "Grr, grr."

"So what did you say was wrong with him?" asked Tante Lina.

"Epiglottitis," said Laure.

"Epiglottitis?" Lina said dubiously. "I've never heard of it."

"*Moi non plus*," said Victorine, as if Laure had invented the condition just to make fools out of them.

"Maybe I'm stupid," Lina suggested. "Stupid, stupid."

"Doo-bid, doo-bid," went Jack.

"*Le petit chou!*" said Lina, even though Jack looked nothing like a little cabbage.

Jack stared up at her. "Tea shoe?"

"*Assez, assez.*" Lina giggled like a child. They often said, 'Enough, enough,' though you could never say it to them, least of all when they were force-feeding you éclairs and other patisseries. If you weren't eating like a pig, you were either ill or extremely rude.

"Nee-nah, nee-nah. Tea shoe!" went Jack.

Tante Victorine giggled, chins wobbling helplessly.

"*Et qu'est ce qu'on t'a dit?*" Lina wanted to know in huge detail what Laure had been told about this mythical epiglottitis.

Laure summarized what she knew. Victorine crossed herself.

"But he was so well that morning," said Lina.

In retrospect, thought Laure, Jack hadn't been a hundred per cent, though he'd had food in each hand, considered a sure sign of health in the Middle East.

"*Le pauvre petit,*" said Tante Victorine.

"*Le pauvre, le pauvre,*" agreed Lina.

Jack stopped racing his tractor long enough to say, "Ge paub. Ge paub."

"*Amour!*" exclaimed Lina.

"*Eh, chérie,*" said Victorine. "*L'hôpital était bien?*"

The hospital had been very good, Laure said, as had the second doctor they'd seen.

Victorine said, "*Que le bon Dieu le bénisse.*"

Laure too wanted God to bless Dr Geoff Taylor.

The aunts were an appreciative audience, tutting at intervals, and clucking their tongues when Laure told them about the first doctor and his near-fatal intervention with a tongue depressor. Both agreed that hospitals were dangerous places, adding that it was a miracle the little cabbage hadn't caught Ebola, SARS, or some other deadly infection.

"The doctors couldn't save my poor Sophie," Victorine reminded them.

At bathtime, Laure's thoughts returned to epiglottitis. One of the doctors had said it wouldn't recur. But that left the field wide open for everything else in the book. At least 200 different viruses caused colds and flu, for a start. Those were just the tip of the iceberg. From the internet she knew there were in all between ten million and one billion different species of viruses and bacteria, many of which had morphed into superbugs and become resistant to everything medical science could throw at them.

Millions of germs versus just one of Jack. She felt her ribcage constrict.

Jack had immune cells to protect him, of course. She wasn't sure what the cells were called, but it was well known that they were immature, like him. Surely his immune cells could barely toddle at this stage, let alone negotiate a hazardous journey without getting run over.

He was so full of life now, strewing the flat with toys and racing his fire-truck all over the walls, but anything could happen. As she got him into his pyjamas, smelling of bath, Laure wondered if she should start breastfeeding again.

She hadn't been producing much milk. They'd been token feeds for a while now.

She tried tentatively that night, before Dan came in. But Jack ignored her nipple and wandered off to do something else.

She thought back to the last feed she'd given him, nearly ten days ago. She couldn't remember it, yet surely it should have been extra special, that final time.

She held him close as she read him *Each Peach, Pear, Plum*. He was growing up, but he was no less at risk.

KAREN

An all-purpose place, Geoff had called it. What kind of purpose could All Bar One have, apart from eating, drinking, and talking?

"I'd really like your advice," he said.

So he didn't want her for her body then. "Sure. What about?"

The waitress hovered until they ordered a bottle of Chablis.

Then Geoff began, "You've got four amazing kids."

Instead of pointing out that Charlotte was precocious, Damon was an insufferable geek, Ashley was besotted with construction, and Edward was a problem, she replied, "Thank you very much."

"Well, you're a lot more experienced than I am. It's all very well reading Bowlby and Biddulph but I don't have your practical know-how."

She nodded. "That's what happens when you're the absent parent."

"Actually, Dave and I never talked much about when I went away to Afghanistan." He paused for a sip of wine. "Neither did you and I."

"That's OK. You did what you had to do." It wasn't OK at the time, but he didn't need to know that.

"There were selfish motives too," Geoff said. He'd gone to get acute experience and get up to speed in critical care. Those were boxes ticked, he explained. He found what he called huge dignity in the serving community. Then there was the realization, too late for many, that the war hadn't been worth the candle.

"But you must have done good work there."

"Yes. But I can do good work here too."

When they'd studied the menu, he continued about Dave. "I've missed out on time with him, what with him being in Australia and me in Afghanistan."

"Yep. It's not just quality time. It's quantity time."

Geoff's eyebrows knitted into a question, so she went on. "I mean the times when you just sit watching TV together. Or doing the weekly shop at the supermarket. Arguing over homework. Making dinner. Throwing dinner away because it's a dish he absolutely hates, and it's all your fault, you did it on purpose. You hate me. You like my brothers more than me. And so on."

"Wow," said Geoff. "I feel like I'm right there in your kitchen."

"All that stuff helps establish boundaries. Shows them what the real world is like." She wasn't convinced about that last bit, but it sounded good.

His mobile pinged and he paused to read a text. "Sorry. So you think I should engineer some really rubbish weekends?" He was smiling now. Was that because of the text, or his little joke?

"No, of course not! Just don't be afraid of the bad times." She paused. "Don't you need to reply to that?"

"It's just a text from someone I used to know." He put the phone back in his pocket. "She's a nurse."

"As I was saying, don't be afraid of the bad times. And especially don't let them get to you."

"You're very confident, Karen."

"Thank you." She felt it. A little red dress from the second hand shop, and a lot of HRT from her doctor.

Geoff was looking at her very differently, she was sure of it. And it wasn't the red dress or the mascara. Respect, that was it. It was more valuable than almost anything.

Was this what it was like, to be a feminist? Karen had always hated the word, along with most other *ists*, but now she was proud of it. The first and second waves might have passed her by, but she was catching the tide now, and it felt good.

By Sunday, Karen wasn't so sure about anything, let alone respect. Barely had the kids dispersed after the final whistle and it was straight to sex on the bench. Only one letter different, yet a whole world away from sex on the beach. Was it worth the effort, now that the novelty had worn off?

Knickers off.

Scrape, screech.

Scrape, screech.

A rattle of the door. Someone after an errant shin pad, perhaps.

Scrape, scrape, scrape. Screech.

Knickers back on. Shoes back on.

"There's no football next week," said Footie Dad without expression.

"I know," replied Karen, already at the door.

GEOFF

He didn't have to wonder how to pass the time in Daisy's absence. Frieda texted again. This time she persuaded Geoff to meet her at a pub in Marylebone.

Frieda was easy to spot, sitting in the corner of the Gunmakers with a large carrier bag. She still had long hair, though she'd always worn it up when she was a nurse on the wards.

"Hi," he said.

She wrapped him in a rich scent of old ashtray and kissed him three times on the cheeks. After all, she was half German.

There was a hint of rosacea on her cheekbones, and a tiny pit on one side of her nose where she used to wear a diamond stud.

"I've never forgotten you," said Frieda.

That much was obvious from her stream of messages over the years, mostly describing every single symptom her kids had developed. The last one, if he recalled, had been *Sick all the time like carrots. Thnk Im going mad.*

He grunted amiably. "And how are things with you these days?" It was obvious she had lost her shape since the kids but was determined to wear a bra she'd outgrown long ago.

"They're OK. My husband makes good money. We have a nice home and nice holidays. I don't want for anything." The way she licked the cider off her lips said she definitely wanted for something.

"And the kids?" This was dangerous ground, an open invitation to bombard him with details of their asthma, verrucas, birthmarks, head-lice, and undescended testicles. Not to mention the contents of their vomit.

But there was no litany this time. "They're pretty good. What about you?" she asked as she put her hand on his, nearly knocking over his beer. Frieda's enthusiasm was more obvious than her grace. As a nurse, she possessed the gentle touch of a Sumo wrestler. When they'd worked together years ago, he'd wondered why patients didn't sue for GBH after one of her bed-baths. He too had suffered at her hands. After a night of particularly rough delights, he'd walked like John Wayne for a week.

"Busy, as ever. There's the practice, and some shifts in A&E. And a bit of teaching by way of light relief."

She was staring right into his eyes. "I always loved you for your brain, you know."

This was a surprise. As he recalled, Frieda normally focussed some three feet below that.

"Don't look so shocked. I really dig brainy men. I mean really, really dig."

He rewound the tape in his head, recalling nights spent in Geraint Griswold House trying to satisfy her overactive clitoris. He didn't have to reply, because Frieda was talking enough for both of them.

Now she said, "You're by far the most intelligent guy I've ever fucked." The two people at the next table found this inordinately interesting. "And the fittest," she added.

"Flattery will get you everywhere."

She tilted her head. "Usually does. Are you going to invite me back for a nightcap?"

"Just a nightcap, then. As you're married."

"I'm not married tonight." She kissed him vigorously before they'd even left the pub.

What the fuck, he thought. Curiosity and opportunity on the same night.

As soon as they got to his place, he excused himself. "I'll get you that brandy in a moment."

He went to the bathroom. The blue pills wouldn't work for some time. Best take two.

Back in the kitchen, he poured her a large Courvoisier and made himself a coffee. For the next hour, he tried to hold her off with cognac and conversation, but it became harder to resist her Teutonic approach. Soon she was undressing him and pummelling his privates.

"Put on a white coat," she ordered. She was down to knickers which bore a strong resemblance to a cheese wire.

"But I'm a GP." He resisted the temptation to say 'just a GP'. "We don't wear white coats. Even hospital doctors barely wear white coats these days. They wear—"

"I know what they wear," she interrupted.

For some reason, she had a lab coat in her carrier bag. Only later did he think it odd.

"Here. I think it'll fit."

He tried it on. It was his size.

She tilted her head and appraised him. "Could you put a book in your pocket, do you think?"

"Everything's online these days."

She produced a well-thumbed copy of *MIMS* from the same carrier bag, shoved it into his pocket, and pushed him backwards towards the wall. Bloody nurses. So damn manipulative.

That brought it all back. Saving lives then dashing back to his room in Geraint Griswold. The phone ringing non-stop in the on-call room next door. Porters arguing outside. A party in a room down the hall. The textbook in his pocket slapping against his thigh. Their grunting as they pounded again and again, Frieda perched on the edge of the basin that threatened to come off its fittings. The towel they'd used afterwards, a stiff square of linen marked *United Hospitals Trust*.

Except one thing wasn't coming back. Silently he urged Mr Wibbly Wobbly to perk up and do his stuff. He had all the side effects. Surely the benefits of the little pills should have been more evident by now.

"It's never happened before," he lied.

Frieda said she was inclined to believe him.

What was it? The booze, perhaps, or not enough time since the tablets? Or maybe he just didn't fancy her anymore.

"I'm sorry," he said. But in truth he wasn't.

CHAPTER THIRTY-FOUR

HARRIET

The book sat on her desk.

Harriet had opened the carrier bag that day almost as soon as Dan had gone. It was a book, as she knew. She hadn't imagined it would be *The Sense of an Ending*.

It was over, wasn't it? He took almost two days to text her, saying he was at the hospital with Jack who was very ill.

There'd been no word since. How could any parent carry on with a fling on the side—which was exactly what it had been—when their child's life was in danger?

She turned the volume over in her hand. Not a very big book, but an important one. It had won a Booker prize.

Chapter One began with a list of things remembered, in no particular order as far as she could tell. A somewhat strange inventory, she thought.

Harriet sniffed the pages and got nothing. No garlic. No sex. No scent of Dan at all.

She didn't shed a tear. Wasn't it always going to end badly, probably with her being dumped?

Here in her hands was his message: a book, just 160 pages long, not even gift-wrapped.

Served her right. She hoped Jack would be OK though.

Normally she admired Julian Barnes. This book she tossed into the corner. It made a satisfying thud as it slapped against the wooden floor.

Back to work, Harriet told herself. There was refuge in writing. She had a commission for a feature on heavy handbags.

"You'll need to do some research," the editor had warned.

As Harriet soon discovered on Google, there were few hard facts. That meant she had to find her own.

She'd already weighed all her friends' handbags.

"I want more data, Harry," said the editor.

The snag, as Harriet found outside Kentish Town tube station, was that women rarely wanted to hand their bag over to a complete stranger, even when that stranger wore her brightest smile and reeled off the health hazards of lugging around unnecessarily heavy objects.

Purse, keys, mobile, make-up, umbrella, tampons, hairbrush and Nurofen. Each item may seem essential, but it all adds up. Throw in a book, e-reader or tablet, and you could be lugging around several kilos.

She forced out another sentence.

Aching shoulders, back pain, neck strain and a lopsided spine. Just some of the things you're risking if your handbag is heavier than it needs to be.

Heartache, sadness, loneliness, and a guilty conscience, she thought.

The stakes had always been high. If she was suffering now, she told herself, it was only what she deserved.

She hoped that child would be OK. Obviously she couldn't get in touch with Dan to find out.

Would the staff at Lolo's know? That was a silly idea, Harriet told herself. It was better to email both Dan and Laure. Then it would look completely normal.

Yes, that was what she would do.

DAN

Fuck! He'd been an etiolated bastard.

The way he'd behaved, *bastard* wasn't enough on its own. Even *cunt* wouldn't have done. He'd been etiolated as hell. Dan had an idea it meant weak, feeble, and useless. Described him to a T.

He checked the mushroom soup and added pepper.

Now that it was over, he still had to keep up the lie. One false move and he could lose Laure. And Jack.

False moves included things like licking your lips when you got rattled. Looking to the left when telling a porkie. Or showing any facial tics. Dan knew all this from being banged up. He'd have to watch the pitch of his voice as well. Make sure nerves didn't send it sky high.

Dan added more pepper.

That was a totally meretricious fling. Another cool word, *meretricious*. For a really uncool way to behave. He was learning a lot of new vocab.

Well, he'd been given a second chance. Not every lag got one of those. Better not fuck up. As the doctors had said about Jack, not out of the woods yet.

He'd start practising right now. So when Fabien the new French lad asked him something about the oil, Dan took care to look to the right and not to blink too much.

"You are OK?" asked Fabien. "Maybe you 'ave *crise?*"

"Nah, mate. I'm fine. Never better."

"But, ze eyes a little...? My sister 'ad same sing."

"Yeah?" asked Dan, keeping his eyes firmly fixed on a pan in the upper right corner of the kitchen.

Fabien replied by spreading out his fingers. "Big eyes like zis. She 'ad to go to 'opital."

"Hope she's OK now."

"She is still in 'opital. 'Ow you say? *Crise de la thyroïde.*"

Fabien shrugged and returned to his chopping.

"That's too bad, mate." Perhaps he should make his eyes a bit less weird in future.

It was an early shift. When he got home, Dan found Jack playing on the sea of toy cars on the carpet, while Laure dozed on the sofa next to him. Jack immediately shrieked, "Dadadada-DA!" which woke her up.

"Hey, how are my special people?" Dan gave Laure a kiss even before she was fully awake.

Laure stretched herself upright and said, "Hi."

Jack went, "Dadada!" and held out his arms.

"Come let Daddy pick you up." He heaved Jack onto his shoulders. Lighter than he used to be. Maybe he'd lost weight in hospital. And Laure wasn't breastfeeding anymore. Dan had no idea if that made a difference.

"Good day?" he asked Laure.

She flicked her hair and pulled her T-shirt down over her hips. "Not bad at all."

"How's Jack been?"

"He was fine."

Dan rubbed his hands. "It's a lot colder today. I'm thinking Jack could use a proper winter coat."

"He's already got that blue one with a tartan lining."

"Oh. Right." He'd forgotten.

"How was your day?" she asked.

"Think I've nailed the mushroom soup. Always thought it could do with a dollop of horseradish. Now the boss says it's going to be the new house recipe."

"That's great," she said.

That evening they managed to sit down to dinner just after putting Jack in his cot.

Over the fish pie, Laure said, "I got an email from Harriet today."

"Oh?" Dan tried hard to keep the pitch of his voice down but didn't quite achieve the desired effect.

She tilted her head. "Is your throat OK?"

"Fine. Why?"

"You sound strange."

He cleared his throat. "Do I? Could be from the spices at work. Or the horseradish or something."

"Don't you want to know what Harriet said?"

"Of course. What did she say?" He made damn sure he didn't lick his lips or suddenly develop a nervous tic.

Laure put down her knife and fork and stared at him. "She asked how our baby was."

"Oh. That was nice of her." A wave of relief washed over him. But not for long.

"I'm wondering how she even knew Jack was ill."

He shook his head slowly and forced his eyes to the right. "No idea. But I did tell a lot of people. Maybe she spoke to one of them. You know what the grapevine is."

"That must be it then."

Laure said nothing more. Now Dan could only hear the sound of his own chewing. The quiet begged to be filled. He should have remembered from his time inside that silence was a trap. But he didn't. He said, "She's very strange, is Harriet."

A bloke would have just agreed and changed the subject. But instead of going, 'You're not wrong, mate,' and moving on, Laure fixed on him and said, "In what way, exactly?"

He did his damnedest not to blush. Or touch his nose or make a move of any sort. Finally he gave the tiniest shrug and said, "Don't know. Just an impression."

"I'm still surprised she knew Jack was ill. And that she even cares. Seeing as she's never shown any interest in him before."

"A mystery then," said Dan, thinking how stupid Harriet was. It was bad enough covering up for his own etiolated fuck-ups. It was a bit of an ask covering up for hers as well.

Laure stacked the plates in silence.

On his way home the next day, Dan gave the matter careful consideration. He still hadn't decided when he got to the shop, so he stood outside for a bit, watching a guy flog *The Big Issue* to people who couldn't give a toss.

A dog tied by the entrance yapped. Dan knew what that was like. Try being in a cell twenty-two hours out of twenty-four, mate, he thought.

Dan nearly bought chocolates. But flowers were prettier. And didn't have to be shared round when someone dropped by.

So. Flowers it was. The bunch he'd got in Harrow a while back was piss poor. All the same, this lot better not be too showy. That would look suspicious.

There was another decision to make, as he discovered when he got to the flower display. He stood and vacillated. Great word. Not so great for making the right purchase.

With roses, the colour was probably significant. The wrong choice could give completely the wrong message.

Dan studied the range on offer and wondered who'd be able to help. Probably not the huge bloke who elbowed him out of the way to reach a hideous cactus thing. Nor the snooty old cow to his right, either. There was a smiling woman pushing a little kid in a trolley. She probably only spoke Japanese.

Daisy would have known. She knew bloody everything. Either that or she gave a damn good impression of it. He hadn't seen her for a while, come to think of it. When had she last visited?

No news of Harriet either. That was a good thing. Laure had probably replied to her email. As for himself, he wasn't planning on mentioning her name ever again.

Dan scratched above his left ear, just where his hat usually sat, and vacillated some more. Over there was a geezer of about his own age, carrying a basket. Maybe him. Then again, maybe not.

He'd have gone online to solve his dilemma but his phone was out of juice again. He vaguely recalled buying roses for Laure a while back. What colour had they been?

In the end Dan stopped vacillating and went for white.

White roses went with everything, he told himself as left the shop. They probably signified purity.

Too late now.

LAURE

Laure twisted round in the driver's seat. Jack's forehead was cool, but his cheeks were a lot redder than when they'd set out. Could this be the beginning of some new infection? There was no chance of checking with the app now, not while she was sandwiched between a Tesco delivery lorry and yet another white van.

At this rate, it was clearly going to take another thirty minutes to get to Willesden. Jack showed his displeasure by kicking the back of the passenger seat and shouting, "Gucky!"

"I know. It is a bit yukky," replied Laure as she put on a nursery rhyme CD. "Just keep calm."

I am calm. I am serene. All is well.

She was doing her best, but the bloody North Circular Road wasn't made with toddlers in mind, nor for this traffic.

She should have gone a different way. And now there were those other people who had no idea where they were going and seemed not to care how much they dithered on their way there. One car had stopped just outside the turning to IKEA, and Laure was behind it, stuck in the wrong lane.

"I think we'll go left here."

"Go leff?"

"Should have turned off ages ago, really."

"CAR! CAR! CAR!" screamed Jack.

It was a transporter, taking up two lanes. His own and hers.

"Gucky guck!" went Jack as soon as it had gone.

"We're just going to leave something. A little present."

"Ess," went Jack.

How exactly did you thank the person who'd saved your child's life? Laure had thought long and hard. Flowers and charity donations were all well and good, but in the end she concluded that they lacked the elegance of a Mont Blanc pen.

The plan was to deliver the little box safely into the hands of a receptionist while the surgery was not too busy, along with the express instructions to make sure Dr Taylor got it.

Now Wembley Stadium towered above them. Was his practice really this far?

Laure found she had driven past the health centre twice without even realizing it. She went back again, but there wasn't a single place to park, other than those marked *Disabled*. While circling for a space, doubts crept in. Wouldn't it have been better to send the thing special delivery or however else people usually expedited valuable objects?

"Mama?" went Jack, as if in echo of her thoughts.

"Nearly there, Jack," she said as soothingly as she could. "Just need to park the car."

Oh, God! What if all the other grateful patients gave him Mont Blanc pens too? She wasn't even sure doctors wrote by hand anymore. They used computers for everything.

No turning back now, she told herself.

Five minutes later, she walked in through the automatic doors. Her hands shook, but that, surely, was from pushing Jack's buggy all the way from the car and then up the ramp to the entrance.

The waiting room, as she'd hoped, only had a few stragglers.

Laure counted an old man coughing into a grey hankie, a child chattering as he worked his way through a toy box, and a huge woman studying a magazine.

The receptionist barely glanced up before asking in a monotone if she had an appointment. Obviously, Laure was simply another patient.

Just as Laure was explaining that she had something for one of the doctors, Geoff emerged from the corridor on the right. He definitely looked at her.

Laure gave a tentative wave. It was an age before a glimmer of recognition crossed his face.

"Ah!" He strode across to reception. He wasn't that good-looking after all, but his hips were slim and his shoulders substantial.

She tried to subdue her speeding pulse. It was Jack he recognized. Of course it was.

"Hello, big boy," said Geoff, bending down to buggy level. His sleeves were rolled up and his shirt was in the process of escaping from the waistband of what appeared to be black jeans.

Jack's face threatened to do the old boot impression, but he didn't cry.

"Um," said Laure, her palms oddly sweaty. "I just wanted to let you have this. As a little thank you."

Geoff appeared mystified.

"You saw my son nearly a month ago. In hospital. Jack had epiglottitis." It was funny how easily the word tripped off the tongue, when a few weeks ago she'd barely heard of the condition.

"Ah, yes, of course. Doesn't he look grand now?"

"Gand," went Jack, no longer frowning.

"He's fine," Laure agreed. Nobody knew how long Jack would stay fine, but Laure did know that, if Geoff Taylor were by her side, she wouldn't be nearly so worried about terrible things happening. She proffered the parcel. "I hope you can use it."

He looked genuinely pleased. "How very kind of you. May I open this a bit later? I still have a couple of patients to see."

"Of course." It had been foolish to imagine he'd have time to chat.

"Thank you very much," he said, waving the parcel aloft as he headed for the waiting area.

Laure beamed at him and beamed at the receptionist, then made her way out down the ramp.

"There," she said to Jack when they got to the bottom. "Job done."

"Jubbun?" asked Jack.

"Yes, job done. Let's go home now."

"Ess."

The drive back was a lot easier and they were back in Hampstead in no time. Laure checked in the mirror. Jack had nodded off.

She parked in the residents' bay in Belsize Lane and opted to let him doze a moment longer. In the few minutes' peace this gave her, her thoughts returned to the health centre. To Geoff Taylor, his crumpled shirt, and his reassuringly broad shoulders.

CHAPTER THIRTY-FIVE

GEOFF

"Hi Daddy!" Dave beamed as he hopped out of Sonya's car.

The whole weekend lay ahead of them, just Geoff, Dave, and the eternal iPad. There were three of them in this relationship, about that Geoff had few illusions, but initial signs were promising.

Dave dumped his bag in the hall. "Can we go to the park?"

"Of course." He vividly remembered Dave (when he was still called Davey) looking for conkers in that same park, and his delight at collecting shiny mahogany treasures, then his disappointment when they turned dull and wrinkly. Geoff had tried to explain gently that was how things were, but at the time Dave was too little for big lessons.

"When?"

"Let me think." Geoff put his fist to his forehead in the manner of a Rodin statue. "How about now? We can have lunch on the way back."

"Ah, yeah!"

They had a good long kickabout, with Geoff in goal.

"How many goals did I score against you, Daddy?"

Geoff put the ball into a carrier bag. It was the safest way to carry it. "Lots and lots. Far too many for an old man like me to count."

"I counted. It was eleven."

"That *is* a lot."

"How old are you, Daddy?"

"I'm thirty-nine."

"Crikey!" At least he didn't say aloud that it was really old.

Going for a pizza was an easy decision. They sat opposite each other at a round marble-topped table, just the two of them studying their menus. For a moment, Geoff no longer felt like a weekend dad in Pizza Express, but part of a normal family.

"Dad, what's the Venzi Fund?"

Geoff checked the menu. "Ah, yes. The Veneziana fund is to save buildings in Venice from getting destroyed by all the water. The city is built on canals, you see, so there's lots of water."

"It's a good thing to give them twenty-five pee," reflected Dave. "Only I don't like anchovy."

When Dave was halfway through his peperoni pizza, he asked, "Daddy, why did they build the city there if there was too much water?"

Even questions that fathers couldn't answer were a good thing.

"I'm not sure, Dave. Maybe they built it before they realized the danger."

On the way home, Dave pointed out the house two doors down from Geoff's. All the curtains were shut, and the shrubs at the front had gone wild.

"Dad?" Dave looked expectantly. "Does someone live there?"

"Not anymore." The old woman had died some months ago. Not one of his patients, thankfully.

"What happened? Did they move out?"

Honesty was the best policy, if you could face it. "In a way. The old lady who lived there died a while ago."

Dave mulled this over. "Did she die inside the house?"

"I don't think so." In truth he didn't know.

"Maybe she did, and her body is still in the house?"

"That's not possible, Dave. First of all, the law says you can't leave a dead person lying around. And secondly, there'd be a really bad smell by now."

Geoff should have guessed that Dave would want to run through the waist-high grasses, brambles, and purple daisies to investigate. The letter box was exactly the right height for his nose.

Dave lifted the flap and sniffed at length. "I think she's gone."

"Let's go home now."

Once through the door, Dave made straight for the kitchen table. A seven-year old could only stand iPad withdrawal symptoms for so long.

"Don't play too long."

Geoff unloaded the dishwasher to the melodious sounds of aliens annihilating one another. Then he checked his texts and emails. There were new guidelines on overweight children, along with the usual offers of penis extensions and sexy Russian girlfriends.

Nothing from Daisy. OK, so she didn't consider herself his girlfriend. He imagined her drawing herself up straight at the very mention of 'girlfriend' and shaking her curly hair into a halo before fixing him with a petrifying look.

"I've finished," Dave announced.

"Killed enough aliens already?"

"Yeah. Ended the world on level eight?"

"Is that a good thing, ending the world?"

"It's only a game?"

"That's a relief. Now, is it too early to think about supper?"

"Got any pizza?"

The freezer was full of pizzas with combinations of toppings that only a child would have touched. Geoff did his Rodin pose again before replying, "As a matter of fact, I think I have."

"Ah, yeah!"

"Pizza it is then."

The crust of the chicken, pineapple, and sweetcorn pizza took a lot of chewing, but Dave managed to eat it all. He burped and said, "Daddy. The lady next door?"

Geoff wiped his mouth. "Yes?"

"Did she know she was going to die?"

"I don't know, Dave. But she was very old, so she probably could have guessed."

Dave frowned. "You're only thirty-nine, right? That's not old, is it, Daddy?"

"Of course it isn't."

SANJAY

He cleaned the cat litter tray and tried Shelley Ritchie's number again. Ten rings then the same high-pitched voice informing him that she would ring back as soon as possible if the caller would be kind enough to leave a message. He'd hoped for something a bit more original, but then there were only so many ways of saying you weren't going to answer.

Sanjay had left messages all over the place. WhatsApp, Messenger, emails—the lot. At first he'd asked about meeting next week, but now a fucking sign of life would have done.

Bloody Shelley Ritchie! Sanjay flung his phone onto the sofa, making the cat jump. All those years to hook up with her again, only for her to go and disappear into a proverbial black hole.

He put on Muse and turned up the volume. Furry Shelley rummaged in her clean tray, as he could hear despite *Map of the Problematique*.

Had he actually imagined those two weeks, beginning with the first meeting over a burger, and ending several shags later with the promise that they'd talk soon?

Shelley Ritchie got in touch on Sunday. Six in the morning wasn't the best time, but that was no reason to let her off.

"Wow. You haven't been kidnapped after all," he said. "How the hell are you?"

Small voice. "Don't shout. I'm OK. "

"I'm not shouting. So, what about next week?"

There was a pause. "Not next week, no."

"OK." He waited. And waited.

Finally she said, "The thing is..."

"The thing is that now that you know me, you've gone off me?" First the beautiful (and possibly rampant nympho) Daisy had turned him down. Now his love from Year Twelve didn't want to know. Fucking great.

"I haven't gone off you."

So she said, but she still didn't sound right. It was as if she had a sleeping baby next to her. He got it. "Someone's there," he said. It wasn't a question.

A pause, then a hesitant "Yes."

"Who?"

Another pause. "Um. Pete."

"Your ex-husband?" He had the urge to fiddle with something. A telephone flex would have been useful.

"My husband, yes."

Fuck! Once he stopped to analyze it, he realized she'd never had said he was ex. She had barely given anything away about her marriage, apart from the fact that she couldn't have more kids. Someone should have kicked him for being so thick. He sighed. "I see."

"I'm sorry," she said.

"I'm only going to say one thing: if he hurts you, I'll kill him." *I will find him. And I will kill him* would have sounded a hell of a lot better, but there was only one Liam Neeson.

"Thanks. I know. Sorry," she said again.

"Me too." He pressed *End* before it got hideously complicated.

There was no chance of going back to sleep now, especially as the cat wanted to play, so he sat and thought for a bit while she attacked his feet through the duvet. Then Sanjay got up and padded into the kitchen. Shelley trotted after him, tail in the air, and jumped onto the worktop. She stared at him from the worktop as he made himself tea, her pea-green eyes wide as if she'd never seen a kettle boil before. Now he wished he'd never called her Shelley, but what did it matter? She didn't respond to her name or anything else for that matter, apart from Dreamies cat treats.

He rattled the sachet of Dreamies and sprinkled a few of them into her bowl.

She leapt down to inspect the offering briefly, then mooched off with her head in the air.

"Hey, what's wrong?" Sanjay picked her up for a cuddle.

She growled.

His cat was giving him the elbow too. Fucking fantastic.

KAREN

The tiles were icy beneath her feet, but then September had already segued into October, and the wind rattled the windows and whistled in through gaps around the door. Karen had been warm enough on the sidelines, in gloves and warm boots as she jumped up and down, clapping herself silly when Ashley's team scored their one and only goal.

Footie Dad and the bench screeched towards the inevitable

conclusion while Karen did mental arithmetic. Twenty minutes until she had to collect Edward. Forty-five minutes until she could be at home in the warmth, slopping around in a fraying hoodie and tartan pyjama bottoms.

Had she gone straight home instead, she could have started on supper, conjuring up a nutritious dish that the kids might or might not eat.

His Brut had worn out, Karen noticed. The predominant aromas were damp sock and disinfectant.

A few minutes later, it was time to leave. He was just looking for his other shoe when *Dr Who* rang out from his mobile. He hopped over to his jeans, extracted the phone from a pocket, and promptly dropped it on the floor.

In that instant before he picked it up, Karen clocked a face in the screen.

He grabbed the phone and rejected the call. "Financial adviser," he explained.

Karen had never had a financial adviser, let alone one who rang clients at weekends. So who was she to say that the moon-faced Asian woman in a sleeveless top wasn't a typical financial adviser?

"Not your wife then?"

"Nah. Anyway, it wasn't a good time," he continued, blushing as he returned the phone to his pocket. "I don't have my facts and figures on me."

Karen pursed her lips as she studied his face. "Why don't you ring her back? I'm going."

"Look," he said, putting out his hand. "It's not what you think. I just—"

"See you around." There was no need for more.

Seconds later, she was out of the door, leaving him among the hooks festooned with unloved jumpers and the noticeboard covered in details of fixtures long past.

LAURE

Jack was a big boy now and slept in his own room. There was no way he was going to succumb to cot death at this age. That didn't prevent all the other tragedies and mishaps that could befall a child.

In the night, Jack sometimes turned black and blue. Or had a broken leg. Or worse.

Laure would get up and pull Jack's covers down and there he'd be, lying there with just one leg. He'd still be smiling and chattering, and oddly enough not crying with pain at all. Sometimes the other leg was gone altogether, or else it was in the bed next to him.

Then she actually woke up, heart pounding, a pool of sweat on her chest. She'd rush to Jack who was still asleep.

Under the covers he looked fine, all four limbs present and correct. Still giddy with fear, she undid the poppers on his vest, checked him all over. No cuts. No bruises. Not even a graze or a hint of a rash. Just soft sweet skin the texture of peach.

The back of his head was OK too. Not bashed in with a club as she'd feared.

I am calm. I am serene. All is well.

Panic still pulsed through her body. She picked him up, held him close, buried her nose in the fine curls on the nape of his neck, and let the tears flow.

"We could try some propranolol. It's a beta-blocker," said Dr Bell. "That should help your palpitations."

"Doesn't that cause vivid dreams?" asked Laure. There was reams of information online about panic disorder, and Laure didn't want her nightmares to get worse with propranolol.

"Occasionally. But I think you'll find it helpful. We can also consider CBT." Dr Bell printed off a prescription and flicked it into Laure's hand.

"Thank you. While I'm here, could you please have a listen to Jack's chest?"

Dr Bell rolled her eyes and fleetingly passed her stethoscope over Jack. "He's fine," she concluded. "As we both knew he would be."

Laure was sure Geoff Taylor wouldn't have been so dismissive, had she consulted him. He'd have been a wonderful GP for Jack, and for her. That would have been impossible, of course. For one thing, they lived miles away from his practice.

She put the propranolol tablets safely away in the medicine cabinet. Jack had nodded off in his buggy. She may as well put her feet up too. Maybe Daisy would pop round and offer to take Jack. It occurred to Laure that Daisy hadn't called round for a while. How long had it been exactly?

The sun was low when Laure woke up. There were flowers on the coffee table and noises from the kitchen.

She sat up. They were white roses without any scent. "Dan? What's this for?"

Dan came in from the kitchen. "I think you mean *who*. Or possibly *whom*."

"That's lovely. Thank you."

Dan smiled. "Jack's awake, by the way. He's on the playmat and I gave him a yoghurt."

"Oh God, the mess!" said Laure.

"Relax," said Dan.

CHAPTER THIRTY-SIX

SANJAY

"You don't have to come." Mum's words may have indicated Sanjay was a free agent, but her tone suggested he'd be mental not to be there for supper.

When he arrived, Dad was already home, but he wasn't in the living room, holding forth.

There were voices from his parents' bedroom.

Sanjay found the room in semi-darkness. There was an elephantine lump under the duvet. It stirred and carried on arguing with Mum. It did not want a special Indian concoction for headache, especially when there was perfectly good ibuprofen in the cupboard. "Besides, it will stink out house, ha."

Dad's face popped out to explain. "Ah, there you are, Sanjay. You see, I don't need medicine. It is only bloody fucking useless people at work. This is what they are doing to me. They are giving me headache."

"But if you still have headache, *beta*..." Mum persevered.

"I have headache in my chest. And my backside. That is what they do to me. Fuck them." He rolled onto his side again.

"Don't be vulgar," said Mum.

"Why the hell not? It is totally British thing."

Dad had a point. Being vulgar, as Mum called it, was as patriotic as you could get.

"I will be up for dinner," he continued. "Don't worry. Now go, both of you."

Sanjay hadn't spotted Sita in the living room. She was entirely curled up in an armchair, playing with her phone and chewing one end of her hair. It was only long on one side. She'd probably shaved the other side. Sanjay preferred not to look.

"Hey," she said.

"Hey." He could see she was thinking the same thing as him. "It's a bit cold for the park. Not to mention practically pitch-dark."

She let go of the chewed bit of hair and got up. "Why don't we go anyway, before supper? I'll put on a parka. Parka, geddit?"

"Nah. Don't get it at all."

She elbowed him in the ribs for that, but he still agreed to go with her.

What trees he could see had lost about half their leaves since they'd last been there. The clocks had just gone back, and the ice cream van had long since given up hope.

"Bit nippy, innit," said Sita.

She was right. Even with coats on, the playground was bloody freezing. No wonder they were the only ones there.

She wiped one of the swings with her sleeve and installed herself on it. Today she was wearing jeans which only had one visible rip. Maybe one day she would graduate to proper grown-up clothes.

"So Dad's been having chest pains as well as headaches," said Sanjay. "Sounds pretty serious."

"I think he's going to have tests."

She was too vague. "What tests?" Sanjay rubbed his hands.

"He doesn't say, innit? But I saw he'd had a letter from the hospital. I recognized it right away cos it was like the letters you used to get. It said he had to see a cardiologist." Sita enunciated every one of those five syllables, as if she was an idiot, or was talking to one.

"Why didn't you tell me before?"

Sita narrowed her eyes. "Bro, I only saw the letter yesterday."

"Mum must be really worried."

Sita nodded and pulled up her hood.

"Guess we'll just have to wait," Sanjay continued. It was as worrying as hell though. "How are things with you?"

"I'm fine," she said.

The whole family always said they were fine, except Mum of course. For a moment he'd forgotten her leg. "What about your guy?"

She made a face. "What guy?"

"You've got more than one?"

By way of an answer, she said, "Give me a push."

"No."

"Give my swing a push and I'll tell you."

Obviously he was going to, because he wanted to know more. Sanjay gave the swing an almighty shove to get it going, then watched as Sita took her time, going higher and higher.

"What about your guy? Or have you got more than one now?" he persisted.

Sita finally brought her swing to a halt and adjusted her hood. "I got less than one."

"Oh, Sita." He let his shoulders droop. How were you meant to respond if you had to show empathy but were secretly delighted? "What happened?"

She played with the zip on her parka, running it up and down at couple of times. "He was boffing someone else, innit."

"Bastard."

"And you know what? He told her I was only his 'financial adviser'. I was so mad. He'd answered my call, but obviously thought he hadn't because I heard him talking to some woman.

It wasn't his wife. Because the woman said something like, 'So it's not your wife,' and he went, 'It's not what you think.' Then, when he called me later, he denied everything. Like *everything*."

"That's so wrong," said Sanjay, although he couldn't quite put his finger on the reason. It was wrong to have it off with a married man. Did Sita have any right to assume she was the only 'other woman'? And what about himself, with Shelley Ritchie who was, as he discovered, still actually married? He found himself unable to get a reading on the moral compass, so he contented himself with saying, "Twat." That man of Sita's was a twat for lying. And an über-twat for messing his sister about.

"Yeah," agreed Sita. "Tosser."

"Cunt." Sanjay breathed on his hands to warm them.

"Dickhead," said Sita.

"Isn't it funny that we have to go to a kiddies' playground so we can swear without Mum telling us off?"

Sita grinned. "Yeah. Fucking great."

"So what happened next?"

"I'll show you the text I sent him." She dug out her iPhone and scrolled to the message. "Here."

Ur so dumped, innit.

"Well done, Sita." He gave her a hug, which she didn't even pretend to resist. Now he could see that the left side of her head wasn't shaved after all, just scraped back with some kind of clip. It was only a small sign, but it told him that she would be all right.

He was less sure about Dad.

HARRIET

Burying your tearful face in cat fur was the number one most soothing thing you could do when you were upset, especially once the cat began to purr. Harriet could have lain for hours, with her cheek resting against that warm flank as it rose and fell, stopping occasionally to wipe her cheek.

But there was no cat. The only cat Harriet saw these days was a lean feral thing that hung around the bins and peed on car tyres. She sat alone on her lumpy sofa, hugging a cushion and intermittently dabbing her eyes with the tissues she'd bought on the cheap.

She was meant to be an adult, for God's sake, and she'd screwed up, so here she was in an emotional stew of guilt, embarrassment, and self-loathing. Maybe listing her problems would help. She found a biro.

Messed up love life
Feeling bad about Laure
Short of work
Short of money
No cat
*Poxy flat above crazy old lady_*

Telling herself sternly to be more positive, she crossed out *above crazy old lady*. A problem that could be resolved with a pair of earplugs was not that much of a problem.

But what about all the others? She blubbed again, aware of how uninhibited she had become. At this rate, crazy old Nora from downstairs would pop round with a cup of nettle tea to cheer her up.

Wasn't there something soothing in the kitchen?

She kept Häagen Dazs chocolate ice cream in the freezer for emergencies like rejections from editors. This was an emergency too.

Crazy old Nora wasn't that crazy. What had she said the day they went to Morrisons? Harriet couldn't recall every word, but there was something about working at it. That made a lot of sense. Obviously Harriet wasn't prepared to learn another four languages, but still.

She scraped the bowl clean and licked the spoon. How long had it taken Nora to learn all those languages?

Language, Harriet had once read, was a set of symbols for communicating thought. Her own writing rarely conveyed much thought, other than the need to pay the bills. Neither did some of her actions, truth be told. That could change, if she worked at it.

This called for a second bowl of ice cream. By the time she'd licked the spoon clean again, she had indigestion, as well as the conviction there were lots of things going for her. Friends to talk to, for one thing.

She corrected herself. Friend, not friends. And she hadn't spoken to Virginia for days.

That day, Virginia was worse off. "It's Robert," she moaned.

Harriet didn't need to ask what the matter was. Virginia's monologue covered everything, including her partner's inability to commit, perpetual lateness, sweet wrappers everywhere, the way he held a knife and fork, laughing at his own jokes, and using WhatsApp instead of actually talking.

Harriet had unlimited minutes on her phone and a Facebook video of penguins to watch while her friend continued with her catalogue of Robert's faults.

"And he borrows my undies." Virginia's voice rose to a wail.

Harriet rewound the video to catch the littlest penguin plopping into the water. "Your bras?"

"I told you. Just my knickers. What shall I do?"

"You could finish with him."

"But then I'd be alone, you know?"

Harriet did know. "That's not the end of the world."

"Maybe he's not that bad," said Virginia.

The baby penguin was sliding all over the ice. "But you just told me he drives you crazy."

"I know. But he's company, you know?"

"I know."

"But I just can't stand him anymore. What shall I do?"

Maybe grow up? "I don't know." Harriet went back to the start of the video, where the mother penguin stood adoring her baby.

The call ended a few minutes later with Virginia declaring she felt a lot better. "I still don't know what I'll do, but it all feels a lot lighter, you know?"

"I know."

"What do you think I should do?"

"I don't know."

Grow up.

CHAPTER THIRTY-SEVEN

GEOFF

Thursday brought with it the unwelcome realization that his annual appraisal was looming. This year Geoff needed to complete a piece of research for it.

That, he thought as he tossed a mountain of post onto his desk, was a fatuous exercise. He was pretty sure his research would show that half his patients didn't need to see the doctor at all. The other half should have attended a lot sooner.

Mr Hilliard was a good example of the first type. He was angling for a new scan he'd read about in a pretentious tabloid paper which carried dire warnings of war, famine, pestilence, and death on every page, interspersed with breakthroughs that could save mankind. Mr Hilliard had been kind enough to bring the cutting with him.

Geoff skimmed the article and said, "I really don't think this new heart scan will help with your knee symptoms."

"But it's supposed to be ever so good. And after all the trouble I had with my gall bladder..."

True, his gall bladder removal had been fiendishly complicated. There had been stones, repeated infections, and, for all

Geoff knew, misalignment of the stars. The surgeon had managed to slice into the common bile duct during the operation, turning a twenty-minute keyhole procedure into a three-hour marathon ending with a scar halfway round the belly, but all that was in the past. "I know." Geoff was placatory. "It did give you a lot of bother."

Mr Hilliard enjoyed his trip down memory lane. "You can say that again, doc. The hospital said my gall bladder was so inflamed, it was almost cancer."

"Hmm." Geoff rather doubted that.

Mr Hilliard was still talking. "So anyway, doctor. What about that new scan?"

Geoff was running late now, but at least Ms Bump would be straightforward. She only had a stye.

"I know I could have seen the pharmacist," she began before she even sat down.

Geoff nodded. Prescriptions were free for pregnant women, whereas she'd have had to pay for an over-the-counter remedy. He looked at her eye. While the printer churned out the prescription, he asked when her next antenatal appointment was.

"Next week." She avoided his gaze. "I missed the last one."

"Hmm," said Geoff. It was shocking how cavalier some patients were, even when it was the first pregnancy. "Mind if I take your blood pressure?"

She pulled up a sleeve and held out her arm.

"It's high." He removed the cuff.

Her face was a picture of unconcern. "My nan has high blood pressure too."

"But she's probably not thirty-five weeks pregnant, is she?" Geoff explained that high blood pressure could seriously harm a baby. "Have you heard of pre-eclampsia?"

"Think so, yeah."

Geoff checked her pressure again. "One hundred and sixty-eight over a hundred. I don't want to alarm you, but you need to go to hospital. Today."

"Can I go tomorrow? Or the day after? We've got house-guests."

He shook his head as ominously as he knew how. "Tomorrow could be too late. That little one in there," he gestured with his Mont Blanc pen, "is your most important houseguest."

"It's my choice, isn't it?"

"Yes. But the choice you make should be well-informed. Shall I see if the midwife is free to have a chat?"

She wasn't sure.

"Let me ask you this. Would I spend all this time trying to persuade you if it didn't matter?"

In the end he gave her a leaflet about pre-eclampsia, and a letter for the hospital in the vain hope she would change her mind.

He wanted to bash his head against the filing cabinet, but there was no time for such luxuries because the receptionist was buzzing to tell him the practice meeting had already started. It was the new male receptionist, whose name was on the tip of Geoff's tongue. What the hell was it? Something like Norman. Not actually Norman, though, as Geoff had discovered last week when he'd said it aloud.

Roman, perhaps?

Geoff settled for, "Thanks. I'll be there shortly."

The meeting kicked off with patient participation groups.

"Right," said the practice manager. "So we invited the PPG to share their thoughts with us, and..."

And the results were entirely predictable. Only a vocal minority of patients ever attended PPGs.

After the meeting, Geoff checked his messages and emails. Nothing from Frieda. Good. Nothing from Daisy either.

She'd said she'd be away for up to ten days. It was over two weeks now. Surely a guy was entitled to care where she'd got to, whether he was her boyfriend or not. Caring, that was it. It was not at all the same thing as being needy. Geoff had never been needy in his life.

There might be clues in Daisy's medical notes.

He locked the door of his consulting room. It was strictly against information governance rules to look at a patient's medical records unless there was a clinical reason to do so. Doctors probably did it all the time regardless, but Geoff wasn't about to be fingered for it. He'd just have a quick look at her notes and get out.

He found her on the database easily. There wasn't much in her records, apart from the contraceptive pill, irritable bowel syndrome, and various immunizations. Some three years ago there had been an attack of bronchitis following a trip abroad. It didn't say where.

Geoff scrolled down as far as he could, then checked her prescription entries. Nothing apart from the Pill and something for hay fever. He went back to the main record and realized with horror that he'd made an entry, just as if she'd consulted him. It was blank, but it had the tell-tale details: today's date and his name.

Shit! He had to get rid of that incriminating consultation, but how? This was the least intuitive software ever. The toolbar across the top had incomprehensible little symbols and the left hand column was filled with verbiage, much of it in pale grey. That meant nothing, as Geoff had found out. The links didn't have to be in black for them to be active.

He tried several clicks but nothing doing. Perhaps he'd have to ask that pious practice manager for help.

Keep calm, he told himself. He took two ibuprofen, stretched his neck muscles, and returned to the screen to try every possibility in turn.

Ah, there it was! A *Delete Consultation* option. Blessed relief.

It was late by the time Geoff left for home. Not-Norman was doing extra hours on reception this week, but even he had long gone.

LAURE

He had brought a rustic picnic. A loaf of bread and a jug of wine, straight out of Omar Khayyam.

Every morning Laure woke up yearning to fall asleep again so she could drift back into a different world. Last night she was alone with him by the banks of a river, but sometimes she'd be at a film premiere or a party, rubbing shoulders with celebrities. In every dream, the same person would be there, just out of reach.

Laure had a book on dreams, among the pile of parenting guides and self-help books.

She checked one of the books. Going to parties and meeting new people meant change, and, unless it was all a load of rubbish, the great outdoors signified leisure or freedom. Food was affection, presumably from the person who'd furnished the picnic.

That would be Geoff. He was in all her dreams, whether they featured premieres or picnics.

She was going to toddler group today and would not give Geoff another thought.

Jack beamed as she helped his arms into the sleeves of his coat, and was still in good humour when she did up the buckle on his buggy. These past nights, Jack at least was sleeping better. Waking up early and noisily, but that was expected. All the books said that. Laure kept the monitor on, though. You never knew when babies would start climbing out of cots.

The minute they got to the church hall, Jack zoomed off to check out the play house.

It was Laure's turn on the tea rota. She kept an eye on Jack as she filled twenty cups with the same murky liquid. He was playing happily in the toy kitchen, his feet planted wide apart while he chatted to miniature saucepans. Was he going to be a chef too?

Laure took a cup and sat near the giant play mat. One little boy was running a toy car all over its road system. Next to him on the soft play area, a little person thoughtfully gnawed on a giant piece of jigsaw puzzle.

A woman sat next to Laure. "We're potty-training," said the woman.

Laure smiled. "Right."

The woman leaned in confidentially. "We're not always getting there in time, of course."

"That must be a problem."

"And we don't want to poo in our potty yet. I'm just hoping that's temporary."

"It's all temporary, isn't it?" Jack was growing up. All children did, eventually.

"Are you potty-training yet?"

"Not yet. Jack is just over a year old."

"You've got all that to come then," said the woman ominously before she got up.

There was a hell of a lot to come. How did people manage to emerge intact the other side?

The child with the jigsaw padded across and offered Laure his soggy piece of cardboard. "Thank you," said Laure.

Jack was still content with his pots and pans until it was time to go.

When they'd got home and she'd given him lunch, Jack lay down for a nap. A morning at toddler group followed by a hot lunch was the perfect recipe for a long sleep. Laure went to the computer as soon as Jack had nodded off.

Her head was swimming as she typed his name into the search engine. It had done that last time too. Today she would study the images, just as when she'd had a crush on Colin Firth all those years ago.

This was how she stumbled on a link to a video Geoff had made. She didn't even know he'd been to Afghanistan. Now it was as if he was in the same room, having a conversation about IEDs and Chinooks the way other people talked about shoes, green beans or potty-training.

Wow. He was even more competent than she imagined.

Jack was still asleep so she watched it again. Geoff was articulate and reserved. The mark of a strong and competent person, she had no doubt. She wished she could be more confident and more competent.

There was a noise at the door. Her heart bounced around inside her chest. Was Dan home early? She shifted to another tab as she called out, "Hello, darling."

No reply.

After a moment, she judged it safe to watch the video again. She was beginning to know the script word for word. How pathetic was that?

This had to stop. Her headlong passion for Colin Firth had come to an end too, eventually. She was now twice the age she had been then, but twice as silly. Surely at forty, and with a child, she could manage to snap out of it and live in the real world.

Unlike Mr Darcy, Geoff did inhabit the real world. If she wanted, she could send him letters, cards, presents. She'd even been on a date with him, just the once, years ago.

He'd written last week, thanking her for the pen, saying it had already become the most prized thing on his desk.

She could write back, couldn't she?

She opened a new Word document and began.

CHAPTER THIRTY-EIGHT

SANJAY

He fed Shelley first thing, as always. She snaked around his legs in the kitchen, rubbing her face against the doorframe to deposit her scent and claim everything in the apartment as her own.

"The whole place belongs to you, Shell," he reminded her. As if there was any doubt when every single surface was lavishly coated in cat fur. At the rate she shed, it was a miracle she wasn't totally bald by now. He should probably vacuum more often, but whenever he brought out the Hoover, Shelley would either hiss then hide under the bed, or, if she was feeling brave, try to attack it, advancing on it sideways, her tail as thick as a toilet brush.

He put some fresh food down, which she ignored, then he powered up his tablet.

Shelley Ritchie hadn't blocked him on Facebook yet. That was a surprise. Even stranger, her relationship status was now *single*. He was sure it had been blank when he last checked. Had that fucking slime-ball husband of hers upped and left?

Shelley jumped up to rub herself on the screen.

"How weird is that?" he asked the cat as he tickled her under the chin.

She responded by purring into his face and shedding a storm of fur. His old laptop had become hopelessly hot and slow, the problem being, as the engineer discovered, hanks of cat fur inside the casing. It figured.

Sanjay would message Shelley Ritchie and find out what the bollocks was going on. What he actually typed was *Hey Shelley Ritchie. Hope you're doing well. Would be nice to keep in touch occasionally, if you're OK with that.*

She replied that evening. *That's OK*, followed by a smiley face. At least it wasn't a fat grey cat sitting inside a box, or something equally cute and inscrutable.

He decide to phone. "Hey, Shelley Ritchie."

"Hey, you." Her voice was flat.

"How's Pete?"

A pause. "He's OK. All's good."

"That's great. So, married bliss and all that? Erin must be pleased too."

"Sure." Her tone didn't convince him one bit.

He began:

But who hath seen her wave her hand?
Or at the casement seen her stand?
Or is she known in all the land,
The Lady of Shalott?

He expected to hear Shelley go, "Onions!" Instead, it sounded like crying.

"Shelley?"

"I'm going now," she said.

"Bollocks, no! Don't hang up on me. Tell me what he's done to you."

She sniffed a couple of times. "Pete's done nothing to me." A pause and another sniff. "He's been living in Spain for years."

"But you said—"

"I know what I said. It's for the best."

"How?" said Sanjay.

"You want kids. And I can't have any more."

Ah. The hysterectomy. "But I don't want kids. Since when do I want kids?"

"I know you want kids."

"I do?"

"Yes, you do. I've known you a long time, Sanjay."

She had it wrong. He'd never wanted kids, family, all of that stuff. Right now all he wanted was the gift of making people do what he wanted, but his skills in that department were sorely lacking. He had no idea how to do that in person, so he hadn't a hope of doing it down a fucking stupid phone line.

"Oh, Shelley Ritchie. You don't know me at all," he said.

"Bye, Sanjay."

It had got dark. Sanjay didn't bother putting the light on. He just sat on the sofa, listening to the Kings of Leon and thinking about Shelley Ritchie and her sad shrivelled womb. Not that it was there anymore, come to think of it. He was pretty sure a hysterectomy meant removing the womb completely. He was less sure about the ovaries and other bits.

Bollocks! She'd seriously led him on that night.

For a moment he went back in time, back to Year Twelve when he used to think that his life would be complete if only he could get into Shelley Ritchie's knickers.

Maybe this was how it was meant to end.

Now, Caleb's haunting voice filled the flat as he went on about using somebody. Had Sanjay used Shelley? The answer was as elusive as the meaning of the song.

Later that evening, he talked to Ben. The lights were still out, and Shelley the cat had installed herself on his middle, which almost made up for the heating not being on yet. She had grown big now, and her fat white paws hung over each side of his belly.

Ben listened before giving his considered verdict. "Mate, which one was Shelley Ritchie?"

"For fuck's sake, you must remember Shelley! Year Twelve, amazing legs, always pretending to smoke?"

"Now I do. Nice."

This was followed by a slurping sound. Sanjay had forgotten that Ben's mouth still drooped on one side from his injuries. "So I thought I'd write her a letter," said Sanjay.

"Don't do that," said Ben.

"But I've got to tell her she's got me all wrong," Sanjay protested, sending Shelley flying off his lap.

"Has she now? You love kids. You're great with kids. You even work with them."

"But I—" Sanjay stopped himself. Fucking hell! Here he was, sharing his feelings with his closest friend. He'd been a bollocking idiot, talking more about relationships in the past few weeks than he had with Harriet while they were together.

"You know what, mate? You should get back with Harriet. You were good together."

"Not going to happen." Shelley was scratching the end of the sofa again.

"You were together a long time. Don't throw that away," Ben said.

Complete bollocks. That was as dumb as saying troops should stay in Afghanistan because hundreds of lives had already been lost there. Now that was something you couldn't say to Ben. "Got to go, mate," said Sanjay.

This bit was sort of true. Sanjay hadn't been to his parents' for days. He was well behind in the ongoing saga of Dad's chest pains and tiredness, not to mention Sita's broken heart.

Sanjay opened the door. It didn't look much like a broken heart from here. More like a blue skirt and a roll-neck top. Her black tights weren't even ripped. What was wrong with her?

"Hey, Sita. Where's Dad?"

Mum scurried out of the kitchen and enveloped him in a haze of spices. "He is at work, *beta*."

"So he's feeling OK then?"

"Yar. He has small bit of diabetes now." She used her thumb and index to indicate just how small. "That is all."

It was hardly surprising, what with his south Asian genes and a waist the size of a hippo. Mum explained what type of diabetes it was by repeatedly making a V-sign.

"Yar. I have a little diabetes," Dad confirmed when he came in from work. "All is OK. There is diet, and maybe less chapattis for me now."

Mum agreed by shaking her head sideways. She had searched online, she explained, and learned that basmati rice was good, but pakoras not so good. Or was it the other way round?

"Basmati rice is low GI," Sita chimed in.

"So." Dad slapped his thighs with both hands. "That is like a plan, ha?"

It certainly was. And Dad liked a plan.

He ate half as much of the starter as he normally did. By the time the main course was on the table, though, Dad had forgotten all about the diabetes and the plan and was in full flow about bloody useless fuckers ("Language, *beta*," said Mum). Although he spent most of the time waving his cutlery about to convey all the irritations he had suffered at work, a lot of food found its way into his mouth.

"Mum," said Sanjay, "that was lovely."

"I'm stuffed, innit," said Sita.

After supper, Dad insisted he felt fine and was not 'bloody cripple', but even so Mum and Sita cleared up while he put his feet up in the living room.

Sanjay didn't need to say much to get the conversation going, because Dad had something big on his mind. He leaned forward in his chair and said, "You know your mother wants bloody eternity ring."

Sanjay nodded. Mum had only been talking about it for twenty years or so.

"And always I joke with her, 'But you wear Calvin Klein Eternity, *beti.'* Anyway, I love her to eternity, I tell her. That is main thing."

Sanjay knew that. How many people as old as his parents held hands?

Dad lowered his voice and leaned further, to the point where the armchair was in danger of tipping over. "Now I have bought her eternity ring. And I will put it in perfume box. Then she will get nice surprise for Christmas, har!" His moustache was seriously grey these days but he was grinning like a teenager.

"Brilliant. She'll love it." Sanjay paused. "Dad? Can you remember the story about the thread? You know, that when God made you, He made two of you, connected by a thread? I think it's a Hindu thing." He couldn't remember who'd told him, but the gist was simple enough. Sometimes the thread was short, and sometimes it was very long, but, whichever it was, you each climbed up your length of thread and ended up together just as God intended.

He explained it in detail to Dad, but just got a blank stare.

"I don't know, *beta.*"

Bollocks! Nobody knew anything about relationships, did they?

GEOFF

Nobody had got the memo.

"What memo was that?" asked the practice manager.

It was a mystery how the staff always took note of the senior partner's memos.

"It was about the two-minute silence," said Geoff. "It's

Remembrance Day. One morning appointment was supposed to be blocked out. So the practice could have a two-minute silence. You know, like the rest of the country."

Cue baffled look from the practice manager before he half-heartedly said, "Sorry."

The nation would fall silent at the eleventh hour of the eleventh day of the eleventh month, if not to stand shoulder to shoulder with those who served, then at least in recognition of sacrifices made and lives snuffed out. Yet his colleagues in the practice clearly thought that losing two minutes was completely out of order, especially when Remembrance Day fell on a Monday and there were targets to meet and hoops to jump through.

Only two of the staff had bothered to wear a poppy. The practice nurse had a crumpled one attached to her right breast, and the male receptionist had one covering his name badge. Was his name Norman after all? He looked a bit like a Norman.

Geoff planned to make his own two-minute break between patients, but he hadn't reckoned on Mr Football booking in as an extra.

He was back, in a Charlton Athletic shirt and the same complaint of groin pain he'd had last year. Geoff overcame the stench of Brut and examined him.

No hernia, or any other visible abnormality, though last time his wife, a nurse, had sent him to the doctor's querying a sports injury.

"I can't find anything wrong. What does your wife think this time?"

Mr Football looked at his feet. "Dunno. The wife's chucked me out."

Then Mr Catarrh couldn't wait any longer.

"My nose is still blocked."

"It's probably a cold."

"Are you sure, doctor? It's been blocked for two weeks now."

So, at the precise moment when the nation honoured the fallen, Geoff was scrutizing the interior of someone's snot-filled nose.

The only good thing was the news of Ms Bump's baby, born by caesarean section the day after she finally decided to go to hospital. The male receptionist brought Geoff the hospital letter, along with a stack of repeat prescriptions to be signed. His poppy had fallen off now, and Geoff could see his name badge.

"Thank you very much, Stuart."

There was still no sign of Daisy. When Geoff got home, he decided to ring her. What harm was there in a quick call? He wasn't sure where she was, or in which time zone, but if she was asleep then she wouldn't answer her phone. Simple as that.

Her number rang and rang before going through to a generic voicemail. It hadn't been a foreign ring tone, though, so she was back in the country. Geoff didn't leave a message. No need to cross the boundary between caring and needy.

The next morning he had a text, saying she hoped to return to the UK in another few days.

He read it again. That was bloody odd.

She wasn't there at the teaching session on the Wednesday, either. During the coffee break, Geoff asked one of the other actors if he knew whether Daisy was due back soon.

"Ah, no," came the reply. "She's gone travelling for a while. No idea when she'll be back. You haven't seen a sugar bowl anywhere, have you?"

LAURE

Dan had left for work almost half an hour ago, and Jack was playing with his cars behind the sofa. Laure had at least twenty minutes before her CBT appointment. Plenty of time to do what she wanted to do.

The folder was password protected, but there was nothing incriminating in it. For over two weeks, there had been just the bare bones of a bland note to someone she hardly knew.

She opened a new tab.

Dan was through the door and behind her before she knew it.

"Hey, gorgeous."

She looked round. "Hi, you."

"Would you believe it? I forgot my phone."

She closed the file. "Have you looked in the bedroom?"

"I'll check. What are you up to?"

"Nothing." There was still a lot more to do, and she wanted to get her thoughts together on her own.

CHAPTER THIRTY-NINE

KAREN

Belinda was upstairs in Charlotte's room where they were plotting who knew what. The boys were in the living room, and there was time for a cup of tea before preparing tomorrow's lessons.

The scene in the living room was peaceful. She would sit down there with her cuppa for a moment.

Edward had spent his accumulated pocket money on more yellow Lego bricks, so all was well in his world. Damon was holding forth while the other two gazed up at him as if he were the Oracle, which was obviously his objective. "Who was the first person to win two Nobel prizes?"

Easy, thought Karen, as well as a chance to make a feminist point. "Marie Curie. Two Nobel prizes in physics."

"Duh!" went Damon. "Marie Curie only got one Nobel prize in physics. The other was in chemistry."

It was some man, apparently, who'd got two Nobel prizes in physics, though Karen had never heard of him. Ah, well. She heaved herself up. Time to prepare those lessons.

Supper brought another torrent of questions. Damon got halfway through the meat-free chili before reprising his interrogation. "Who here knows how many galaxies there are in the universe?"

"A million billion zillion squillion gazillion!" squealed Edward.

"I've told you before," said Damon. "Those aren't numbers."

"One. I gave the other one to Belinda," said Charlotte.

"Ha, ha," said Damon. "So funny I forgot to laugh."

"I don't know, Damon. How many?" Maybe if they all went off to keep a tally of stars, she'd get an extended period of peace and quiet.

"It's over 200 billion," announced Damon.

"But how did they count them?" asked Ashley.

Before Karen could hear how galaxies got totted up, Rose appeared at the door.

"Bad time?" asked Rose.

"Dinner time, but it's fine."

"Just quickly, then. I forgot to tell you, my cousin Roland's here from tomorrow. He's a very nice man, a widower. He's staying for just under a week."

Karen made a face. 'Very nice' meant soporific. Besides, Rose should have known better than to set her up, especially within earshot of the children.

"Anyway, drinks tomorrow evening, say six o'clock?"

"Sure," said Karen, trying to mean it. "I'll figure something out for the kids. Looking forward to it," she added as an afterthought.

She'd have to farm the kids out for the evening, even though this Roland was going to be a crashing bore. Karen just knew it.

DAN

He was getting home early all this week. Even more amazing, Laure was smiling when he came through the door. Three days running, that made it. Jack was whizzing round the carpet with his favourite toy bus. And there was Laure, sitting at her laptop instead of following Jack around the flat with a worried look on her face.

He kissed her on the head. "What have you got there?" he asked, gesturing at the screen.

She snapped it shut. "What have you got there?" she countered.

He put down the carrier bag. "This? It's dinner. No peeking."

Tonight he was going to make her a lovely meal. With delicate flavours. And some clandestine ingredients. Fennel from Italy. And broccoli raab from the old biddy's allotment.

Jack had a smashing time in his bath, then went to bed like a little angel. "Ni-nite," he said as he shut his eyes tight. Clutching his blankie in one hand, a toy car in the other. Typical.

Laure loved the dish Dan cooked. It was the dog's bollocks, if he said so himself.

Afterwards was even better. She'd avoided it for months. All summer, the weather had been too hot for sex. She kept reminding him it the worst heatwave in decades. Then autumn arrived. Too cold for anything but cosy nightwear. But tonight it was just right.

Goldilocks sex, he told himself as he kissed the back of her neck, ran his fingers through her lovely hair, felt her warm body. Not as firm as it was before Jack, but actually sexier.

He didn't remember her being this warm.

He didn't remember being this wanting.

A long time since they'd been this loving.

He hung back as long as he could. Concentrated on pain instead. Like when his tooth got knocked out all those years ago. But even the memory of Maxy thumping him in jail couldn't stop the inevitable.

"Oh God," she went.

And he erupted, parting with a wave of molten lava.

Why did people mention God at a time like this, he wondered as he drifted into sleep.

Jack woke early and babbled happily. Dan got up and gave him some more toys and went back to bed.

Laure was still asleep, one arm over her head, displaying the curve of one breast. Very Grecian. Like the statues in the British Museum, only warmer.

He inched towards her. Got as close as he could without waking her up. How close would he ever really get? You couldn't ever fuse as one with somebody. Even when you loved someone as much as this, stuff got in the way. Clandestine stuff. The worst kind.

A bit later, he made scrambled eggs for the three of them. She was taking Jack to toddler group that morning. Better ask her before she disappeared, and before he went to work.

So he dried his hands and said, "What do you say we get married?"

She gave him a strange look. OK, maybe he could have been more romantic. Or chosen a time when she wasn't unfolding the buggy.

"I'll rephrase that. Will you please marry me, Laure Dimmock?" That was better. Even if he was still holding a tea towel instead of a ring.

She pushed a strand of hair out of her eyes. Although she gave him the most gorgeous smile followed by a hug, all she said was, "Let's wait and see. I might have other plans."

HARRIET

Cheese on toast for supper again, against the backdrop of a gameshow from Nora's TV. At least a payment was on the way.

She'd already had the remittance advice, telling her it would be another two days, maximum.

Harriet checked on the bread in the grill.

You had to get out there, all the articles said, including the crappy ones she'd written herself. There was a whole world waiting to meet a newly single woman. All she had to do was get out of her comfort zone and herself into bars, onto websites, and use apps like Local and Looking, or DingDing.

Harriet got the toast out and spread butter thinly onto it. She didn't want to look for someone funny, smart, and good-looking. Not when she already knew where he was.

What harm could it do if she called him? Besides, she still had a couple of things she'd left behind at his. He'd probably be at home right now.

Or out with a new girlfriend.

Only one way to find out. She pushed the toast away and looked for her phone.

She didn't need to call. The phone rang in her hand. And it was Sanjay.

"Hey," she said.

Sanjay asked how she was, and she said, "Fine. How's Shelley?"

A pause then he said, "What do you mean?"

That was odd. "Well, how's she eating these days?" It was too weird to ask if she'd stopped clawing the sofa. It was also pretty unlikely.

"How am I supposed to know?"

"Er, because she's your cat?" Christ! She hadn't gone and died on him, had she?

"Ah." He swallowed audibly. "Yeah. The cat's fine."

"Phew. You had me worried there."

"Just got the wrong end of the stick, that's all. Shelley's great. Still clawing the sofa. In fact everything except her scratching post."

"Par for the course, eh?" Harriet was aware her responses were exaggerated, but that didn't stop her giggling like a fool.

"Yeah." His voice was deadly serious. "It is."

"I miss her." It was marginally less obvious than admitting she missed him.

"I think she misses you too. She's been weeing over the side of the tray a lot. That's probably telling me something."

Probably telling him to buy a tray with higher sides. "I didn't know she was that attached to me."

He chuckled, and she visualized his dimples. "Guess you don't know everything then. So how's work?"

"Good," she said. "I'm doing a piece on Army reservists and all their different professions." Put like that, it didn't sound exactly thrilling, but it marked a new and more serious direction. Tomorrow she was going to interview some of the medics who'd been deployed. She also had a commission on women in London Fire Brigade.

"Heavy stuff," he said.

Words did a little dance in her head but all that came out was, "I suppose." She cursed herself. She wasn't sure why he'd called, but time was running out, and she'd look back and realize that her last conversation ever with Sanjay had been about his cat scratching the sofa and peeing on the floor.

Then he said, "I don't know if this is strange, but I was wondering whether you'd like to meet sometime. It could be a coffee? Or, I don't know, a tea or a hot chocolate?"

"That's a thought," she said, as if he'd just shared a hugely original idea.

They agreed to meet next week. It was that simple.

Now the call had ended, but the phone was still in her hand. She smiled at the handset.

When you knew, you knew.

CHAPTER FORTY

GEOFF

On Saturday, Dave practically bounced out of Sonya's car and into the house with, "Hi, Dad? Can we go to the park? Can we have pizza?"

Geoff went in goal, as usual. The grass was damp and covered in leaves. He slipped and slid, and let through an inordinate number of goals as a result. During one of his many tumbles, he managed to invert his ankle. It wasn't puffy yet, but it made him wince with every step home. He paused and checked his phone while Dave watched a squirrel deal with a nut. Three weeks now, and still nothing from Daisy.

They got to the small square of grass by the roundabout when Dave put him straight. "Daddy," said Dave with the seriousness only a seven-year old could carry off properly. "I'm not sure football is really your game anymore."

"I see. And what is my game then?" Geoff tried to keep a straight face.

"I think you should try crickid."

"Well, if you say so." Cricket was inordinately dull, he'd always thought at school. "But my ankle's a bit crook and I don't have a bat."

Dave's face cracked open. "Aw, Dad! I can get you a bat." It sounded like *bet*.

"How so?" Geoff didn't want to borrow anything of Drew's.

"I got some birthday money saved up." Dave tapped the side of his nose. "*Dave* does rhyme with *save*, ya know."

"Does it, now?" Geoff would have winked back if he could have done. He made do with contorting his face, then covering one eye with his hand.

Dave exploded into laughter. "Aw, Dad. Everyone knows how to wink." With that, he fell onto the grass, clutching his belly.

"I don't know how to wink."

There were lots of things he didn't know. On the other hand, there were lots of things he was learning, like how to be a dad.

LAURE

Laure clutched her briefcase and patted her pocket to check that nobody had lifted her phone. The tube train was packed again today. No seat for her, and barely any elbow room. How did people manage to read books and play with their phones when they could hardly breathe?

It had been almost eighteen months since she'd last been to the office and back on a daily basis. Literally a lifetime away. Could she get used to leaving Jack, even part-time? It was brilliant that her aunts could look after him. That was going to make her decision so much easier.

Today was about finding out what her firm could offer, if she returned. She probably would, but she wasn't going to rush.

Three people got off at the next stop, leaving Laure enough elbow room to re-read the response she'd had from Geoff.

You asked for advice. I don't have all the answers to happy healthy children, so this is simply what I know. Yes, eternal vigilance is the price of health, just as it is for freedom. On the other, anxiety can cripple. All I can suggest is that you know the facts, but then try not to worry until you have to.

You seem to me a wonderful mother, and I wish you much happiness.

She put the phone back in her pocket and got out at her stop.

I am calm. I am serene. All is well.

That was a lie. All could not be well all the time. Even so, she knew she could cope. It was a huge step, this going back to work. But it was the right time for today's discussion at the office.

SANJAY

"Let's go to the park before dinner," said Sita. She was wearing dark blue jeans and a kind of blazer that Sanjay had never seen before.

"I don't feel like the park," he said. "It's warmer here."

"I know," she hissed as she grabbed a thick scarf and wrapped it around her neck three times. "Come on."

She had probably had man trouble again, he thought as he reluctantly followed her out of the front door. If there was time, maybe she'd sit on the swing while Sanjay brought her up to date with Harriet. Wasn't that much to tell yet, but they were talking again and trying to see if things could work.

In the playground, which was every bit as cold as Sanjay had feared, Sita turned to face him. "I've been checking what Mum and Dad said," she began, her breath condensing in the evening air. "It's not a small bit of diabetes. It's every bit as bad as the other kind, because it affects the blood vessels, like in the heart and the kidneys."

"No, it isn't. Diabetes makes blood sugar go up." That much he knew.

She put her hands on her hips. "You better believe me, bro. I've read all about it."

"What are you getting at? Dad seems fine."

"Maybe he does. But he's not fine. He's overweight, and the diabetes makes heart disease worse. Anyway, point is, he's been told to ease off a bit to prevent a real problem. But he doesn't want to."

"Ease off how much?" If the business needed looking after, Sanjay could ask for time off work so he could step up to the plate to help his dad. He'd do whatever it took. Dad's life was the most important thing. "I'll have to see what I can do."

Sita nodded. "That would be cool, but not necessary."

"What do you mean? He's my dad, and——"

"You're forgetting something. He's my dad too. I will look after the business."

She had a real stubborn set to her jaw as she said this, but it made perfect sense. She was the fully qualified chartered accountant, and probably the one who knew most about Dad's company.

She added, "Not forever, right? Just till he's stabilized."

"Have you said anything to him yet? And how would you find the time?" It was great that Sita could take charge, but a load of practical questions were falling over one another.

Sita waved her hand at him. "Not yet, no. But my job's totally shite. I was thinking of leaving anyway. Let's go talk to Dad now."

That sounded like a plan to Sanjay. Like his dad, he liked a plan.

Sanjay used his key. Dad wasn't in the armchair in the living room.

"Noises in the kitchen," Sita pointed out.

Dad was lying on the kitchen floor, with Mum kneeling on the floor next to him, mobile phone in her hand.

"Hey, Dad. What's happening?" For a moment Sanjay thought Dad wasn't breathing, but he was. He made a moaning sound and his skin was clammy.

"Ambulance on its way," said Mum, her voice rising. She was wearing a favourite old apron covered with turmeric stains, and looked terrified. Suddenly the kitchen of thirty-two Cornwall Gardens, once the safest place Sanjay had ever known, had become the scariest, most dangerous place on earth.

Sanjay held Dad's hand and Sita put her arm round Mum.

Dad moaned again.

"OK, Dad," Sanjay said, without a clue what his dad was trying to say.

"Your father was about to lay the table," Mum began, but faltered.

Sanjay had done some first aid once, but he couldn't remember a thing. Were you somehow meant to check your father's pulse when he looked like he was dying? "How long will the ambulance be?" It was a stupid question to which nobody had the answer, but he had to say something.

DAN

Laure was going to bring work home sometimes. Dan knew she would have to, if she went back to work.

She had brought home a pile of documents just from today's one meeting. Before putting them away, she found a blank piece of paper for Jack who began to scribble all over it with a fat crayon.

"So who shall we invite?" she asked.

"All your ex-boyfriends?" When Dan saw she wasn't

laughing, he added, "Sorry. Joke."

"We'll have to have people from work, and their kids," she pointed out. "Seeing as Lolo's has plenty of room, we'll obviously need to invite all your ex-girlfriends." She grinned, but that was even less funny.

"Yeah, right," said Dan. The celebration was going to be tricky, if Sanjay was going to be there with Harriet. "Are Sanjay and Harriet an item again?"

"No. But they're talking, which is good."

"Yeah. Talking is good." Depending on what they actually told each other.

Laure clicked her briefcase shut and installed herself at the table next to Jack.

"Anyway, I think he's bringing Harriet," she said.

"Right." That was going to lie like a stone—no, a socking great boulder—in the middle of his gut. Well, he'd just have to circulate with trays of food and keep it all light despite that lump of stone inside.

Dr Geoff was invited, of course. You couldn't celebrate Jack's life without the geezer who'd saved it, could you? He was bringing his son Dave (nothing to do with the prime minister). Plus someone called Karen who was just a friend and had loads of brats. Laure reckoned Dan had met her at speed-dating years ago. Her four kids were coming too, and they were semi-vegetarian. The children's menu would have to satisfy some pretty discerning critics.

There were going to be loads of people from Laure's firm, a bunch of lawyers who brayed and wore red socks. Lolo's always had lots of types like that in anyway.

Dan checked his list again. It was actually two lists. The other list had things like balloons, paper tablecloths, and Smarty Marty. The top children's entertainer in the whole of North London, apparently.

It wasn't just a party for Jack. It was to celebrate Dan's new column. In point of fact, *What's Cooking* wasn't just his new column. It was his first column ever. Looked like he'd have total freedom to write whatever he wanted about food.

Freedom was fantastic. And scary. Gave you lots of ways to get things wrong.

Just like the tray puzzle Jack was now doing. He used to get it wrong more ways than you could imagine, but now he'd totally nailed that farmyard, putting the sheep, horse, and barn pieces in the right places. Only one way to do it right.

Jack beamed when he'd completed the puzzle.

"Well done, Jack," he said.

His little lad was teaching him to be a grown-up.

KAREN

Karen waved goodbye to her kids as they clambered into her ex-husband's SUV, Edward still clutching Mr Cow.

She changed into an emerald green dress, new to her, and patted it down, hoping that the side seam she had taken in would lie flat for the next hour. Although the dress was on the thick side for the weather, that was less of a worry now she was on HRT.

She took off her furry slippers and tossed them into the corner. Tonight the silver ballet pumps would be perfect.

Rose's cousin Roland had postponed his visit. Just as well, as it gave her a chance to tee up Thomas for some childcare.

Yesterday she'd seen Roland arrive in a VW of some sort. He looked nice, smiling as he gave Rose a hug. Not that it meant anything.

What would they chat about? Small talk could be tricky, especially with Rose's narrow take on life.

By the time she'd shut the front door behind her, Karen's

mind was made up. She didn't give a fuck what Rose and her husband thought. If the evening went well, Karen would ask them all the riddle about the man out driving with his son.

And if it went badly, she'd ask it anyway.

SANJAY

They were working on him now in resus. Sanjay could hear them talking, just on the other side of that door.

On this side of the door, there was only space for one relative to sit staring, waiting, hoping, praying. Sita did her bit by taking Mum to the canteen for a coffee that neither of them wanted.

Near silence now. Sanjay strained to catch a series of regular beeps. Even irregular beeps would have done, come to that. But the door was too thick.

He would have to wait till a doctor came out. Then he would know. Sanjay could read doctors like a book. Hadn't he spent eighteen months having a cancer hunted down and blitzed, followed by treatment for TB?

Then he heard it. The whoosh that came fractionally before the door swung open.

A doctor emerged. Latex gloves. A badge that said *Dr Geoff Taylor*.

"Mr Shah?" began the doctor.

In that instant, Sanjay caught a string of regular beeps from the monitor.

CHAPTER FORTY-ONE

DAN

"Chérie, chérie," went the aunts, distributing kisses. They were the first to arrive, so they could help with Jack. They wanted to know what smelled so tempting.

"It's Lolo's brand new children's menu." Dan showed them the newly printed card.

Today was a bit of a road test of that as well as a celebration. The gaffer wanted a new kids' menu. He was sick of little tykes who only picked at their food. Or asked for fish fingers. Or got bored and lay face down on the table, like the toddler last week who demolished the entire stock of sugar packets.

Dan couldn't see how a new menu was going to make Hampstead brats behave. But it was a great chance to show what he could do. And today was a mega celebration.

"Mais c'est superbe," said aunt Lina.

"Il est très fort," Dan heard Victorine say to Lina. He had an idea she was talking about him. Hadn't a clue what it meant, but it sounded good.

The place was filling up. Smarty Marty had set up in the corner, Jack was working his way through the chicken tenders, and the lawyers had swooped down on the filo parcels. Dan was pleased with those parcels. Not greasy. Not heavy. Just right.

"Like my mum's samosas," said Sanjay between mouthfuls. "Only different."

So Harriet obviously hadn't said anything to him. Dan hoped she would keep it that way.

Eliot from next door arrived with some nieces and nephews in tow, as promised. He said Daisy had moved out and he didn't know where she was. Didn't matter right now. Everyone was having a good time.

Dan checked his denture with his tongue then had a quick chat with Geoff. Met his kid and Karen too. He remembered her after all. Pleasant face. Full credit to her for raising that brood.

He managed to avoid talking to Harriet. Just offered her a glass of Prosecco from a tray and moved on. Hoped that didn't look too obvious.

Tante Lina tapped him on the shoulder. "*Il y aura un* speech?"

Crap. He hadn't planned on a speech. "No speech," said Dan.

"*Quel dommage*," she replied.

He had an idea what *dommage* meant. There'd be a lot more *dommage* if someone got up and said the wrong thing.

"Hey." Now Laure was tapping him on the shoulder. She gave him a kiss and a massive smile. "It's all looking good, isn't it?"

"Yeah," said Dan. He checked the fishcakes, vegetarian sausages, pizzas with funny faces, beanburgers, and halloumi kebabs.

What would he have said, had there been a speech? For one thing, he'd have talked about all the support he'd had from Laure and her aunts.

About his love for Laure and Jack.

About how great it was to work at Lolo's, and what it meant to him. Leaving aside the gaffer and his tantrums, obviously.

About how amazing it was to have a second chance. He wouldn't go into details.

You couldn't predict the future, but hard work always gave you a leg up.

"What's this?" asked Eliot, grimacing at his plate.

"That, my friend, is *rapini*. Aka broccoli raab," said Dan.

"I love it," said Eliot.

Dan had no idea why more restaurants didn't serve it. He was going to write about new vegetables in his column, but his first *What's Cooking* article was going to be about children in restaurants.

Smarty Marty was making himself useful in the corner creating a whole menagerie of balloon animals. The grown-ups had taken over most of the tables. They also stood around and milled, balancing their plates. Everyone raised a glass, or two.

Dr Geoff was talking to Sanjay and his sister. Turned out he'd saved their father's life as well. Top bloke.

Dan got himself his first and only glass of fizz. He was going to be abstemious. Wouldn't do to get hammered.

He didn't have a word of the day today. If he'd had to choose one, it would have been *family*. You didn't always need fancy words to say complicated things.

Sita had moved on to Karen. Talked and laughed like they knew each other. Then Sita went and sat on the floor and played with Jack. Nice woman.

The world was full of nice people, thought Dan as he got himself a glass of water. He already felt light-headed. Went to see how Laure was. Smiling at everyone he passed on the way. Getting clapped on the back.

In a way today was also to celebrate Laure going back to work. He didn't want to revel in that too soon though. Let her find her feet again and feel good about it. Course, he'd always known she'd go back when the time was right for her. That CBT helped. The other thing that helped was time. And hard work.

OK, so that was at least two things.

DAISY

Whoever said you couldn't fool all the people all of the time obviously didn't know her, Daisy Isabella Long. She was at the height of her powers.

She said this to herself as she continued her brisk pace to the station. "At the height of her powers," she repeated, making it sound Nigerian.

Some African accents pleased her greatly, though, truth be told, she could pass herself off as almost anything: Welsh, Arab, Indian, Pashtun, Geordie, American, Jamaican. She could play many parts, as Laure had remarked.

There was no need for Daisy to look back as she went down the escalator. She wasn't being followed.

This was a real Daisy day. After today's meeting, she would play the most important role of all, one that had nothing to do with bipolar patients or bereaved mothers. Teaching the doctors of tomorrow was all well and good, but not as vital as protecting the nation in a constantly changing world, as the government website put it. She was proud to have made the grade, and looked forward to deploying her talents.

The Shadows' *Apache* filled the air as she got off the escalator and joined the seething humanity on the platform. A minute later, a rush of air and singing of the rails foretold her incoming tube train.

She smiled and grabbed a strap hanger. Her journey would stop short of Vauxhall. The building had not of course been destroyed. It was still very much there, despite the need for extravagant effects in Bond movies.

Others might make fun of the service's headquarters, calling it Legoland or the Hanging Gardens, but she was proud of her association with it and appreciated the architecture of the vast building.

Was Daisy being contrarian again? That too was all part of her act.

THE END

ACKNOWLEDGEMENTS

Special thanks to Jane Davis, Liza Perrat, and Katharine D'Souza for editorial help, to my proofreaders Catriona Stewart, Dinny Lovell-Pank, and Neil Browning, to Jessica Bell for cover design, to Jane Dixon-Smith for production, and to my husband Jeremy Grundy for his encouragement and amazing cooking.

Published in 1832, *The Lady of Shalott* is by Alfred Tennyson. Any errors are mine.

THANK YOU FOR READING

Feedback keeps authors going, and makes a huge difference to readers looking for their next book. If you enjoyed *Hampstead Fever*, please take a moment to leave a short review on the website where you bought this book, or on your bookseller's site. Facebook and Goodreads are also great places to share your opinion. At the very end there are some questions as discussion points for book clubs.

FIND OUT MORE ABOUT THE AUTHOR

Website: www.drcarolcooper.com
Blog: pillsandpillowtalk.com
Twitter: @DrCarolCooper
Pinterest: drcarolcooper

Also by Carol Cooper

ONE NIGHT AT THE JACARANDA

One young man dying of cancer.
One struggling journalist.
A group of single Londoners.
One night that changes everything.

The trouble with speed dating is that three minutes can last a lifetime, and, ever since he was diagnosed, Sanjay doesn't have a lifetime to waste.

For one booze and hope-fuelled night in London, the lives of a group of thirty-somethings criss-cross. As well as Sanjay, there's lawyer Laure, divorced doctor Geoff, newly single mother-of-four Karen and traumatized ex-con Dan all hoping to find love, solace or amazing sex.

Undercover journalist Harriet is after a by-line, not a boyfriend. She's a struggling freelance with a live-in lover, but soon she has to choose between the comfortable life she knows and a bumpy road that could lead to happiness.

As they each discover, relationships aren't just about finding someone special. They're about finding yourself.

Praise for One Night at the Jacaranda:

"A blinder of a tale" – *The Sun*.

"The dialogue is pitch-perfect, the sex scenes amongst the best I've ever read." – Liza Perrat, *Bookmuse*.

"At times dark, at times laugh out loud funny, this snapshot of dating in London stays with you long after the final page."
– Martel Maxwell, author of *Scandalous*.

"Sassy and classy in equal measures. A must."
– Dr Pixie McKenna, media doctor and TV presenter.

"Contemporary romance for intelligent grown-ups. The characters are real, the medical details are spot on, and the sex scenes are utterly believable. An absolute joy"
– Christine Webber, author and psychotherapist.

An excerpt from One Night at the Jacaranda

Already Simon was giving Harriet a special face to remind her he was infinitely superior. At what point had he stopped being just a music critic and branched out into criticizing everything?

"Just don't miss your deadline this time," he sniffed.

Long ago, he would read her articles with interest. Back then she'd also jot down the humorous things he said, sometimes weaving them into her pieces. Until Harriet realized they weren't witty epigrams but actually snide comments at someone else's expense.

They ended up having sex because he wanted it. She was curious to know if it was as good as it used to be, which was stupid, because that was impossible. It never would be again.

Years ago, Harriet would go with him on the foreign jaunts he made to discover new music and find old instruments. These were trips when they couldn't wait to get back to their hotel room, lift, wherever. She would sit waiting for him in some dusty café under a wide-brimmed hat, pretending to write as she sipped an over-priced Fanta. In reality she was rewinding the last tape of their love-making in all its knee-trembling, pelvic-clenching glory, complete with the after-burn in her lower belly that would last hours but was totally worth it.

HAMPSTEAD FEVER
QUESTIONS FOR BOOK CLUBS

To come up with thought-provoking questions for book clubs, it is necessary to reveal certain aspects of the plot. For this reason, we suggest you finish the book before reading this page.

What was your overall experience of *Hampstead Fever*?

What was your main emotional response to the book? Did you laugh? Or cry?

Did the book take you out of your comfort zone?

With an ensemble novel and multiple points of view, it can be hard to become immersed in all the characters' lives. Were you engaged right away, or did it take a while?

How well do you think the book portrays North London, and Hampstead in particular?

Which of the characters (including minor characters) did you enjoy most? And least?

Which of the characters did you have most empathy towards?

Did any of the characters make you feel closer to their particular worlds, for instead freelance journalism in Harriet's case, restaurant work with Dan, and medicine with Geoff?

Did some of the medical details seem too much, or were they interesting?

Were the characters' actions justified? Dan's excuse is his partner's loss of interest. For Harriet, it's loneliness along with chemistry. Karen doesn't want a proper relationship, but is that a reason to have an improper one? And was it acceptable for Geoff to tail Daisy?

How much impact do you think Laure's previous termination and her abuse as a child had on her parenting style?

If some mothers are helicopter parents, how would you best describe Karen's parenting?

Why is Daisy's behaviour so erratic? Did you believe she had taken drugs the day she visited her agent?

Were you satisfied with the ending?

Did the book leave more loose ends than you'd have liked?

Will Laure and Dan stay together?

What do you think will happen to Karen next?

Had you read any reviews before reading this book? If so, did you agree with them?

Had you already read *One Night at the Jacaranda*, which features many of the same characters and is set two years earlier?